BUTCHER RISING

The After War Series
Book II

BRANDON ZENNER

Dedicated to you, the readers, who push me to continue writing.

All of you out there can sign up for my email list on my website, and you will receive the short story, "Helix Illuminated," for free.

http://www.brandonzenner.com/contact.html

Prologue
Marianna

In the low of the valley lay a pond, whose brackish water veined into the soil to make the bowl of land fertile against the harsh desert terrain. Upon society's collapse, people gravitated to this land to possess the water for whatever length of time their fate would allow, before hostilities put them at odds against their fellow man.

A soldier named Gerald White led a disorganized flock of survivors, who thrived for peace amid the carnage of the world, to construct walls out of scraps of wood, road signs, and fallen trees around the pond. They claimed the water as their own, and cultivated plots of the fertile soil to support the agriculture needed to feed their feeble numbers.

Dour men stood guard at the walls with rifles and blades, many adorned in biological protective coveralls and face masks. Towers were in the midst of construction, when on one early morning, an armed horde appeared on the horizon like an army of ghosts. They were covered in the white dust of the desert wind, and dressed in a nightmarish array of spoils: army fatigues, construction helmets, and hazmat suits torn under the masks so that they fluttered over their backs like surreal capes. The adversary marched to the defenses and broke down the walls in a clatter of gunfire and explosions. Gerald White died on the battlefield, lanced through by a bayonetted rifle. He would perish before seeing the face of his enemy's leader, Nathan Clemens, once a soldier in the Canadian Royal Forces, who had armed and trained these people to fight.

The barriers were reconstructed tall and strong, with cement bunkers and hardwood walls, and lookout towers were erected in haste. The flimsy huts made by Gerald White's people were torn down and built anew, designed by an engineer who went by Georgia. This man was second in command under Nathan Clemens, and a skilled architect.

The settlement was christened as New Faith, and in time it would grow to an avenue of homes, a clinic, and a plank-board saloon that served whatever was plundered or fermented by the townspeople. The strumming of guitars could be heard at night, mixed with the crackling of the bonfire in the center of town, and for a long duration, peace endured. Even the occasional drifter who would chance encounter their walls, begging for food and water, was allowed entry and made a part of their citizenry.

In a dusty pit of desert, two towns over, was the Haddonfield Maximum Security Prison. The guards had disappeared or perished long ago, as had much of the prison's population of rapists, serial murderers, gang leaders, perverts, and the insane.

The cell doors were unlocked after society's collapse, and a stew of starved human filth stumbled into the dismal halls. A thick smell of rot permeated the building from the many doors that opened on the long dead and decomposed.

Old affairs were settled with fists, pipes, and knives, and the guard's armory was sacked. The small yet formidable population that remained in Haddonfield Prison fell into isolated groups that waged conflict with each other over the more valuable real estate—the kitchen, bathrooms, and offices—and eliminated any of the more peaceful and terrified survivors.

On a cool fall day, a man came galloping to the prison on horseback, with two dozen armed men following his lead. The prison population knew this man, for he had been one of their own: a death row candidate who'd been transferred many months ago. His deep, dusty words echoed in the halls with the promise of reward. He brought the divided groups out of the shadowy corners to stand united, as he belonged to no single ideology, but created his own, and gave the starved and crazed assemblage new purpose. This man called himself the *General*.

Far in the deep, dark recesses of the solitary confinement wing, the General searched for and found his old cell neighbor: a man whose crimes were more appalling than the worst among them. This man had been hiding alone and feral in a cell, with only a candle for light against the crushing darkness. Neatly organized in the surrounding units were the dissected remains of the prisoners the man was able to trap like a spider and drag back to the depths to feed on.

This miscreant was taken out of the darkness and made the lead physician to serve among the other officers, who each in turn had a storied past of comparable villainy.

Under the General's control, the various gangs and ethnic groups took up arms together. Neighboring army barracks were looted, the soldiers who had guarded the posts no more than weathered hide and bones. With some training, the General's men became a formidable fighting force.

On a crisp morning, the gates of the prison were thrown open, and the army spilled forth to desecrate all they trampled upon. The General had adorned himself in full riot gear, and led the procession into the desert, riding his muscular steed. A few who could ride were at his side, but the majority of the men stayed on foot in the rear of the cavalcade. They marched across the desert and to the edge of New Faith, spying the tall lookout towers looming over the surrounding trees. It was the water they desired. It was water they would kill for.

Shrill whistles blew behind the walls, alerting New Faith's occupants. The General's prison army came snarling out of dawn's early shadows to flood like a burst dam against New Faith's defenses. Many fell before the boundary, but soon the gates were reduced to splinters by a shoulder-mounted rocket. The murderous horde swarmed the townspeople, shooting, hacking, and leaving trails of gore in their wake. The General rode into the melee with his officers, his stout lieutenant beside him, striking down the fleeing townspeople in experienced fashion.

New Faith fell. The engineer named Georgia was struck dead early on in the fighting by a barrage of bullets. Nathan Clemens lost a finger and sustained injuries before his capture. He was bound and blindfolded, and later brought to the inner depths of Haddonfield Maximum Security Prison.

Those who remained of New Faith's population when the fighting ceased were consumed in an orgy of brutality. The more desirable among them were shackled and showcased as trophies of war. One such woman was Nathan Clemens's young wife, Marianna, who wailed at the carnage displayed all around her and flinched under the filthy hands of her captors. Many men lusted for her, but the officers kept them away, as she now belonged to only one.

In the midst of this revelry, a dozen of New Faith's detained officers were brought before the General and his lieutenants and made to kneel. The General sat on a wooden chair at the bank of the pond, a cigar clasped between bloodstained fingers, and watched as the enemy officers were executed by knife or bludgeoning device. One of the executioners dipped his palm in the blood of his slain and held his red hand high, swearing an impromptu oath to the brotherhood. The man slapped his wet handprint over his chest and smeared some of the gore over his face, howling mad in the debauchery of victorious warfare, his brain sparkling with narcotics.

After the man's oath, others followed suit, raising their soiled palms and reciting ritualistic pledges. Alcohol and various substances fueled the celebration, either brought along or plundered from the homes they conquered.

The General produced great white clouds of smoke from his cigar and drank from a bottle of something brown. The more attractive prisoners, whom the soldiers had not yet hidden away for themselves, were led out single file, their hands bound, and chains around their necks. They were presented to the General as his trophies and made to sit at his side. The slim girl named Marianna, with fire-red hair, was displayed at the water's edge. A soldier stepped forward to cut away her torn summer dress for the entire frothing congregation to witness. Tears rolled down her cheeks, yet she did not speak or cry out, but stood solemnly, glaring at the General and each of his vile officers in turn.

In a dash of movement, the young girl struck her elbow deep into the stomach of the soldier beside her, and twisted the blade out of his hand. She ran half-naked, palms clasped, into the frigid water of the pond. A few soldiers lunged to grab her, but stopped waist deep in the lapping water to laugh along with the others as the young girl cut at her wrists and stumbled beyond the murky shore, using the weight of the chains around her neck to hold her head below the water's surface.

The General watched, sipping at the bottle and inhaling the rich smoke.

The next day he christened the land inside the walls as the town of Marianna.

Chapter One

Rock Forrest

Karl Metzger, along with a six-man exploratory team, traveled west, bypassing Albuquerque, where the racket of warfare could be heard from miles away. Flashes of light strobed on the horizon from explosions in unceasing intervals, like a storm of great magnitude.

In Arizona, the terrain became harsh, and his stout second in command, Captain Liam Briggs, asked, "What the hell type of rocks are these?"

Karl looked at the ground and then out to the far scope of the land, scanning the arrays of fallen pillared stone.

"Petrified wood," Karl said. "This was once a forest. Look out at the valley." He pointed to the basin of land, where the circular stones lay flat, all facing the same direction, as if some force had knocked the whole forest down in unison.

"Never seen nothing like this," Liam said, and scratched at his developing beard. His voice was hoarser than normal, scratchy from the dry desert air.

"It's a sight," Karl said.

Before evening approached, they set up camp beside a dry gulley, and the men wandered about before darkness set in. Liam played with a small crank-powered radio, scanning the static for voices, while Doctor Freeman examined pieces of colorful stone by firelight, taking notes and making sketches in a worn leather-bound binder. He stopped to whittle a strip of charcoal with a razor blade, and Karl nodded to him. "What you got there?" he asked, looking at the half-moon-shaped rock held delicately in the doctor's palm. The round side resembled bark cast in stone, yet the inside was far from any wood found in nature. It swirled in brilliant shades of red, purple, and black, with pockets of pure white. "I do believe the process of petrifying wood is called permineralization," Karl explained. "Mineral deposits form internal casts of the organisms, much the same as dinosaur bones."

The doctor looked up at Karl with dark beady eyes and pushed his glasses farther up his nose. "That's right. Where'd you learn that?"

"In my travels, good doctor."

Karl leaned back, leaving Doctor Freeman to his studies, and watched the first stars shine out from the darkening sky. Soon, the stars would appear in such numbers as to make the heavens a tapestry of sparkling white.

Numbers and quantities went thought his mind in endless loops as the night wore on, causing pangs of anxiety. Marianna was little more than a small pond with a few buildings, surrounded by a tall fence. The population—*his* population, the prisoners, wanderers, and drifters he determined to be worthy of inclusion—numbered far more than the little plot of land could sustain. Haddonfield Maximum Security Prison housed the overflow, but transporting water and food back and forth was burning through their scarce supply of fuel.

It was his second in command, Captain Liam Briggs, who offered the solution: "Let's just expand Marianna's walls."

Karl answered, "Expand to what? To encompass more dust?"

The only land fertile enough to grow crops in Marianna was near the water's edge. Farther out, the soil became desert sand. Maintaining crops had proved a difficult process.

These people, he thought. *They couldn't make a seed grow in the best of conditions.*

His men were trained for warfare, pillaging, looting—not maintaining gardens. Keeping the vegetable plots required constant attention and instruction from the few able gardeners. But farming would be essential in the coming months and years, as looted supplies would become scarce and increasingly difficult to plunder with the absence of fuel, and even canned goods would expire.

In the early morning, after a few hours of sleep, Karl announced to the men that their journey would go no further than this eastern section of Arizona. Before they left, they boiled strong pots of coffee over the campfire, and Liam reheated the charred remains of last night's bean dinner, which had been left overnight in the pot. A thick layer of crust had developed, and Karl picked away bits of blackened soot and flakes of ash with his spoon.

"No more beans," he said, "for the rest of the journey."

A scout named Terry looked up from his bowl. "That's all we got."

"I don't give a damn. No more beans."

"Sir—"

Karl locked eyes with Terry, a young ex-con from Haddonfield who had a knack for scouting. "Did you not hear me?"

"Y-yes, sir. No more beans."

"What was it you were in for? All those years locked away; it was murder, right?"

"Um, aggravated manslaughter is all."

"Is all? Well then, how about you do what you're good at, and slaughter some man for his food?"

The others laughed.

Karl tossed his plate into the sagebrush. "Let's go. Saddle up."

Terry chewed at his burnt beans. "You not gonna eat?" he asked.

"One more word—one more word, Terry, and it will be *you* being served tonight."

Karl and Liam saddled their horses as the rest of the men gathered their gear.

"There's a pinyon pine up on that bluff," the Captain said. "Want me to take a look?"

"Finally"—Karl looked down at Terry, who was retrieving Karl's discarded plate—"one of you has a notion of how to survive out here. Leave the plate."

Terry did as instructed and the men mounted their horses.

The entourage consisted of Captain Liam Briggs, the scout Terry, Doctor Freeman, two able hunters, and a man named Bishop, who had grown up in the Southeast and knew several varieties of edible plants. He was also the most experienced scout in all of Marianna, and could walk silently through any wilderness like an apparition.

As the afternoon wore on and the sun blazed down from a brilliant sky, the men fanned out and spoke in quiet conversation. Liam cleared his throat and fussed on his saddle, adjusting his pistol belt around his stocky midsection.

Karl spoke without looking over. "What is it, Captain?"

"Sir?"

"You're fidgeting."

"I was just thinking, it's not gonna go over well if we return empty-handed. The men are down to half rations as it is."

"What would you have me do? Turn these rocks into meat?"

"No, sir." He adjusted his wide-brimmed hat against the harsh sun. "Maybe we should take a closer look at what's going on in Albuquerque?"

"War is going on in Albuquerque, Mister Briggs. Six of us riding headlong into a battle will see us all dead before sundown."

"I'm just saying, maybe we should get a bit closer. There could be spoils to be had at the edge of town, a wayward brigade we can swipe food off of, or some dead ones still with gear. It's worth inspecting."

A pang of fear struck Karl's mind as he envisioned himself addressing his near-starved men after another fruitless excursion. Keeping them happy, willing to fight, murder, even die under his command, was a pressing objective. He turned to his scout. "Bishop, what are your thoughts?"

The lean man stroked his beard and said, "We got nothing to lose, as long as we stay clear of the fighting. The way I see it, if we don't bring *something* back to the men, they'll be rioting over the smallest crumbs in due time. Finding anything—booze, tobacco—might appease them until our next foray."

Karl paused, and then said, "Well put. All right then, we march to the edge of Albuquerque."

The general unfolded his map from his breast pocket and held his compass to the page. "That way," he said, looking out over the boiling desert landscape of dead trees turned to stone.

8

Chapter Two
Edge of Town

The scouting party followed the interstate and soon passed through the deserted Zuni reservation, where the corpses were weathered bones and dried strips of flesh. The area saw little travel since its collapse, but still, they found nothing but rancid and rotten stores of food in the few homes and pueblos that hadn't been wiped clean.

In an eastern section of the reservation, a few miles from the mountainous woodlands thereafter, they rode to a stretch of buildings no greater than a block in length. Before the doors to a small clinic, among the line of boarded-up and broken storefronts, were piles of remains, some in body bags, others wrapped in stained sheets.

Karl sent Bishop and a hunter named Marshal inside, as the others stayed mounted on their listless horses. After some time, the two men appeared at the doorway with wayward expressions and a small canvas tote.

"Well?" Karl asked.

Bishop opened the bag. "Got some codeine and oxycodone. Not sure what the others are. We took everything in the cabinets." Bishop rattled a bottle, then dropped it back in the bag. "It's hell in there. Bodies piled waist deep. We couldn't get to the basement. Opened the door, but it's full to the top step."

Karl took the bag from Bishop and tossed it to Liam. "Let's move."

A mile out, they stopped at a modest pond to fill pots with water and then boil them before filling their canteens. They spent an hour fishing to no avail before venturing into the wooded and mountainous terrain.

Bishop led them through dense pockets of pines and firs, over rolling valleys of bright pink wildflowers growing out of the volcanic soil, and across narrow basins. The two hunters discussed a time and location to meet, and then disappeared around a cluster of sandstone bluffs to look for prey.

"I grew up only a stone's throw away," Bishop told them. "South of here, by Highway sixty."

"Hot as the devil," Liam said. He pinched a portion of chewing tobacco from a tin and tucked it under his bottom lip, then spat a dark trail into the brush.

Near evening, they made camp and gathered wood, waiting for the return of the hunters. They were eager for any sort of meat, be it squirrel or possum. As the sky darkened and the hunters still hadn't returned, Liam approached Karl, who was sitting with his back resting on his saddle and his long legs stretched out toward the dancing flames. "Should we send Bishop to look for 'em?"

"No, Mister Briggs. We wait. If they don't return by morning, we move out."

Doctor Freeman was studying the rocks and minerals he'd taken from Arizona, and the men in turn asked him questions about their geology. He begrudgingly answered, and pointed out the black carbon and the green and blue copper.

"What's all that red there?" Liam asked.

"Iron and manganese," the doctor said. "The rock itself is primarily quartz, a colorless silicate. The different elements in the waters and muds have contaminated the permineralization process and stained the rocks the various colors."

Liam tossed a twig in the fire. "I'll be damned," he said.

A half an hour passed, and Liam ordered Terry to heat up a can of beans. Karl kept his gaze trained on the young man as he emptied the can's contents in a crusted pot and set it on a rock before the flame. Terry kept glancing up as he cooked, and Karl did not break his stare. When the pot began to bubble, issuing pockets of steam, Terry asked, "You-you want some, sir?"

Karl didn't answer, but Liam let out a laugh and said, "Of course he wants some. You don't think the man's hungry? Give 'im a heap."

Terry doled out small portions, setting a plate beside Karl, when a disturbance in the brush caught everyone's attention. The two hunters came leading their mounts out of the shadows and into the firelight.

One raised his hand, displaying a wicker basket. "It ain't much," he said, opening the lid. He removed a small rabbit by its hind leg and passed it to the other hunter. "Not much meat on it, but we did manage to get this." He reached into the basket and began pulling out what looked like a thick cord. "It's small for a bull snake, but we'll get a meal's worth."

"Terry," Karl said. "Give these men your utter thanks and appreciation."

Terry looked from the hunters to Karl, then back to the hunters.

"Yeah, of course."

"They saved your life."

The hunters skinned the animals and cut the flesh into chunks to roast before the flame. The smell of meat cooking made Karl all the more hungry, and he was given the largest section of snake meat, charred at the edges. The immediate rush of warm juices in his mouth, laden with protein and calories, sent pangs of pleasure throughout his body. A veil seemed to lift from his eyes.

"Eat up, boys," he said. "Eat up."

***

Bishop and two of the hunters took the lead as they neared Albuquerque, scouting for signs of warfare or trouble. They were out of the woods, and again on dry, barren land. The horizon was free of the explosions they had witnessed several nights earlier, giving Karl some hope that fighting would not see them all dead before midday. The desert offered little cover as they approached the far cluster of homes. From a half mile out, Bishop returned with his horse at a trot.

"Sir," he said, within earshot of Karl. "We got a live one."

"Where?"

"By the barn, up a ways. That one plumb center."

Karl squinted and shielded his eyes from the sun. "Is he alone?"

"It appears so. And injured. He was pulling himself along with a crutch or a branch, until he saw us."

"He's seen us? What's he doing?"

"Took a seat on a rucksack he was lugging. He's just sitting there. Want us to gather up what he's got?"

Karl strained his eyes in the direction of the barn, which he could see far off on the flat land. "No," he said. "We'll go together."

They cantered their horses, and it wasn't long until Karl could see clearly. The man was staring in their direction and did not move as they approached, but stayed sitting upon his rucksack. When Karl was within speaking distance, he said, "Hello there."

"Go on," the man said in a booming voice.

Karl didn't reply. The man was covered with grit from head to toe, making his worn military fatigues the same shade of gray as his hair. A stained bandage was wrapped around his right thigh, and his shirt had torn open to reveal scrapes and lacerations all along his chest.

"You found me," the man continued, "so go on and kill me. I won't make it much farther anyway. Get on with it. Haven't had a lick of water in over a day. By God"—the man looked to the sky—"I'm coming home."

Heat rose in Karl's chest, and he could feel the stares of his men, feel them recoiling in expectation of his typical reaction when faced with a man of ideology. But instead he took a deep breath, cooling the flames in his heart, and said, "Perhaps. Please do inform me: who is it that you believe we are?"

"One of them." The man motioned with his thumb behind him.

"From Albuquerque?" Karl shook his head slowly. "I'm afraid not, my good man. Just passing by."

"Passing by? You're not planning on going in there, are you?" He motioned again behind him.

"The barn?" Liam asked.

"Albuquerque." The man ran his palm over his hair, shaking out some of the dust. "It will be the death of you, by Lord, I swear it."

"You swear what now?" Liam said.

"Death. It will come swiftly."

"How the hell do you know?"

"Because I've fought and failed to claim it as my own, and witnessed firsthand the ruination of my comrades. By God's good grace, my life has been spared."

Flames shot up again in Karl's heart. Grainy images, so old that it was like looking at an ancient video reel and not his own memories, flashed across his mind. Gray-haired men in black priest robes, their faces so stern it was like they were chiseled out of granite. The smell of cologne. Breath laden with coffee and whiskey.

Karl suppressed the fire inside him and let his throbbing vision clear. He was the leader of men, and managing his thoughts in a calm demeanor was imperative. He looked at the flatland all around. "You alone?"

"You going to kill me or not? I see you eyeing my bag."

Karl could feel the silence of his men waiting for his command. This gray man wouldn't make it much farther the way he was looking, and especially without any water.

"Perhaps," Karl said. "Or perhaps not. We passed north of Albuquerque not long ago and witnessed war. What part did you play?"

The man swallowed but didn't answer.

"You have nothing to gain by not speaking up. From the moment we laid eyes on you, your life was forfeit."

Liam spat tobacco juice in the bushes and said in a rasp, "Want me to end this?" He unsheathed a combat knife and brushed his thumb over the blade. "We can't be standing around all day. He's injured. People are after him, and I'm assuming it's whoever's defending that city."

"Point taken. Mr. Briggs, please—"

"We came here two hundred and fifty strong," the man cut in. "We approached from the east with the full might of our colony, of which I've grown weary. From what we'd gathered, the city wasn't supposed to be so heavily fortified. We expected maybe a few dozen behind the walls, but no more. We were nearing the defenses when they opened fire, and the superiority of their armaments became apparent. I implored our leader to order a retreat, but my words fell on deaf ears. Must be hundreds in there. Yet, we furthered the advance. Marcus Johansson, our ill-fitted commander, held out the belief that the enemy's strength was less than we were seeing, that they couldn't endure ... but then their artillery opened up and hell rained down. We lost over half our men in the first twenty minutes of battle. Gone. Vanished to ash in pillars of fire and smoke. In the end, with Marcus missing, we fell back. The doors to the city opened, and a great mass of men spilled out. Soldiers, by the looks of them. They came running after the retreaters, shooting and clubbing us down. I managed to slip away, crawled all through the night, heading southwest instead of east, like the rest. If they had any inclination that I'd escaped, I do believe they'd have caught up to me by now. Don't go in there, for the life of you."

"There were two hundred and fifty of you, you say? Why attack Albuquerque?"

"Why do men fight? For survival. We need fuel. We need water. The city center has running, filtered water, and we've all but run dry."

Karl lifted an eyebrow. "Running water? You don't say."

"By my reckoning, I do."

"Where did you come from?"

The man opened his mouth and then paused. Then he said, "Please, in all that is holy … could you spare a sip of water?"

Despite the man's injuries, he was well-fed and strong. Karl nodded to Bishop. "Give it to him."

Bishop passed his canteen and the man grabbed it, closing his eyes while taking long pulls.

"Hey." Bishop reached for the canteen. "Easy now."

"We have plenty," Karl said. "Go on. Drink."

Water washed down the man's chin, trailing dark rivulets across the dust.

"How many of your people survived?"

The man finished drinking and wiped his mouth with a sleeve.

"I don't know. A few dozen, maybe."

"My name is Karl Metzger. I lead this contingency, and we number in the hundreds. Tell me, what are your plans?"

The man shrugged. "To survive, I guess."

"Do you aim to go home? You say you've grown weary; why is that?"

"Can't rightly say."

"Can't or won't?"

The man shrugged.

"What is left of your home? Your leader is dead, and you rode out with over two hundred men—how many now remain in your colony?"

"What are you asking me?"

"A proposition. You strike me as a man who knows how to brave this world. A man who knows when to take advantage of a situation to his benefit."

"I follow the Almighty. I am but his servant."

"Come now, let's get you bandaged up and feed you something proper."

The man found the branch he'd been using as a crutch and slowly got himself to standing. He took a stiff step, then said, "I trust in the Lord to guide my steps, and I can tell you that our meeting here today is by no means a coincidence."

"What's all this about God?" Liam asked. "You a priest or something?"

"Sir," the man said, "I was and always shall be. My name is Dietrich."

Chapter Three
Ravaged Youth

The horses took to the wet terrain with ease, but the same could not be said of the army marching through the mist behind the officers.

"They'll be needing a break soon," Liam said, looking over his shoulder to the three hundred plus men. A ragged bunch that belonged to the desolate landscape.

"Captain," Karl replied, sitting tall upon his buckskin horse. "The men are hearty, and the evening fast approaches. They'll be fine, I assure you."

The army had been marching east for days, and the going was slow. Karl rode with Liam and the Priest at the head of this cavalcade. The scenery had been magnificent at times, despite the rain, with overlooks of lush mountains and valleys of pines. The Priest whistled a melodic tune as they neared the wooded section of a mountain pass, and Karl could feel through the pace of his men a lifting of spirits.

The rain tapered off as they reached the lowland, and the Priest said, "We should make camp. It's another full-day's ride tomorrow."

Karl nodded and issued the command to Liam. "You heard the man."

Liam turned his horse and spoke to the sergeants. The army fanned out, and tents and tarps were raised. Soon, a dozen campfires pockmarked the terrain.

"No fires," Karl instructed Liam. "There could be scouts around. We don't need our army blinded in the middle of the night if we come under attack."

"Yes, sir."

The order was repeated down the line, and Karl began unfurling his own tent.

"Dietrich, Briggs," he said with his back to the men. "Get the maps."

"Yes, sir," they replied in unison.

A moment later, the three men sat hunched over a map. *America Southwest* was printed in bold letters at the top. The paper was lined and zigzagged with black and red marker, and a small dot of green forestland was circled. On the map's border were tallies of numbers.

"You do realize what will happen if we reach your destination and find nothing?"

The Priest looked at Karl through a placid gaze. "Sir, I echo again the words that I've spoken … it was divination for us to meet. You saved me in my time of need; found me injured on the battlefield, and delivered me to salvation. I've healed on your bed, and have eaten your food. It's my turn to return the favor. I had no inclination of returning to the bunker, and to the imbeciles who reside in hiding, waiting for death to take them. I was going to venture into the world alone before you came to my aid."

"Don't know about any higher power," Karl said. He'd become so accustomed to hearing this man go on about God that the fire inside him had simmered to sparks. "Luck had us find you, and I'm taking you at your word."

"You will see when we arrive," Dietrich continued. "I cannot promise you numbers, only attest to what we left behind in defense—an exact fifty. I suppose some more will have made their way back from Albuquerque, but not many. There's no way of knowing if those bastards killed them all while they fled, or followed them back to the bunker. If they did follow them, they wouldn't have gotten inside easily. The hatch is over a foot thick, solid steel, and once inside, the entry shoot is a straight hallway going down. There are three remotely controlled turrets at the bottom, and room for a dozen armed men behind reinforced walls. Anyone invading has one option—straight into gunfire. And there are explosives planted in intervals along the way. Once we get the people settled under my leadership—*your* leadership—I'll call a meeting with our allies in the north, as promised."

"Your people, they'll follow you?"

"Most will. Some will resist. Those who can't decide can stay and do as they please. There's nothing left for them—little clean water, and the fuel was so low when I left that only the emergency lights were burning. And with the floodwaters rising, they won't have a choice but to venture out. There is only so long a person can stay confined to four walls."

Karl snickered and traded glances with Liam. "Most of us can attest to that."

"I am their priest and a leader among the community. They have always heeded my counsel. I have no doubt they will continue to listen."

Karl nodded, tracing his finger idly over their marked route.

"Yet they didn't listen to you when you gave pause in Albuquerque?"

"Many wanted to. You must remember, Marcus Johansson was the commander of the colony, and his words were held in high esteem."

"Okay then. Let's get some shut-eye. We march at dawn."

***

Scouts were sent in advance of the army, and in the early morning, camp was broken down and the men moved out.

The Priest rode beside Karl, and as the day warmed under a clear sky, Karl patted his front pocket and found a cigar. He offered one to the Priest, but the man declined.

"Not a smoker? That's a rare thing these days."

"Never been a smoker," the Priest said. "Vices do not attract me."

Karl eyed him up. "You don't drink either?"

"Not in excess."

Karl lit his cigar and issued huge plumes of smoke to waft behind him into the trailing Liam Briggs, who found and produced his own cigar.

Toward midafternoon, the Priest fell back and took up riding beside Doctor Freeman, who was reading a paperback novel as his horse clomped on. "If you don't mind me asking," the Priest said, "how is it he got to be the General? He kill someone for the title?"

"Kill who?"

"Whoever the General was?"

"What makes you think there was some other general?"

"Leading men in a military fashion suggests so."

The doctor glanced behind him at what he could see of the horde: men marching in loose columns, grumbling to one another about their aching feet, the weight of their packs, and the ammunition they carried. Even the wagon drivers, who sat atop the carts full of implements, cast their eyes to the ground.

"Do these men appear to have any semblance of military fashion?"

The Priest didn't look back, but said, "No. Still, they march. They follow orders. They're prepared to fight and die."

"What differentiates these men from others is that they long for the plunders and the euphoric rush only warfare can provide—and which Karl Metzger can offer. Individually, each of them would have died a long time ago. But together, under Karl's leadership, they have the world at their disposal."

"That brings me back to my original question—how'd he get to be their leader?"

Doctor Freeman thumbed his place in the book.

"Karl and I were cell neighbors for over a year, deep in the pits of Haddonfield Penitentiary. For about six months, we were completely alone, with only an occasional guard walking by to smack at our cell doors with his baton. We had plenty of time to talk in the timeless solitude that was death row, and he took to telling me things about his life. He thought of me as something of a psychiatrist, despite me telling him I'm a surgeon by trade. But he kept talking nonetheless. Perhaps it was the loneliness that came from being locked away for so many weeks and months, with no windows, no sunlight. But whatever the case, I think to better understand Karl as the General, you need to process his childhood experiences, of which he's told me every last detail, down to the mundane. At a young age, he was deemed unfit to mingle with the rest of society, and was locked away in a detention center."

"For what?"

"Burglary. It was in that detention center—a Christian-based detention center—where he learned the true depravity of mankind. He witnessed what the violent and carnal desires of adults could impart on the innocence of youth. After his release, he told his father what they had done to him—the counselors, guards, and priests—and his father did nothing but say he hoped it taught Karl the ways of the world. A few years later, the police found him responsible for the string of missing pets in the neighborhood, and he was sent to the same detention center. He served some more time, and when he was released, his father beat him at first sight, although the man was barely sober enough to hold the belt. But Karl did not cry like he used to as a little boy. Pain, anger, gratification—they were all blending together in the chemistry of his young subconscious mind. His own family called him a monster; said they wished he'd been aborted. His father yelled at him through whip-strokes in breath that reeked of hot beer, saying, *'Cry, dammit—why won't you cry?'*

"He wasn't such a child then, and at some point in the beating he decided he wasn't going to take it anymore. He turned around and punched his father hard. He expected to feel relief, but he didn't. He felt nothing. His father hit him back, but Karl stood his ground. His mother hollered, and attempted to break up the fight that had destroyed the bathroom before flooding out into the living room, toppling chairs and lamps. At some point, Karl's mother twisted her heel and her ankle snapped. But that didn't stop the two men from fighting—it was the police who arrived that stopped their scuffle and put Karl in handcuffs once again."

Doctor Freeman paused, looking at Karl riding up ahead. The Priest was about to speak, but then the doctor continued, "That was the last time Karl saw his father until years later, when he bashed in the man's head with a baseball bat, nearly killing him. That one got him locked up in an adult detention center, despite him being little more than a teenager. More grown-ups used their power and influence as advisers, both spiritual and mental, to inflict sadistic aggression and pleasures upon him. Being locked up for most of his youth had taught him that the pain a person inflicts on others is the pain of the world. Humanity at its core is a wretched entity, and could be no other way. He vowed in his late teenage years to inflict that same pain he had experienced onto the rest of humankind, as it is the essence of a person's purpose on this earth to be vile. Man, woman, boy, girl, cat, or dog. It doesn't matter. He feels no remorse, no pleasure. All he wants is to see the world turned black. He has no desire to live or die. He is simply *here*. Existing."

The doctor paused to take a sip from his canteen. In the silence, the Priest said, "My God."

A stray drip of water trailed down Doctor Freeman's chin as he continued. "During a transfer from Texas to … wherever … Karl managed to escape, and he ran off into the world a crazed and angry man. He stole, raped, and killed whatever and whoever was in his path. For years he eluded the authorities, taking on different identities and working small jobs when he couldn't steal enough to get by. It took a considerable amount of investigation for the police to catch up to him and realize the scope of his atrocities—the trail of mutilation and debauchery he'd left in his wake, from coast to coast. When the police approached him in a small studio apartment, it took six officers to subdue him, and he left two disabled in his wake.

"A cell in death row, deep within Haddonfield Maximum Security Prison, was his new home. That's where we had the pleasure of meeting. It was only through rumors that we heard of the war being waged around the world. The disease had not yet come to fruition, but some of the atomic detonations had. Convicts were offered the choice to participate in the *Freedom to Fight* campaign, and Karl joined without hesitation, knowing full well that the inmate brigades would be sent to the front lines. He also knew that if they were soliciting death row prisoners, the state of the conflict was dire, and his time to prosper could soon come to actualization. Before he left, he promised me he'd return, and when he did, it would mean the world was ripe for us to devour. It would be our time to rule. No more jail cells. No more solitary. The nooses would be cast for the wicked who'd imprisoned us."

"So he was in the army?"

Doctor Freeman nodded. "He's had some training. It was during boot camp that he met Captain Liam Briggs, who is an honest-to-God captain, and can steer any vessel, be it canoe or warship. They both escaped before seeing any action, with much aid of the disease that was wiping out the armed forces.

"Know this, being that you are a man of God—it is *your* God who spared him from the disease. It is *your* God that spared him from the electric chair, and from various deaths a million times over. He is the General because he is the strongest, toughest, most wicked man you will ever encounter. Killing Karl Metzger is no easy task. Many have tried; all have failed."

The Priest scratched at the stubble on his chin and said, "Hmm."

"Now, I got a question for you," Doctor Freeman said. "Why is it that you decided to join us? You belonged to a colony, much as our own. But you've chosen to join our ranks and solicit your fellow men without their consent. It spells death to those who oppose us."

"Well," the Priest said, "that's simple. It's the same reason that you, and all the men, are following General Metzger now; and it's not just for the thrill of warfare and the plunder to be had. As I see it, we all stand to live another day if we fight with Karl rather than against him. The people in the bunker have survived for so long because they had enough money, back when money held power, to afford a room in that costly silo. Their time on this earth is coming to an end. The strong will rise; the weak will perish. All who oppose Karl won't stand a chance. In order to survive, we must choose our paths wisely, and I choose to follow this man who had the opportunity to kill me for my meager possessions. He sees something in me, and I will prove my worth."

Doctor Freeman nodded. "Fair enough. It's for similar reasons that I followed him out of Haddonfield Penitentiary. To be honest, I was perfectly happy down there in the darkness. But in time, my food and water supply would have run out, and I'd have been forced to eat rats or venture into the world alone. Joining the brotherhood of the Red Hands was my best option for survival."

"You were happy staying in a cell, with no light, no moving air? You're a study, doctor. I'll give you that. You *all* are."

Doctor Freeman opened his book. "A study of what?" he said, and cast his eyes to the pages.

Chapter Four
Faith

Karl Metzger, Liam, and the Priest stood atop an expansive flat rock perched high on a mountain bluff, surrounded by thick pines. Through the circular peripherals of binoculars, they could make out portions of the rectangular structure jutting out from the ground in the valley below, beneath a sea of wavering treetops. Karl stopped his wandering view and focused on the dozen or so fully decomposed corpses nailed to crucifixes or hung upside down so that only leg bones remained attached to ropes.

"Quite a civility you got here, Dietrich."

"I never aforementioned anything in regard to my people being civil."

"Do you not belong to the same barbarity as your fellow man?"

"I've done what I need to survive; call it what you will. As far as myself belonging to my fellow man, I have made my opposition to their style of governing clear. On my accord, we would have opened the gates months earlier to scout for a new settlement and not attacked the closest colony, regardless of their military prowess. If I felt attached to the leaders of these people, I would not have directed you here. Those who I hold dear will follow me—follow *us*—and I do believe, most will follow. I am their spiritual advisor, after all, and have served as an army chaplain for a short duration of my youth. And these bodies," the Priest waved his hand dismissively toward the line of corpses, "they're only to scare off any wanderers."

"In a world where death is dominant, a few corpses are nothing to be frightened of."

"It's not fear of the dead, but rather what the living can do to make them that way."

"An astute observation, Priest."

There was no indication that the people from Albuquerque had marched to the settlement. The grass leading to the bunker looked lightly trod, and there was no movement in the nearby wilderness. Karl lowered his binoculars and said, "All right. Let's get on with it."

The Priest took lead down the mountain pass with the army in tow. Once at the edge of the valley, they halted and Karl dismounted his steed. "Look alive, Briggs," he said to his captain.

"Yes, sir." Liam dismounted and adjusted his pistol belt before finding the two officers selected to join them as envoys. Sergeant Iain Marcus, a gray-haired soldier with deep scars and a disfigured hand, had proven himself as one of the fiercest fighters among them, despite being one of the oldest. The second officer, Sergeant Novell, lacked the finesse associated with military order, but had displayed himself as a valiant leader on many raiding trips.

The men were gathered, all dressed in relatively clean olive-green army fatigues, and with fresh red handprints over their hearts.

"Priest," Karl said. "We follow your lead."

The Priest nodded and adjusted the strap of his shouldered rifle before turning into the thicket of wilderness. Karl followed, trailed by Liam and the two officers.

"General," Liam said in a near whisper. "I implore you to reconsider your tactics. It's not too late. The doctor's got enough amphetamines to dole out to the troops; we could have this bunker before nightfall. If we go in alone— if we even get in—what's to say they'll let us out?"

Karl opened his mouth to respond, but the Priest spoke up without turning to face him. "Mister Briggs," he said, "nothing in life is certain. Sometimes a leap of faith is in order. Perhaps you don't have faith in me, and to say you should think otherwise would be a fallacy. If I were in your place, I would not trust myself either. But you have already taken a leap of faith by not killing me when you had the opportunity. Instead, you gave me a proposition on which I have continued to deliver. I prayed for salvation in my darkest hours as I skulked wearily down the bitter avenues of Albuquerque, collapsing at times to go at it at a crawl. The duration of my people's time on this earth ceased when we marched to the gates of that city, fought, and failed. It occurred to me during that battle, as I watched my people disappear in gusts of fire and bullets, that they had become an extinct civilization. Hope was fading, but then on the outskirts of town, you appeared and delivered me."

"Never offered you any fucking salvation," Liam said. "Saying so is deceptive. And don't think for a minute that we've passed the opportunity for killing you."

"Gentlemen," Karl said with a laugh. "Enough. Perhaps a leap of faith is indeed called for."

"Faith?" Liam said. "You're starting to sound like him. Crazier than a shit bird."

Karl laughed again, then took a deep breath and exhaled it slowly, listening to the wind play with the leaves on the trees and the crunching of their boots on the ground.

"Don't know how you're laughing," Liam said.

"Captain, life is but a gamble, and I aim to win every hand. Amnesty, trust, and devotion—these things can be had through the selection of the right words and the correct presentation of assemblage. Also, having an army in waiting helps."

"But what's to say—"

"That will be enough, Briggs. The bunker is in sight."

After a brief pause, Liam said, "Yes, sir."

The concrete structure loomed larger as they neared. The front was a set of double doors, the same gray as the concrete, and wide and tall enough to drive a work truck through. The building extended backwards for many feet, and then sloped into the ground.

"We've passed the motion sensors," the Priest said. "They'll be watching us."

The corpses on either side of the entrance were so weathered that they resembled thin saplings. Karl looked up at the bulking size of the gates as he stood before them, and scanned the concrete and cement walls for the several cameras mounted inside protective cages and behind thick shields of smoky glass. The air was still, peaceful. The Priest went to the side of the door, where a keypad was built in, and typed in a code. The keypad beeped, and a moment later he leaned in close and spoke, "Hello? It's me, Priest Dietrich. I've returned. Hello?" He retyped the code and again it beeped. Then he stood back, facing the cameras one at a time.

A screech emitted from the keypad, and then a ruffled voice spoke out. "Dietrich, is that really you?"

The Priest laughed. "By God's good grace, it is. Parker, is that you?"

"No, sir, it's Ritchie."

"Ritchie, my boy. I'm alive. I've been spared. Open up."

The voice returned, "Who's with you?"

The Priest turned to face Karl and the men. "These men are responsible for my survival. They saved me from the edge of battle and patched my wounds. I would not be here today if not for them. How many returned from Albuquerque? Did any make it back?"

There was no response.

"Ritchie—"

"Dietrich, look," the voice crackled, "you know the rules. We can't let outsiders in."

Dietrich took a deep breath and exhaled. "Ritchie ... who's in charge? Are you going to refuse me entry?"

"N-no, sir. Just those men. The rules—"

"Ritchie, you can kindly go fuck the rules for once. Marcus Johansson, our blessed leader, has died on the battlefield. I don't know who's left in there, but I am most certainly among the ranking officers."

"It's Seth, sir. Seth Cross took charge."

"Cross?" Dietrich exclaimed. "Why in God's good name would you ..." He paused. "It makes no difference."

"I'll go talk to him. Give me a minute."

"No, Ritchie."

"Sir, it will only be a moment."

"Ritchie, I'm ordering you to open this door this instant. When I get in, I'll explain everything to Mr. Cross. His leadership is debatable, being that we hold the same rank. If I say these men are welcome inside our home, you had better follow my command. Have I made myself understood?"

The radio was silent. Then it crackled. "Yes, sir."

With a mighty groan, the left door creaked to life, and inched inward. The

Priest guided it back as its mechanical hinges swung open. Karl took a deep breath and exchanged glances with Liam at his side. The stocky man looked at him with large eyes, a sheen of sweat on his forehead and face. Then he looked back to Sergeants Marcus and Novell and motioned with his chin for them to follow. Karl stepped forward, trailing behind the Priest, who had disappeared into the black recess.

Chapter Five

Flood Waters

A green light shone from the bottom of the entryway, reflecting its neon color along the downward ramp and boxlike walls and ceiling. After a few steps inside, more hazard lights turned on in intervals along the hall, and at the bottom, a brighter light emanated from a room. A trigger of memory came to Karl: the crushing feeling of walls encroaching on every side.

Jail, he thought. *This place is a tomb.*

Their footsteps echoed in the enclosed space, joined by the creaking of a door below. A voice rebounded. "Dietrich, that you?"

Two forms emerged. The half wall the Priest had described was clear to see with the light on behind. The front was lined with sandbags, with cutaways for rifles to stick out while offering some degree of protection. The shadowy form of the three turrets also loomed—one near the landing in the center of the ceiling, and two more against the far wall. All three were unmanned Miniguns with protective shields, capable of firing something in the ballpark of three thousand rounds per minute.

"Parker, that you?" the Priest called out.

"Yes, sir," the man said, and continued up the passageway to meet them. "Goddamn, it's good to see you." Parker hugged Dietrich, and then the man behind stepped up to do the same.

"Ritchie," the Priest said. "I wasn't sure if I'd ever see you boys again."

"Welcome home, sir."

"Come, come," the Priest said. "Let me introduce you all in the light."

The massive door atop the passageway began to shut with the grinding sound of gears. Karl turned to see the slit of sunlight dim until it disappeared entirely. The door slammed closed and locked with a mechanical noise.

They were led to the entrance at the bottom, where Parker typed a code into a second keypad. A green light on the console blinked, and the metal door opened. The room inside was bright in comparison to the hallway, yet only a line of unmanned computer monitors illuminated the space. A rush of cool air played at Karl's hair from a vent above, and fed into his nostrils. Fake, acrid, temperature-controlled air. On the far wall was a small armory, with an organized line of machine guns and pistols on racks. Ammunition boxes sat on a table beside it, along with a number of handheld radios on chargers. Two grenade launchers with circular magazines lay behind the ammunition boxes, and beneath the table were a number of drawers. Karl was counting the rifles … *seven, eight, nine …*

"General Metzger," the Priest said, snapping Karl's attention away, "please let me introduce you to Ritchie Smith and Mason Parker."

"My pleasure." Karl extended a hand and bowed slightly, shaking first Ritchie and then Parker's hand, offering a wide smile. Ritchie was just as young as his voice indicated over the keypad radio. Parker was older by a number of years, and stood as tall as the Priest. They wore similar attire: green army jumpsuits and leather boots. The Priest went on to introduce Liam Briggs and the two officers, and gave a hurried tale of their exploits, starting with the battle for Albuquerque and ending with them standing there in the entryway.

"Parker here was left in defense of our fine establishment while our army marched," he told the officers.

Parker nodded. "Until Seth Cross returned," he said. "We marked you off for dead, Dietrich."

"Back on the battlefield, I had marked myself off for dead as well. How many have come back?"

"Thirty-four came back in one group, which included Seth Cross. Donaldson and Freddy showed up together an hour later, and a few others trickled in throughout the night."

The Priest shook his head. "We lost over two hundred … what are our numbers? Where do we stand?"

Parker eyed Karl and the officers. "Sir, maybe you should discuss this with Mr. Cross?"

"Nonsense. But please, let's go inside. I'm starved." The Priest unslung his rifle and handed it to Parker, who placed it in an open rack. He then unclasped his pistol belt and passed it over.

Karl felt Liam's stare in the corner of his eye as he swung his rifle off his shoulder and took his pistol out of the holster, handing it to Parker handle first. He nodded to his officers. Liam made a low grumbling noise and handed over his weapons.

"Sir," Ritchie said. "We're going to have to pat you all down. It's the rules, sir." He glanced to Dietrich, who stood looking down at him. "Not-not you, sir. You're an officer."

The Priest smiled. "Of course."

Karl lifted his arms, and the man named Ritchie gave him and his officers a quick inspection, finding nothing in their empty pockets. Afterwards, the next door was opened, revealing a stairway. Ritchie stayed behind to watch the monitors while Parker led them down a flight of stairs and through another doorway at the bottom. This door opened to reveal a tubular hallway. The entrance they had taken was a two-story buried structure, which served as the gateway. Below the monitoring room was the bottom story, containing holding cells and a guard post. The hallway they were traveling now was the main entrance, connecting to the subterraneous silo.

The Priest had told the officers the complete layout of the bunker on the second evening of his journey with the Red Hands, and explained the story of his people. Seated around a campfire, he tended to the wound on his leg while saying, "The bunker withstood the destruction of warfare and kept the elite who had the money for a room safe from harm. However, it did not stop the spread of the disease, which was unknown when the doors were sealed shut. We brought it down with us and only enjoyed a week of the bunker running at maximum capacity before people started falling sick. Out of the fifteen hundred residents and five hundred employees, who also had to pay for entry at a reduced rate—myself being one of them—under four hundred survived. The disease took a few days to wipe out over fifteen hundred people. Those days were marked by an insanity that I do not think I'll ever witness again. Those who were healthy panicked at the grisly sight of their fellow man being turned inside out. Whole floors were sealed off and never reopened.

"A meeting took place to see if we should open the front gates, but we started hearing over the radios that the disease was not limited to the bunker alone. It was everywhere, killing without discrimination. Marcus Johansson decreed that the bunker would remain shut. But several dozen of the residents disagreed with this choice and made an effort to storm the armory. Armed security forces met the resistance before the depot doors, and twenty citizens were killed before the rest were subdued."

It was on the other side of the tubular hallway that the men were now crossing where the door to the armory was located, and where the fighting took place.

As they crossed the hall, the Priest's story continued in Karl's thoughts. "The morgue wasn't suited to hold the number of bodies piled up. There's a crematory down there, but it was a pointless task. Several of the bottom living quarters were designated as burial grounds, and the dead were sorted in rows, and sometimes piled in heaps. The floors were then sealed, the oxygen vents shut down, and the electricity turned off. I led many gatherings in prayer over the dead. Not one of the survivors was without loss.

"In the aftermath—after weeks of recovery, of cleaning, disinfecting, trying as we might to overcome our losses—people began to once again have a positive outlook. We survived war and disease. We would prosper, and we had more than enough supplies. Our water came from a well, with hundreds of gallons stored as backup, sealed away in containers. We had enough packaged food to feed two thousand for a year, a fully operational hydroponics garden, and enough fuel to keep our worries low. But the world is not without its constant woe. A pipe in the fuel tank sprung a leak and it took days to repair. We had lost the architect, the foreman, and dozens of our mechanics to the disease. Once fixed, the loss of fuel was declared slight … then it happened again. Another leak. It was a reoccurring problem, caused, we were told, by faulty washers. But even without fuel, the mechanics informed us that we could continue to run the bunker at low power from the small solar array high atop the mountains—enough for the emergency lights, the ventilation, and water line, so long as the panels remained clean enough to receive sunrays.

"Our genuine troubles came a short time later, from the water pump. It broke down and it was beyond the capability of our men to fix it, although they never stopped trying. For weeks they labored down in the inner workings … but still not a drop. It was said that the construction of the bunker was rushed in the face of the impending war, and our misfortunes were blamed on the already dead. As for who is to blame, I think naught for the consideration, as it is all a test from the man high above. His plan shall be revealed one day; but until that day comes, I will follow the path He lays under my feet."

Liam spat a dark trail of tobacco juice into the campfire. "So you don't got any water?" he asked.

The Priest shook his head. "Too much, actually. Our misfortunes hit a perilous climax early one morning over a month ago. The people blamed it on our mechanics lacking the proper experience, but whether that's the case or not, we'll never know. There was an explosion and the pumps blew out, spewing water in such volume that the three mechanics drowned before they could reach the stairway. Their labored screams came from over the radios until their voices disappeared. The whole floor was sealed. And when the water found its way up to the next floor, it too was sealed. Again, the rushed construction was to blame, for we were told that the structure had been designed to stop such an occurrence. Sometimes it took weeks, days, or only hours for the water to take over whole floors, one at a time. The lower levels, where the dead had been interred, were the first to flood, and the water that now comes up is septic. The floor devoted to growing our gardens is destroyed … row after row of tomatoes, beans, strawberries, and even corn. All gone. So are our medical offices. The water will reach the upper mechanical wing soon, taking out our electricity and fresh air. Eventually, we'll all be squeezed out the door like a cork from a champagne bottle. And so, it did not take much deliberation for Marcus Johansson to decide on invading Albuquerque, where we had intercepted a limited number of radio communications, and sent scouts to survey the land."

The Priest told them all he knew of their leader, Marcus Johansson, a retired prison guard before the war, and many of the other people living underground. Seth Cross was mentioned, and he was not a beloved member of the community. The man was known for his rash decision-making, like pressing the battle onward in Albuquerque, straight into machine-gun fire, when it was evident that the fight was lost. How many lives the man was responsible for taking would never be known.

The Priest spoke late into the night, and no one interrupted his stream of conversation. Karl poked at the fire with a stick, watching swirls of escaping embers drift into the air like fireflies. It was the next part of the Priest's speech that interested him the most—more than all of the food and ammunition in the bunker combined.

Several months earlier, the Priest's people met a group of marauders who had established a small colony to their north. They were quick to make an alliance; however, the group was not keen on invading Albuquerque along with them, and did not see eye-to-eye with the former leadership. They offered little help with the bunker's impending destruction, stating they didn't have the resources. Their relations had been strained, but not broken, and the Priest promised he could establish a meeting. Even more, this other colony knew about another civilization, far away on the East Coast: a town named Alice, which was the largest and strongest force of men that was known. Clean water, the Priest had told him, and food. Enough to feed a city. At this, Karl's ears perked up, and the Priest told him all he knew about Alice, which was minimal. But all the same, Karl said, "Enough food, working gardens, and fresh water to feed an army indefinitely?"

The Priest shrugged. "It would appear so. You'll have to talk to our colleagues in the north."

"What do they go by, what are they called?"

"They don't call themselves anything. Many were bikers back when there was enough fuel. Belonged to some gang or another. The man in charge is named Mark Rothstein."

"I want to meet them. Immediately."

The Priest promised again to send an emissary, and told them all he knew of the bikers' leadership. When he'd finished, Karl asked him, "Your people, and yourself being a man of God, does it not bother you to kill others?"

The Priest answered without the slightest trepidation. "My hands are guided by the Lord's intentions. The same is true for the people that I muster. We are His weapons, His design. No different than Templar knights, only we brandish rifles, not swords. Those worthy of inclusion to His kingdom, killed by my hands, will rejoice at having found majesty. Those who deserve eternal damnation will get there either by my method or some other. It makes little difference how death finds them."

That night by the campfire remained in Karl's mind as they marched across the hallway in the underground silo, nearing the far door. It opened before they reached the handle, and a man appeared, stopping short before Parker and the Priest.

"My God," the man said. "I just heard the news … I thought you were dead."

Two men followed, wearing identical tan jumpsuits and baseball-style hats that indicated they belonged to the security force. They exchanged handshakes and hugs with the Priest.

"Mr. Cross," the Priest said. "Praise be it, I've returned. And I've brought salvation with me." He motioned to Karl and the officers.

Seth Cross broke off his embrace with the Priest to offer a cold stare in their direction. "Who authorized these men to enter? We're at war."

"From what I've been told," Karl said, his deep voice reverberating in that circular space, "your war is over. You've fought and lost. I am here as a comrade, adviser, and friend. We have much to discuss."

Seth Cross opened his mouth, but before he could speak, the Priest said, "Now, now. Let's talk inside. Please. I'm starved."

"These men aren't to step another foot onto our property. They are to be returned to the entrance and processed in a holding cell until I'm briefed on the whole scope of events."

Two guards stepped around Seth Cross, but the Priest raised his palms. "Now you wait just a minute. Who are you to issue me a command? We are of equal rank, Mr. Cross. Don't think any other way. If I deem these men worthy, then my word is law."

"I've been declared leader—"

"Only because I had not yet returned. If you want to put it to a vote, so be it. Parker, hear my words—we will vote, if Mr. Cross so wishes. We will let the people decide. The people whom I've consoled for months at a time. The people who have told me their fears, their worries, and to whom I have lent a guiding hand in their time of need. Who do you think they will vote for? You are a man of the system, a product of the machinery that has turned the world into what it is today. The people, they don't know you. They don't trust you. They do not heed your words as they heed mine." The Priest exhaled a breath and his face softened to a smile. "All I'm asking is that you listen to me and trust what I'm telling you. Let these men inside, for as we will discuss, I owe them my life, and all they have to offer for you—for us— is hope and prosperity."

Seth Cross brushed his hair back with a palm, his other thumb tucked in his pistol belt. Karl noticed the man was wearing a sidearm, though the Priest had told Karl no one was allowed to carry firearms inside the bunker. The security force carried Tasers and batons only.

"All right, Priest. We can talk in the cafeteria; get you something to eat." He looked at his watch. "We're between meals. It will be quiet enough."

"Excellent," the Priest said, issuing another smile. "I follow your lead, sir."

Seth Cross turned and led the men into the inner workings.

Chapter Six
Company of Murderers

The air was cool and steady, a constant light breeze flowing from overhead. Still, the men at the table were sweating, sipping coffee—real, fresh coffee—and picking at plates of heated up MRE meals.

Karl touched his lips to the hot side of the tin mug and sipped at the steaming black coffee inside. Dietrich was explaining to Seth Cross the story of his encounter with the Red Hands, and a brief assessment of their manpower.

The warmth of the caffeinated liquid in Karl's stomach sent pangs of pleasure through his body. He glanced around the cavernous cafeteria, extending, he was told, nearly the entire diameter of the circular silo floor. Three out of every four lights were extinguished to save electricity, yet still, it was easy enough to see the scope of the interior. Table after table sat in rows, many with shadowy faces staring back at him from some of the farther reaches. Although the atmosphere was pleasant, the walls painted a neutral tan shade, the environment was similar enough to prison.

As Dietrich emerged from the entry hallway, more and more people had gathered, shaking his hand, offering him the highest praise. Many greeted Karl as well, thanking the man who had brought back their beloved Priest. Seth Cross's security detail kept the crowd moving so they could be led toward the cafeteria, one floor down. From the entry hallway, they passed the armory. Karl could see the lobby, with the bulletproof glass reception area, where firearms would be doled out from inside. Based on the Priest's assessment, they had lost a great deal of their firearms in Albuquerque, yet their armament remained impressive. Dozens, if not hundreds, of brand-new rifles, hand grenades, some plastic explosives, a few shoulder-mounted rocket launchers, and more importantly—what his men always needed—ammunition. Enough for a small brigade.

Before going downstairs to the cafeteria, they passed straight across the bunker's reception room. Dozens of plush couches sat atop thick carpeting, and a massive, yet dark, chandelier hung in the center of the room from a domed ceiling that was painted to resemble a clear blue sky with wisps of soft clouds. With most of the lights off, the ceiling gave an odd juxtaposition: a sunny sky turned dark.

People emerged from doorways and shadowy corners as word of the Priest's return spread through the bunker. The population was a gloomy and mourning mass, like frightened animals, grieving over the deaths that befell their community, and terrified of their future prospects. Children were among them, aged from the very young to teenagers, and there were elderly and women. The throng followed them down a flight to the cafeteria, where Seth Cross's guards kept them back from the table so they could conduct their meeting in peace. Parker drifted away to leave the men to talk.

"Are you and your men military?" Seth Cross asked over a spoonful of what looked like lumpy mud.

"Some," Karl replied. He kept his palms cupped around the metal coffee mug, absorbing the warmth like a lizard on a hot stone. "I myself had a brief foray in the armed forces."

"What branch?"

"Army."

"Where'd you serve?"

"Didn't see any action. The virus saw my unit dead before deployment. Captain Briggs can attest to that; he was one of the few survivors."

Seth Cross sat hunched over his plate and tapped the edge with his spoon, holding the handle like a child, with his thumb on top next to his knuckles. "Hmm," he said.

After a period of silence, with Seth Cross lost in thought, his gaze trained on Karl, the Priest cleared his throat and said, "We've traveled here along with a small contingency of Karl's men. A dozen in total. We left them a half mile out so we would have the opportunity to speak to you first and not present a threat at the front door when we arrived. What they have with them is an answer to our prayers. Water. Fuel. They carry an offering, a show of what they have available at their disposal and what we could share if we join forces. They've carted two barrels of clean, fresh water all this way."

"There are streams and lakes all around. Water is everywhere. What makes yours so special?"

The question was meant for Karl, yet the Priest answered. "The same thing that made Albuquerque's water special. The same thing that so many of our men and women died to take as our own. Their water is filtered and abundant."

Karl cut in, "There's more than enough for my people and your own. Our water is free from radiation and the terrible biological impact of so many corpses being thrown into many of the water supplies, which, if you had spent more time outside, you would learn to be a problem. It makes the water undrinkable for a duration, depending on severity. You can take your chances, move your people out of here when the time comes to live beside some stream; or we can share my fresh and filtered water." Karl glanced at his watch, then crossed his legs and rested his palms on his knee. "In only a matter of minutes, the twelve men that we traveled with will make themselves visible on your monitors. You can see the barrels for yourself."

Seth Cross said nothing. He brought the spoon back up to his mouth, slurping up the brown mass.

"Where'd you say you came from, Karl? Originally."

"I didn't say."

"Perhaps you could tell me now."

"Perhaps I could."

Seth Cross laughed and wiped a drip of stew off his chin. "Maybe you just look like someone I once knew." He paused to take another slurp. "Or maybe not ..."

"Seth," the Priest said, "what are you getting at?"

"General," Seth Cross said, turning to face the Priest. "It's General Cross. Please address me by my title."

The Priest said nothing.

"What I'm getting at is that I know you," he said.

"We've met?" Karl pointed to his chest with a thumb.

"Not face-to-face. But I know you. I know who you are." He glared across the table. "I remember the newspapers. I grew up in Stone Acre. The papers said you were moved to Haddonfield to face death row. You were all over the headlines. The butcher, they called you, or something like that."

The guards around the table tensed, and the few who were leaning against neighboring tables or sitting in chairs stood rigid.

Karl sipped his coffee. It had cooled significantly. He kept his stare locked with Seth Cross, despite seeing Liam looking his way from the corner of his eye.

"Look," the Priest said. "What's done is done. The world is a different place. We have all committed crimes against our fellow man, and in this time of peril, is it not met with absolution? I can attest to my own atrocities, and yours as well, Mister Cross. We have executed our enemies in brutal fashion. Left them outside the bunker doors to wither upon the implements of their demise. My hands have seen their fair share of blood, as have your own."

Seth Cross brushed him off. "This man," he continued, "has massacred women and children alike. His atrocities are extreme. He lacks any semblance of human emotion, and seeks pleasure in killing."

"Correction," Karl said. "I take no pleasure in killing. It is but a thing to do. A thing that must be done."

Seth Cross eyed a guard at his side. "Take these men to holding. Don't open the bunker door for any of their people." The guard nodded, and the throng closed in behind Karl.

The Priest said, "Seth—"

"Dietrich too."

The guards exchanged glances. "Sir?"

"He's in the company of murderers. Take him away." Seth Cross made a shooing motion with his hand, and scooped up the last trail of stew.

"You're making a mistake," the Priest said. "A terrible mistake."

Karl took a final sip of the coffee and placed the mug on the table. He felt hands grabbing his shoulder, his arm, but he stood on his own. Liam and the two officers did the same, their chairs scraping against the concrete floor. "A fine cup of coffee you brew here, Sir General. I thank you for your hospitality. I look forward to many more cups." He bowed his head and then turned to the guards behind him. "I follow your lead."

Chapter Seven

Uprising

Before being led away from the cafeteria, Karl saw Seth Cross stand and issue commands to the guards beside him, while wiping his mouth on a crumpled napkin.

"Send a team to the monitoring station, weapons free. Those doors are not to open," he said. "And get these men processed as fast as possible."

The guard responded, "Even Dietrich?"

"Especially Dietrich."

The guard removed a pair of handcuffs from a pouch on his belt, but Seth Cross said, "No. Not here." Karl turned to see the man looking around at the people at tables nearby, all craning their heads to see or hear what was going on with their beloved Priest and the strangers who were allowed entry. "Just take them to the cells."

Two guards led the procession, with Karl and Liam behind, followed by Dietrich, Iain, and Novell, and then four more guards. In the far rear, Seth Cross followed the entourage. The guards kept their hands on their holstered stun guns and extendable batons, but none drew to keep their profiles low.

People gathered at the sight of the Priest being led through the lobby toward the entry hallway, and the Priest called out to them, "Seth Cross has betrayed us!"

"Dietrich, what's going on?" The voice of Parker shouted from the crowd.

The Priest pointed back. "He has betrayed me! Seth Cross has betrayed us all! I am being sent to jail for no other reason than that I have questioned his leadership! I have returned from battle only to be faced with tyranny! Am I not your leader? Am I not—" His words were cut off in a huff, from what Karl imagined to be a shove.

The hallway door opened, and the entourage entered. The circular passageway was wide enough for two men to walk shoulder to shoulder down the metal catwalk.

"Pray," the Priest said as they neared the end of the hall, his words echoing. "You, Mister Cross, must pray for redemption! It is *your* actions that will see our people dead!"

Seth Cross's voice could be heard saying, "I don't—" before the Priest spun around. His hand grabbed the snub-nosed pistol concealed in the rear of his pants, and he aimed and fired point-blank into the face of the escort behind him. The noise was deafening, and the entire group recoiled as if they were standing atop an explosion. The man who'd been shot splattered red in all direction, and the guard standing behind him fell to his knees. His hands clasped at his throat where the bullet had pierced straight through the first guard's head before lodging in his neck.

The two lead escorts turned, batons drawn, as Karl and Liam sprung upon them. Karl grabbed the man before him and pulled his head into his chest. The man's eyes were huge and pleading as he scratched at his holstered stun gun. Liam wrestled with the other guard, who was swinging his baton, but their close proximity made his efforts futile. Another shot rang out, and then another. Karl lifted the guard off his feet and pressed his forearm tight against his throat. The man grabbed at Karl's arm, kicked his feet, and sputtered out strings of saliva. All it took was a mighty shake and a twist, and Karl felt and heard the rewarding sound of something break. He dropped the guard in a heap and turned to see Liam raining down blows on the other escort, who was lying curled up on himself, as Sergeants Marcus and Novell stomped him with their boots.

Behind them, Karl turned to see three more guards either dead or dying, blood pouring from the metal gangway to pool in the rounded floor below. Seth Cross and the last guard were scrambling to the far door, both yelling, "The alarm!" The Priest fired again, and Seth Cross slammed against the wall, blood rushing from his shoulder. He was crying out in pain as the door opened and the guard shoved him through.

"All right then," Karl said, feeling the smooth cold grip of the security baton in his palm. "Quick now."

The slain men were relieved of their weapons. "I've got one bullet left," the Priest said.

Karl turned with his officers toward the far entrance. "Not to worry."

They raced through the doorway and up the stairs, approaching the monitoring station. As the Priest typed a command into an electronic keypad, a red strobe light began flashing in the hallway.

"They've sounded the alarms," the Priest said, and pushed the door open. "They'll come flooding in soon."

Ritchie turned from the monitors to face them, recoiling back. A second man was by the armory, fumbling to put the magazine in a machine gun. Karl and the Priest stepped toward Ritchie while the others dealt with the man with the gun. He was sliding back the bolt when they were on him, ripping the rifle out of his grip and forcing him to his knees. Displayed on the monitor behind Ritchie was the scene from the hallway: the dead guards, and one crawling across the catwalk. On another monitor, a dozen Red Hands were assembled outside the gate, removing two fifty-five-gallon plastic drums from a horse-drawn cart. Karl glanced at a clock on the wall above the monitors. They were right on time.

"Ritchie," the Priest said. "Easy now."

Ritchie swallowed. "I-I didn't sound the alarm." His eyes were huge.

"Okay," the Priest said. "I believe you, son."

"I don't know w-what's happening ..." His rattling knees shook his whole body.

Liam and Iain approached Ritchie's side.

"I ain't," his voice quivered, "gonna fight you."

Karl signaled his men to stop. "All right," he said. "Then open the door."

Ritchie exchanged glances with the Priest.

"It's okay," the Priest said, and reached to a corded microphone on the control terminal. "Hear me out, son." A red light came to life on the console, and the Priest began to speak over the bunker's public-address system. "As many of you have already heard, I—Priest Dietrich—have returned. I must be quick with what I tell you. Seth Cross has betrayed me, and all of us in turn. He had the chance to help our colony, help our people, and has decided to turn down a proposition we need to ensure our survival. Just moments ago, he issued the command for my immediate incarceration, based solely on the

fear that his leadership will come into question. His decision has resulted in the death of several of our comrades; and for that, I am truly sorry. I didn't want for anyone to get hurt. I tried to explain to Mister Cross that there is a way for us to be free of our impending doom at the raging flood that will see us all drown in the coming days.

"Our people died on the field of battle, slaughtered like a swarm of ants. I did not return to live out the remainder of my days waiting for death to take me. When *we* made the decision—and may I remind you that it was cast to a vote—to march to Albuquerque, *we* decided to do what must be done to endure, even if that meant spilling blood. We were to become conquerors, invaders, and we were at peace with that resolution if it meant our endurance. Today, I had to make that judgment once again. Our battles are not over; they have just begun, and this next battle is happening on our turf."

The Priest paused to study Ritchie.

"I have not returned alone," he continued. "A brave group of fighting men found me on the outskirts of Albuquerque and patched my wounds. They offer us a proposition that Seth Cross has cowered from. These men know how to endure this violent new continent, and they have extended their hand to unite our two tribes, so we can become the fighting force needed to ensure our survival. Our numbers have dwindled to a skeleton crew; but together, with the might of the Red Hands, we will live not only to see another day, but thrive for years to come. Seth Cross had an opportunity to see our communities come together, but instead, he sentenced me to rot in a cell out of fear that his leadership would be questioned. Because of his unwillingness to lead our people, I declare his control revoked. You now have the chance to stand with me, along with the wise General Karl Metzger, leader of the Red Hand brigade. I swear my allegiance to the General and the Red Hand army, and in all that is holy, I encourage you to do the same. All who follow me will prosper. All that oppose me will be left to suffer, to face this world against the raging tide of what's left of humanity beyond these walls. You will find nothing but a quick death. That, I assure you."

Ritchie's trembling subsided to something barely noticeable, but still the boy was pale.

"You are free to make your own decision," the Priest proclaimed. "Do not fight for Seth Cross. Do not rise up against the Red Hands: either stand down, or join us in battle. You will be rewarded, in this life and the next."

The red light on the console turned off, and the Priest lowered the microphone.

"Ritchie," the Priest said. "I apologize for sneaking the gun in past you, but it was necessary. Everything that I said is true; I never wanted anyone to get hurt or killed. Please open the gates, or we will do it ourselves, and I will again have to lament the brutality you will endure. What you are presented with is an opportunity. A chance to prove yourself."

Karl watched the second hand tick away on a large clock behind Ritchie. On the monitor below the clock, he could see the sergeant in charge check his own watch and then issue commands to the men beside him. They were quick about it, removing plastic explosives and the RPGs from the barrels that he told Seth Cross contained water. In the bottom of each was more C4. In the event the doors would not open on their own, the army was to blow them to shreds, and then roll the barrels down and detonate the explosives to take out the Miniguns and anyone defending the bottom of the ramp.

Behind the twelve-man unit, Karl could see his army approaching through the veil of the thick pines. Over three hundred seething and frothing men were ready to rip the colony to shreds if he so wished.

The sergeant was helping a soldier arm an RPG when he stopped and looked at the doors. They had opened.

Chapter Eight
Smoked Oysters

The tin made a sucking sound as the airtight seal opened, and a drip of oil trickled out as the lid was peeled back. A musty combination of smoke and the ocean rose to meet Karl's senses, and he savored the strong aroma. He pierced one of the smoked oysters with the tip of his combat knife and marveled at its glistening round form before biting it off the blade and sinking his teeth into the rich mollusk.

"It's funny," he said to Liam, who was sitting beside him on a granite boulder. "People have fought and died over tins such as these. One little can has enough protein and minerals to fuel the desires of man."

Liam examined a chunk of shellfish meat between two fingers, the oil dripping to his knuckles, and said, "Sure. I guess."

It was while they were unloading the second crate of canned goods from the storage room that Seth Cross had emerged from the depths of the bunker. Those loyal enough to fight on his behalf were fewer in number than anticipated, and the Red Hands had dealt with the pockets of opposition quickly, sweeping from one floor to the other. The Priest had led the advance, calming the fears of the more alarmed citizens of the bunker as they passed, and giving celebratory handshakes to others.

They encountered the majority of resistance in two areas: first, before the doors to the armory; then again three floors down in a wing of living quarters that was converted into offices and an infirmary after the primary medical wing was flooded. The armory took little manpower to overtake, as it was at the entryway to the bunker and Seth Cross's men were still scrambling to assemble. A larger group had gathered in the medical wing, and were attempting to flee farther belowground. The Priest had called out to them over the exchanges of gunfire, "It's not too late! Lay down your weapons and join us! Rejoice at having deliverance find you in a time of peril! You will not win this battle; do not fight for a man who cannot lead!" Some heeded his words, laying their weapons down, and emerged after two dozen of Seth Cross's soldiers were slaughtered. They rose with shaking hands held high. Some were injured, many splattered in the gore of warfare, and all were wide-eyed and terrified. They were patted down and made to stand facing a wall. The Priest reassured them their digressions would be absolved, and they would be allowed to rejoin the citizenry. When all were assembled, the Priest and a handful of Red Hands aimed and fired. "They'd never have followed us," he'd told Karl. "God is a better judge of a man's soul than myself. He'll sort them out proper."

Karl allowed for Seth Cross and his one or two remaining loyalists to further flee down into the depths. Guards were put at the doorway to the stairwell, and the rest of his men began mixing with the citizenry of the bunker, exchanging plundered goods for new knives, boots, and whatever else they could trade. Karl emerged aboveground, along with a dozen of his men, and some of the spoils of victory began to appear. Crates of high-calorie survival bars, industrial-sized cans of beans, and boxes filled with smoked seafood were piled outside, awaiting transport.

Word of Seth Cross's reentry preceded his appearance, and Karl had been peeling off the lid of the first of many cans of oysters when the man approached. Soldiers pressed in from all directions, forming a circle around the meeting.

"Karl," Seth Cross said in a low voice. "Karl Metzger, sir."

Karl turned to face him, biting a mollusk off his knife. "Good afternoon, Mister Cross. Please, no need to call me sir. General will suffice."

"Y-yes, sir. General."

Karl chewed. The rush of calories made him feel giddy.

Another man stood beside Seth Cross, dressed in similar attire: a military jumpsuit, pistol belt, and black boots. "Please allow me to introduce Lieutenant David Brown." The man named Brown nodded. There was a trace of red at his hairline, and Seth Cross's jumpsuit had a light mist of the same.

His shoulder was bandaged, and he wore his arm in a sling.

"You did not think it appropriate to wash and change before coming out to stand before me?" Karl asked. The men looked at each other. Seth Cross was about to speak when Karl continued, "Please, do go on. What would you like to say?"

Seth Cross stood tall. "We've come to discuss terms."

Somewhere to his side, Liam laughed.

"Terms, you say?"

"Yes, General. We've—"

"Terms of surrender?"

Seth Cross swallowed visibly. "Sir, it was a poor decision not to hear you out before acting in such a rash manner. I had the best intentions for my people."

"Mister Cross." Karl paused to chew an oyster, and then continued. "Please tell me, why on earth should I consider terms with you? Your own people have willingly sided with Priest Dietrich. You have nothing to offer." Karl tossed the empty tin to the ground.

"My-my people." He swallowed visibly again. "I have been a good leader—"

"They are not your people any longer. You stand before me armed. I ordered my men to allow you to remain in such a manner because I believe in having a fair fight ... most of the time. You should have come out shooting."

Seth Cross looked to David Brown, and in a fast and practiced motion, Karl unholstered his pistol, aimed the long barrel, and pulled the trigger. Seth Cross's head snapped back and he fell violently backwards. David Brown's eyes shot large. In a twitch of uncertain movement, he wiped at the red splatter covering his eyes with one hand and scratched at his holster with the other. He stopped short of drawing his weapon, contemplating the press of Karl's men. Some were laughing, and a few clapped. The man's knees appeared to be giving out.

"Mister Brown," Karl said. "Do you have anything to say?"

The man opened his mouth, but as he said, "I—," the Priest came up to his side and shot the man square in the temple. David Brown toppled over, and did not move.

"He'd never have followed you," the Priest said, wiping the blood off the barrel of his pistol with a rag. "He'd try to slice your throat at first opportunity, and flee into the night. No need to try and rehabilitate him."

Karl holstered his pistol and sat back down on the boulder. "Pass me another tin, would ya?" he said to Liam.

The last reserve of soldiers approached through the brush, along with the motorized brigade. Doctor Freeman was among them. He unsaddled his horse. "Ah! Good doctor," Karl said. "Please, sit. Celebrate with us." Karl motioned with his knife blade toward the box of canned goods.

The doctor blinked his beady eyes, looking at the bodies of Seth Cross and David Brown, and then settled on Karl. "Are those oysters?" he said, and took a tin from the box.

Liam was chewing through the soft flesh of the smoked creatures, making a sour expression. "Never had a taste for 'em," he said, and offered the rest of the tin to Karl.

Karl motioned with his blade to Doctor Freeman, who took them eagerly and said, "You shouldn't turn down such a delicacy."

Liam took a swig of water from his canteen and laughed. "Delicacy? Don't smell as such."

The doctor shook his head and chuckled. "All we need are a few crackers, a touch of caviar, and a wedge of lemon."

Liam stood and dusted his pants. "Keep it all," he said, and walked toward the open entrance of the bunker, where the Priest was going over papers and ledgers with an officer from the Red Hands and a member of his own community. The captain kicked the booted foot belonging to Seth Cross out of his way as he passed, and shouted to a group of soldiers who were idling about in a circle, finishing tins of their own. "Hey," he said. "Clean this shit up."

The soldiers responded, "Yes, sir," and finished eating as they moved toward the corpses.

"Set 'em up proper. How the people here are accustomed." He motioned toward the woods, where the old tortured and crucified bodies still lined the entryway to the bunker. "Do onto others as they would have done onto you, right?"

"Sir," one of the soldiers said, reaching down to grab Seth Cross's

shoulder. "I think it's do unto others as you would have done unto you."

Liam scratched the stubble on his chin. "Same sh:t. String 'em up." He turned and disappeared into the bunker.

Two ropes were thrown over branches of nearby trees, and Seth Cross and David Brown were strung up by their ankles, where they remained for the rest of time.

Chapter Nine
Meeting of Three

The Red Hands remained in the bunker, removing box after box of food and supplies. There were stores of preserved vegetables from their gardens, hundreds of boxes of MREs, bottled water, gauze and bandages, pills and medications, and even stores of hard alcohol.

Karl stood beside a soldier taking inventory as a procession of men loaded the crates onto carts and vehicles. The Miniguns from the hallway were dismantled and brought outside. He sipped from a bottle of brown liquor and offered it to the Priest, who declined with a wave of his hand.

"You know," Karl said, "we can't take them all."

The Priest nodded.

"The women, the children; it's been hard enough keeping the men away for this long. And there's fear in many of their faces. Distrust."

"Yes," the Priest said. "Some. But many know that this is the next step in our evolution as a society, and are eager to step out from the abysmal underground. The bunker is little more than a tomb. A reminder of what they have lost. It's time to start over."

Karl patted his front pocket and produced a cigar. He bit into the end and rolled the wide tip over a flame. "I've held counsel with Mister Briggs and several officers. It's decided that some of the more concerned citizens will relocate to Marianna when we move out, along with the supply wagons and the bulk of what we can't carry on our backs. They can tend to the withering crops, and receive some training in the form of warfare. Those who can fight and are eager to explore this world will advance with the main expeditionary force of our army. The others, the more desirable … nothing can be done to protect them. If there are some you wish to spare, I'll allow you to quietly escort them away from our proximity. They will have to brave the world alone. Please know this is not an offer I have given in the past. You have delivered on your word. Our numbers have grown, and we will not go hungry for many nights. This is a one-time deal to show my gratitude."

There was a brief pause in their conversation. The loud din of the soldiers working, or drunk, was all around. Then the Priest said, "We shall endure," and nothing more was discussed.

In the three days that the Red Hands occupied the bunker, mingling with their new brethren and sharing in the spoils of alcohol, tobacco, and painkillers, the water flooded two additional levels. Karl estimated they would get one more night, maybe two, until the electricity would cease. In the dark, that's when his command over the men would lessen, and they would become the demons they desired to be. There would be no stopping the angry brood from taking their earthly pleasures while hiding in the shadows. One night in the dark would be permitted before moving out and sealing the doors shut for good.

Although the inventory of fuel was plentiful, many of the barrels had expired, despite the Priest assuring Karl that the drums had received large doses of stabilizers. It was decided to send everything of value back to Marianna, and scout the road ahead far and wide, before all the fuel spoiled. Despite the abundance of food, Karl knew that it would not last forever. The army needed its strength. They needed all their might for what was in store for them. There were still battles to wage—large battles—and cities to topple if his people wanted to endure for many years. All the canned goods in the world would not stop Karl's anxiety over knowing that it would eventually run out, spoil, and his army would starve.

As the Priest and a small unit traveled to the delegates in the north, a dozen motorcycles were sent out to snake the land, reporting the occasional warehouse of goods and the more abundant tractor-trailer still with its cargo. Some of the exploratory scouts rode along with flatbed trucks, with barrels of fuel tied on the backs to expand their reach. On one occasion, they returned with news of an entire field full of brand-new and never used military jeeps and hummers, dozens of them. The location was marked on a map, along with every known military base and area of prior operation, and the looting there turned up vast armories. Some of the smaller hauls included a trailer full of cigarette cartons, which the men applauded and took greedily as they were handed out from the back of the truck.

Reports came from Marianna, the scouts recounting that the gardens had all but given up producing crops, and that before the haul of goods from the bunker had arrived, the stores of food were so low that on four occasions fights had broken out to stop the near starving men from overtaking the warehouse. On the last occasion, a man stabbed a guard in an attempt to steal food. He was brought to trial on a makeshift stage, and an explanation of his crimes announced to the attending audience. His wrists and ankles were stretched out, tied to beams of wood on both sides, and a butcher stood behind him with his collection of blades. He cut the man from the base of his skull down his back, then across each arm and leg, flaying the wailing man alive before the spectators. The loose skin was nailed to the door of the warehouse, and no further attempts at stealing were reported.

Karl heard this news in the cafeteria, and thought long and hard.

"We need some damn farmers," he said to Liam. "Even the few from the bunker who claimed to know their way around crops have only dealt with hydroponic systems. Not one of these morons knows how to plow a field."

"Do you?" Liam asked.

Karl stared at his captain. "I know how to lead men and punish those who disobey."

"Yes, sir." Liam looked to the ground and fidgeted with his gun belt.

"Stop that," Karl said.

"Yes, sir."

Karl left his captain in the cafeteria to go to his dormitory. His men were spilling out from the doorways of the rooms, and the red carpeting with its ornate patterning now held trails of grime from their boots.

He glanced at his watch, then stopped walking and tapped at the weathered crystal display. The time hadn't changed since he'd last checked.

Great, he thought, and changed his course to the storage rooms to see if he could find a spare watch, or a new battery. On the way, he passed a group of soldiers sitting around a table in a foyer, a half bottle of dark liquor passing between them while they played cards. A nearby doorway belonged to Doctor

Freeman, and the stench of decay drifting out was undeniable.

The men nodded to Karl as he passed, saying, "Sir." Karl addressed a soldier slumped in a chair. "You there," he said. "What time do you have?" The man looked at his watch, but before he could respond, Karl said, "Give me your watch."

"My watch?" the man said in a slur. He examined Karl's wrist. "What's wrong with the one you got?"

Karl stared at the man, and the others around him inched their chairs back. A few turned and walked away as Karl's hand moved to his pistol.

A voice behind him shouted, "Karl, they're back!"

Liam caught up and repeated, "They're back, sir. The Priest, and maybe a hundred more."

Karl turned and began walking as Liam strode behind him.

"Are we all set?"

"Yes, sir."

They proceeded down the hallway toward where the officers resided. They ducked into an office room, and Karl went to take a swallow of whiskey from a side bar as he heard the commotion of the visitors being led to the meeting room a few doors down. He poured another swallow and drained the glass, then turned and left.

At the meeting room, he swung the door open and everyone turned to face him.

"General." The Priest smiled, his hand on the shoulder of a short and stout man wearing a weathered leather jacket with a long, scraggly red beard. "Please, let me introduce you to our colleague from the north: Mark Rothstein."

"Ah, Mister Rothstein. The pleasure is all mine. Please, sit." He motioned to the chairs around the circular table, and pulled out one for himself. Liam sat beside him, and three of Mark Rothstein's companions sat along with them.

Full introductions were made, and then Mark said in a gruff bark of a voice, "I see you did away with the women and kids. Smart move. I told Marcus Johansson as much. All they bring is unwanted attention, if you ask me."

"I couldn't agree more. They've been moved away for now. Only, Mister

Rothstein, we *are* the unwanted attention. Don't think any different about it. If you're going to take up with us, you should better understand the desires of my organization."

One of Mark's men spoke up, "What's that gotta do with women and kids?"

"They are but playthings, if my men wish it so." Karl waved his hand dismissively. "In this particular case, I will allow the good priest here to move them from the vicinity in order to qualm any griping we might encounter from the peasants we're allowing into our ranks."

The man nodded and said, "Why not just kill *all* the people and let your men have their ways?"

Karl rested his elbows on the table, his tall knees brushing the bottom. "What is your name again?"

"Michael," the man said.

"Michael?" Karl leaned forward. "Michael what?"

The man glanced around at his fellow soldiers, but no one looked his way. "Rogers. Michael Rogers."

"I wasn't asking your last name. It was *sir* I was looking for. You are to address me as such at every available opportunity."

The man smirked a nervous smile and again looked to his fellow soldiers, but no one offered him assistance.

Karl then said, "In just a moment, I will begin bashing your head in with this chair that I sit upon, and I won't stop until your brains speckle the floor like a Jackson Pollock painting. Your friends will offer you no aid, for if they do, I will deliver to them the same treatment. Your shattered body will then be tossed to my men for further insult, perhaps to be cut up and braised in a stew, or to be used as a toy while you're still warm. Do you understand?" The man's eyes were large, and Karl said in a hiss, "*Do ... you ... understand?*"

"S-sir. Yes-yes, sir."

Karl watched Michael's face beat bright red under his dark stubble. He could feel through the trembling in the man's eyes his pulse hammering fast, his skin breaking out in sweat, his bowels on the verge of releasing.

Then Karl averted his gaze to Mark Rothstein.

"Tell me about the towns."

"Yes, sir." Mark cleared his throat. "I, um ... we had a previous treaty with

Marcus Johansson, for our mutual benefit. We raided a few settlements together and shared in the plunder."

"And yet you left him high and dry in Albuquerque? And offered him no help as this establishment began to drown?"

"No, sir. It was nothing like that. I told him—warned him—that Albuquerque wouldn't fall. We'd sent scouts thataway, four in total. Only one escaped after being taken in, and the defenses he described there were beyond our capabilities. Hundreds if not thousands of strong, well-fed soldiers. Hardened bunkers with a network of trenches, and dozens of guard towers. They were wearing matching, clean uniforms, suggesting military order. The city is impenetrable. Yet, Marcus's scouts had not gone far enough into the city, and didn't see the true size of their forces. In the end, he relied on his own intelligence over ours."

"You couldn't sway Marcus not to attack?"

"No, and for the life of me, I don't understand why." Mark's voice did not waver under Karl's inquisition. "There are three establishments where we know that water flows freely. Albuquerque is the closest march. I pressed Marcus to reconsider and attack the smallest of the three settlements, but he thought it wiser to go straight for the more ambitious and lucrative victory. I told him he'd lose, but he simply dismissed me. He was sure of his men's abilities, despite my telling him he'd be fighting alone. Think he was more frightened of the long march, of facing the world. Being in this bunker warped his perception. The largest of all three of the settlements, and the farthest away, is on the East Coast. Alice, it's called. That one wasn't even considered, although it offers the best possible chance for long-term survival. They're bigger than even Albuquerque, and by all assessments, they got enough gardens to feed thousands if maintained proper. Acres of crops: apple orchards, cornstalks, zucchinis ... you name it. And an operating reservoir with a water filtering plant. We know this 'cause they exiled one of their own, many months ago, for causing a fight that saw one of their men dead. His name is Jacob, and he stumbled on us after roaming the woods for over a month, nearly starved. He hates their leaders so much for kicking him out that he wants to see them crumble—by any means. He knows the layout of the town, and has drawn us some good maps."

"Yes," Karl said. "I'm eager to know more about Alice. But getting back to your previous engagement with Marcus Johansson, could you not offer them a home as the bunker here was flooding?"

"Sir, I say in all confidence that there was nothing that could have been done. Marcus's blood is not on my hands. The deaths of his people rest entirely on his shoulders. My current settlement is small. We don't stay in any one location for long. It's been our way to travel from area to area—wherever there's food and water. When it's dried up, we move on. They could have joined us to do the same. Marcus, and then Seth Cross, they didn't agree with those conditions. Living in this bunker for so long gave them a sense of security. They believed that walls could keep them alive. I believe that if you stay anywhere long enough, some other group will come paint a target on yer ass."

"What good was your treaty then?"

"I guess …" Mark paused to scratch his beard with grimy fingers; his thick knuckles were covered in faded tattoos. "I guess in the end it didn't amount to jack."

"And here you are now, seeing if I'll agree to the same terms?"

"Well," Mark said, and nodded to the Priest, "from what Dietrich described, you and me, we want the same thing. Something that Marcus and Seth didn't so much as care about."

"And what is that?"

"… The world."

Karl reflected for a moment and then looked right into Mark's eyes. Mark seemed to quiver, and then Karl let out a laugh that made everyone at the table jolt.

"Ha!" he exclaimed, and patted Mark heavily on the shoulder. "Right answer, Mister Rothstein. Perhaps we can work something out. You have a head on your shoulders; I'll give you that. I'll need a full assessment of your numbers, armaments, and available resources. As far as treaties, I will dictate the terms, and you can either accept them or decline. It's as simple as that. They'll be fair, I assure you."

Mark exchanged glances with his men and said, "We'll listen."

"But first," Karl continued, "tell me about the other town, the one that's closer, with running water."

"I think it would be best for these men here to tell you." Mark motioned to his two colleagues, sitting beside the silent Michael Rogers. One was a wretched-looking man with deep scars running down his face and a chewed-up ear, named Laurence. The other was a tall black man with long, skinny dreadlocks tied together at his shoulder blades. "Laurence here was a citizen of that town, but for all intents and purposes, they believe he has disappeared while scouting for supplies. What he found was us, and we share an opinion about what's best for his establishment, which his people will be opposed to."

"And what opinion is that?" Karl asked.

"Laurence, and many of his colleagues, believe survival can only be had through aggressive tactics and campaigns. Others don't see it that way."

Laurence nodded and said, "I know the ins and outs of that town like the back of my hand. If I was to come back, they'd open the gates for me, sure as shit."

"And why is that?" Karl asked. "I would think it suspicious if one of my men up and vanished, and then came back after we presumed he'd disappeared."

"They'll open 'cause I'll tell 'em to open. I was one of the original founders, under command of President Clark."

"President? Ha! Who would want such an archaic title?"

"They're not a soldiering bunch," Laurence said. "Beyond some defenses, they don't amount to much in terms of fighting. They've been lucky. The way the town sits, in the middle of the woods and far from cities, it hasn't seen extensive combat. That's made them think they're impervious to attack. They got scouts that go out to round up anyone they can, even the weak and frail."

"So tell me, Laurence, why are you leaving them? It would seem you have a good thing going. Plenty of food and water, shelter. But yet, here you are, betraying the security of the people you've lived with."

"Those people," Laurence said, crossing his arms over his chest, "don't amount to nothing. I helped found the settlement, and instead of President Clark listening to me, building our fighting force, scouting for arms and supplies, he cowers behind the walls. The way I see it, I have two choices: either wait for a force such as yours to invade and slit my throat; or, I can be on the winning side of the battle, and partner with the likes of your people here. The president and his men, they got brains, they're a sharp group, but they know nothing of warfare. Very few behind those walls do. Over half are elderly, sick, injured, or maimed. He's running a charity, where the majority of the people can't contribute."

Karl nodded. "So tell me, what are their numbers?"

"Last I knew, close to six hundred. About half are the cripples and such. About two hundred, a little less, see things our way. Despite the large stockpile of food, we're just waiting for someone to come steamrolling through, taking it all and leaving us dead. The rest are loyal to the president. Some can fight, but most are soft and meek people who belong behind desks. They survived this long by riding on the backs of hardworking people like you and me. They can design walls and keep the water running, but they can't protect any of it."

"All right," Karl said. "So the ones who see things our way, will they join us? Will they give it all up; fight against their fellow man, such as what has happened here in the bunker?"

"Sir." Laurence leaned his elbows on the table. "If they got something to fight for, someone to lead them, they're ripe for it. It ain't natural living behind walls like that, just think'n about death and knowing how fragile life is. Aside from the scouts, the rest of those people never venture out. They've grown stir-crazy. If we don't invade and lead them in mutiny, they're liable to revolt on their own for no other reason than they've gone plum mad, and burn the place to the ground. Many of them, and I know this for a fact, can't wait to see President Clark dead. They'll take up arms against him without hesitation."

Karl nodded and the table went silent. After a moment Mark spoke up. "And that brings us to our next subject." He motioned to the dreadlocked man, sitting beside Laurence. The man leaned his muscular forearms on the table, smiling a mouthful of blazing white teeth.

"What was your name again, King or something?" Karl asked.

"Sultan," the man said. "And what I got for you, General, ohh ... you gonna like it, my man."

"Sultan," Mark Rothstein cut in, "is a delegate from another settlement far to the east, closer to Alice. His brigade is perhaps the largest force we've yet encountered. He is here with a hundred and fifty of his soldiers, camped with ours."

"We hold a military shipyard," Sultan said.

"All right, Sultan," Karl said. "Go on."

"Us at the docks, we've been aware of Laurence's settlement since its inception, and of Alice a short ways to our south, although we're pretty sure they know nothing of us. We've even sent small expeditions up against both of their defenses, to see how they'd manage. Alice is impenetrable, for now. But Laurence's town, we know their strengths and weaknesses, and our little melees have softened them up a bit. Remember, they're not getting any bigger. But us, the three of us here in this room, well, we got numbers. Real numbers. Together, we'd be unstoppable."

"I'm listening."

"What we need," Mark said, "is a plan. You and Dietrich, you took this bunker with minimal casualties. You fight not only with fists, but with your minds."

Karl nodded but didn't answer.

Mark continued. "Together, we can take Laurence's town, no problem; but we're hoping to do it with minimal bloodshed. That's why we want to discuss a strategy with you."

"After the town is ours," Sultan said, "I'll take you east, to my people. We got things to discuss there." Sultan went on to explain his colony and gave a brief overview of why they wanted Karl to meet them, although he knew little of their actual proposal.

When he was finished, Karl said, "Alice ... is what I want. Alice is what we need to survive. It is the end result of everything else that we do. We can enslave their people to maintain the gardens, and live a full and prosperous life."

The men all nodded.

"Give me the details of this town we're to attack first."

Laurence stood and unrolled a map on the table, holding the bounding corners.

"There." Mark pointed to a black dot surrounded by green woods. "Odyssey."

Chapter Ten
Harvest

After an hour of respite following the miles of marching, the army was back on its feet, continuing east. On Mark's advice, Karl decided against scavenging in Nashville, which was out of the way.

"Nothin' there," Mark said. "We spent a week goin' street to street. Even the bones are picked clean by the crows."

The march continued for days, passing through small and dilapidated towns, nothing more than morgues, and across large patches of previously farmed lands. In the evenings Karl, Liam, the Priest, Mark, Sultan, and Laurence went over maps and strategy, until the layout of Odyssey was burned into their memories.

On a flat stretch of land, they came to a field of wheat grown wild. The lead scouts swung machetes to hasten their pace, and the men behind collected the dry, chest-high stalks. In similar fashion, the army found fields of corn, but to their dismay, the ears were rotten and infested with plump white grubs and patches of mold. Some in the group ate the kernels anyway, and succumbed to stomach cramping and diarrhea. A few experienced varying degrees of hallucinations along with pangs of both pleasure and dread that were surreal in nature.

"Ergot," Doctor Freeman said, examining a patient's eyes. "Don't eat the corn."

A field of soybeans offered the largest reward, despite the majority of the plants having withered. The ones that were still alive were ripe with plump, elongated pods.

A day's march after harvesting the soybeans, the army came to a flat field that stretched to the horizon, covered in low shriveled plants set in rows.

Karl smiled.

"What are you so happy about?" Liam asked. "They're all dead."

"That building there." Karl pointed to a barn the size of a warehouse and tugged at his horse's reins. They rode to the building and dismounted as a soldier pulled the sliding door open. Before he took a step inside, a pungent odor drifted out.

"Ah, would you look at this?" Karl said, going to a large bale of dried and brown leaves. More sat in orderly piles, and even more hung from drying racks and from the rafters.

The officers entered first, and then the men pressed eagerly forward.

"Tobacco," Liam said.

"Yes, Mister Briggs. All of it."

"Holy mother of God."

Karl crumbled a leaf in his hand and took a deep breath.

"Open the doors at the opposite end, and let the men pass through in a line to take their fill. There's enough to last a lifetime."

When Karl and the officers had taken all they could manage to stuff in their sacks, the men made their pass, and all began attempting to roll the tobacco, mostly to fruitless frustration. Those who knew how to do it began rolling cigars of various sizes, and the men removed their gear and sat around like children playing with a new toy.

Karl lit a cigar and inhaled the rich smoke, sitting with his back against the side of the barn. A moment later, a man came running through the company.

"Sir," he said, out of breath, "we got movement."

"Where?" Karl was on his feet so fast that the man stumbled back.

"Th-there. Up there, by the shed."

Karl looked to a modest wooden shed, where a group of his men were standing in the doorway. He stomped to the building, Liam and Mark at his side, all three men trailing tobacco smoke.

The soldiers parted for them to enter. The walls were lined with an assortment of old and rusted shovels, tampers, and rakes. Spider webs connected one tool to the other. In the middle of the floor, before the circle of men, was a metal trapdoor. Loose hay and straw was swept aside.

Karl bit at his cigar, rolling a loose strand of tobacco around on his tongue.

"We saw something up by the house," the soldier said. "Just a flash of movement. By the time we realized he wasn't one of us, the guy was at the door to the shed."

Liam leaned over and grabbed the handle, but it didn't budge. "The metal is thin," he said. "Wasn't built to withstand a bombing."

"What we have here is homemade," Karl said. "Open it."

A man came forward holding a pry bar, his hands and face covered in layers of grime. The rest of the men readied their guns and scuffled about in anticipation. The end of the pry bar fit in the rut between the door and the floor, and the soldier pressed his weight down, his face contorting with effort. Another man joined him, and they pressed and lumbered their weight against the metal rod. The door creaked and bent.

"Oh, for Christ's sakes," Karl said, and flung his still burning cigar out the door. A soldier at the doorway ducked as it trailed by. "Move." He pushed the men out of the way, feeling their body heat radiating from the effort. He gripped the cold metal, gritted his teeth, and pressed down. Every muscle in his body flexed, and the bar seemed to bend as he strained. The dry heat inside the shed was stifling, and a layer of sweat rose fast on his skin.

Without warning, the door popped free and the pry bar hit the floor, scraping Karl's knuckles. A metallic clinging sound echoed up from the hole, as what Karl guessed was the padlock dropped down the entry shoot. The men aimed their rifles and stared into the foreboding abyss.

Karl tossed the pry bar and patted his pockets for a roll of tobacco leaves.

"Well?" he said, maneuvering the leaves between his fingers. "Get on with it."

The men looked to one another, then someone produced a flare. He sparked it to life and tossed it down the hole. Without hesitating the first man descended the ladder with a second fast behind him. The lead man called down, "If you got yourself a gun, you'd better aim it elsewhere." Before reaching the bottom, they jumped to the ground and swung their rifles around. A third and fourth man followed, and then Karl stepped to the ladder. He heard shouting as he went down, his men yelling, "Drop it! Drop it!"

Flashlights were turned on, and as Karl stepped over the burning flare, he lit a fresh cigar, rolling the end in the flame to get an even burn. He stared at a filthy, feral man at the other end of the narrow enclosure, holding a bolt-action rifle. The man looked back at him, his eyes twitching from one soldier to the other, his mouth agape behind a scraggly beard.

"Who-who …" was all the man could say. The rifle trembled in his hands, and his whole body shook. A dark spot spread from the front of his pants.

"Easy now," a soldier said.

Liam and Mark joined Karl and stood behind him with pistols drawn. The soldiers continued to press in, and the man paced back until he hit the wall.

"Oh, for the love of …" Karl stepped forward and snatched the barrel of the gun, twisting it from the man's grip. The man just stood shaking, his eyes fluttering as if he'd pass out. Someone found a lantern, and the small room illuminated. There was a dingy couch beside Karl, and a table with a folding chair further in the room, with a hot plate and a mound of crusty cookware atop. A cot hung on the opposite wall, with a soiled blanket and pillow. The bunker extended about twenty feet to a door in the rear, and the men approached it with guns at the ready.

"You know," Karl said to the man, "this didn't have to go all that bad for you. What's your name?"

The man opened his mouth and then closed it.

"If you had displayed yourself in a more courageous demeanor, then perhaps you could have joined rank with the brotherhood."

The man looked at him, his wet eyes pleading.

"No," Karl said and grabbed the man's bicep, his fingers touching around the thin bone. "You're not worth the effort to beef up."

"I-I can fight."

Liam began to laugh and so did the rest. Karl pressed against the man's chest until he sat backwards onto the couch.

"Stay there," Karl said. "Don't move."

The soldiers who had entered the rear room returned.

"Some supplies and a generator. No fuel. He's got a mess of bullets for that rifle, but nothing more."

"Food?"

"Some shelves of canned goods, and plenty of water for one person."

"If you have all that," Karl said to the man on the couch, "why not eat it, put some meat on those bones?"

"Not-not enough."

"Not enough what?"

"Food."

"You have plenty."

"Gotta make it last." His filthy shirt bobbed up and down with his sporadic breathing.

"There's never enough, but if you'd ventured out farther than this little shithole of a room, you'd know there's always more. Just a day's ride west are acres of soy."

"I ... never, never enough ..."

"You've gone plumb mad, haven't ya?"

The man didn't respond.

Liam spat to his side. "Can I just fuckin' end this?" He patted his combat knife.

Karl laughed and said, "I might just take him along for entertainment. Keep him trailed to my horse."

"You ... no, please ..." the man said.

Karl stood in contemplation, everyone watching him.

"What the fuck are you all doing? Get moving. It stinks down here."

All at once, the men began filling boxes with the bottles of water, cans of peaches and beef stew, the bottles of propane, the ammunition, and the man's rifle. They found a .22 pistol and a box of bullets in a kitchen cabinet, and Karl inspected the barrel and cylinder before tucking it in his belt. When everything had been ransacked and removed, with the man not moving from the couch, his head hung low, Karl tossed his cigar to the floor and twisted it out with his toe. He waved his hand at the drifts of smoke.

"Leave some water," Karl instructed. "And a sponge, right next to that bucket there."

The soldiers looked confused, but did as they were told.

"Why ... what are you going to do to me?" the man asked.

Karl walked to the ladder.

"Me? I'm not going to do anything. If it weren't for the pressing need of my men's satisfaction, I would simply toss a beam of wood over the door and nail it shut. See if being caged alone in the dark for eternity makes you become something of a man and muster the strength to break free of your confinement."

"No. My God … please."

"Relax," Karl said, and went up the ladder followed by the rest of the soldiers. Liam turned to close the door, but Karl shook his head. "Leave it open. Let the stink ventilate out a bit. He likes it as fresh as possible."

Karl issued a command to a nearby soldier, and ordered everyone to clear the area. He puffed at another cigar as he waited, enjoying the burn in his throat. Across the field, by the mass of his army, a single man walked toward him. When he was in earshot, Karl said, "Right here, ol' sport."

"Sir?" Doctor Freeman walked up, clutching his satchel.

"As part of our continued pact, I present you with an offering." He motioned toward the bunker door. "Bob is down there, awaiting your arrival."

"His name's Bob?"

Karl shrugged. "Sure, why not."

"Is he clean?"

"I left a bucket, sponge, and water at the base of the landing. There's a lantern, and his propane stove still has some fuel."

The doctor moved his satchel to his other hand.

"You have one hour until we move out," Karl said. "Make the most of it. He's all bone anyway."

Doctor Freeman nodded and swung his feet onto the ladder. He proceeded down the entryway, and Karl watched the glow of the lantern illuminate from within. A moment later, a quiet trail of violins and cellos rang out from the doctor's portable stereo.

Karl turned and left, joining his officers beside the field. He was passed a bottle of dark liquor, and took a hearty swallow. For a moment, he thought he heard screaming in the distance, but it might have been a flight of birds.

***

The exhilaration was palpable in the increased conversation and quickened pace as the army entered the lush, green terrain of the mountains.

They slept that night in the deep thicket of woods, and Karl ordered no fires to be made, as they were within a mile of Odyssey. In the morning, a blanket of fog hugged the earth, rolling through the trees on the mountain like something alive.

The officers proceeded on foot into the wilderness. The earth swept up and down over hills both shallow and tall, and it wasn't long until Laurence whispered, "Quiet now," and they climbed up an embankment to an overlook at the top.

They crawled on their bellies, each man holding binoculars. The thick canopy of pine trees worked as cover.

"That's it," Laurence said. "Odyssey."

Chapter Eleven
Hellfire

The town of Odyssey was nestled in a valley, surrounded by tall mountain peaks as if it were inside the basin of a bowl. From their vantage point, Karl and the officers could see a good portion of the layout.

Whispers of smoke rose and dissipated in the air from a dozen campfires hidden from view behind buildings, and men carrying rifles were visible on rooftops beside the main road and bordering the vicinity in a ring. Makeshift bunkers were constructed on the taller buildings, with many additional lookouts extending from the tops. From what Laurence reported, there were a total of six towers, complete with snipers and machine-gun turrets. An assault from over the mountain could be effective, but they would be exposed on the sheer mountainside, and it would be slow to climb down.

"Liam," Karl said to his captain. "What do you make of this?"

Liam cleared his throat, peering out from the binoculars. "There's no easy way in. It's best to stick with the plan that we got."

They reversed down the embankment and made their way back to camp.

That evening, as Karl held counsel with his officers, a hunter returned holding the back legs of a plump raccoon. He proceeded to skin and butcher the animal, and the meat was roasted in chunks over a small flame, issuing dark swells of greasy smoke. The officers ate with appetite, tossing the little bones into the brush.

After their meal, the campfire was smothered, and soon Karl fell into a fast and deep sleep. At dawn, a young private named Ryan Pechman came into his room, saying, "It's time, sir."

The man was shooed away, and Karl stood and stretched. He dressed in clean, dark-green army fatigues and polished his boots before stepping out into the damp morning air.

Laurence waited outside along with the Priest, and when Karl arrived, they nodded.

"Sir," they said. "The men are ready."

Karl yawned. "Let's get on with it then. Are you prepared, Laurence? If you feel this plan is at all in folly, this is our last chance to reconsider."

Laurence shook his head. "It'll work. Like I've said, President Clark and the counsel are a soft bunch. They know nothin' of fighting. Hell, they dress themselves in button-down shirts and running sneakers, like it's just another fuckin' day at the office. Never venture outside the gates themselves. He'll send the army out, practically delivering them to us, if I tell 'im it's worth it."

"And he'll be willing do that, sight unseen?"

"It'll be seen, 'cause I'll tell 'im it's seen. That's my job, to scout out anything worth lootin' and send the army to go forage."

"Very well then."

Laurence turned and began his trek alone toward Odyssey. The officers turned the opposite direction to lead the army back out the way they'd arrived, to the pre-determined clearing right outside of the entrance to the woods. Laurence had a lot to accomplish in a short period of time. First, he had to convince the leadership that he'd been lost out west, to justify his absence. Then he was to persuade President Clark that he'd seen a group of vile men camped beside a broken-down convoy, which appeared to have been transporting fuel. Laurence was to explain that he'd seen from afar that the group of men, about thirty or so, had prisoners, women and children tied with ropes, disheveled and downtrodden. Appealing to President Clark's good-natured disposition, Laurence would convince him to send out his loyalist army to eradicate the miscreants, free the prisoners, and take the fuel. Out in the open, Karl's army could deal with the more experienced soldiers away from the town's defenses before storming the gates.

As President Clark's army was being mustered, Laurence would then have to find and organize the citizens he knew would rebel against the current authority. Their numbers would be low, not enough to take the town on their own; but that was not their objective. They were to wait until Karl and the

Red Hand army were near the gates, and then help eliminate or subdue the soldiers standing guard in the lookout towers, machine-gun posts, and atop the walls. To aid them were the dozens of snipers who had left in the night to scale the surrounding mountains, and were sitting high atop rocky perches.

Before sundown, Odyssey would fall.

***

The horses snorted plumes of steam that evaporated in the damp morning air. Karl Metzger sat atop his pale stallion on the crest of a hill that overlooked the advancing army, just a twinkle in the far distance emerging from the woods. Beside him, Mark Rothstein stroked his long red beard.

"They're coming right at us," he said.

Karl turned to Liam. "Ready the men."

"Yes, sir." Liam tugged at the reins. "Come on now," he told the stallion, and trotted down the embankment.

Karl raised his binoculars and watched the kicked-up dust on the horizon, trying to estimate their numbers and machinery. There were vehicles, but he assessed by their slow advance that most were on foot.

"All is not lost until pale death lays its shadowy fingers over my eyes," he mumbled to himself, surprised at hearing this strange verse come up from the depths of his memories. He chuckled and turned to the officers waiting behind him. "Keep watch," he said, and led his steed down from the crest until he came to a ridge of land overlooking his army in the gull of the rocky terrain. They were a scramble of activity: dusty glooms going this way and that, preparing trenches on either side to stop the enemy from flanking their position. Taking up the rear was Doctor Freeman with the rest of the medical brigade, double-checking their pouches of gauze and painkillers.

Karl guided his horse through the throng, some of the men stopping to say, "Sir," as he passed. When he reached the doctor, he strode up beside him.

"Arthur," he said. "We'll be seeing a fair share of bloodshed. Are your men ready?"

"Yes," the doctor replied.

"Good." Karl sighed and let out a low laugh. "It's funny," he continued, "just a moment ago I remembered something my grandfather used to say."

"What's that?"

"All is not lost until pale death lays its shadowy fingers over my eyes."

The doctor stopped checking his gauze pouch and looked at Karl. "Your grandfather told you that?"

"The man was a religious fanatic. If it's from the Good Book, the verse is unknown to me. By all accounts, he enjoyed making up his own spiritual acknowledgments and played them off as something wholly divine."

"Hmm," the doctor said.

"You know, that's why I always liked you—you're a hell of a listener."

Doctor Freeman pushed his glasses up the bridge of his nose and looked at Karl through his dark eyes. "You got any family left?"

"No, Arthur. No family."

"No one has any family left."

"Not true, sir. Not true. Here in this valley are our brethren. Better than the family we were given at birth. Am I wrong in saying so?"

Doctor Freeman shrugged.

Through the cluster of men, Liam appeared, trotting his horse up to meet them.

"We got less than twenty minutes. Let's get in position. What the hell are you guys talking about?"

"Aye aye, Mister Briggs," Karl said, pulling the reins of his horse.

A command was shouted from the front and repeated down the lines.

"Position check! Position check!"

The men stopped digging their foxholes and jumped into the shallow depressions, feeding their assortment of large caliber machine guns, and pulling back the bolts to arm their weapons.

Karl heeled his horse and hurried back up to the crest of the rocky hill to check the advancing party, with Liam in tow.

A shot fired out from the valley, and Sergeant Novell, standing two over from Karl on the vantage point, dropped. More shots rang out and the men recoiled. "They're breaking off their approach," Karl issued. "The main attack will be from the north, but they will flank both sides of the hill. Fall back into position. Everyone." He turned to face his army, hiding behind the massive rock formation, waiting for the enemy brigade to come around the bend and find themselves at odds with the force of the Red Hands.

Karl took up position on the front, and looked to his rear to see Mark and his army holding the opposite flank. They were a rough assortment of outcasts, most of which belonged to various biker gangs that had squashed their rivalries in the face of mass-extinction, and came together under Mark's leadership and authority. They lacked the finesse of military order, but took to violence with a particular revelry that made Karl know their virtues.

"Hold," Karl said, hearing the roar of the coming army. Bullet shots echoed from the snipers scattered atop the mountainous rock and from the invading men shooting back at them.

The soldiers at Karl's side and all around him squatted low, pressed to the walls of their shallow dugouts, their teeth clenched, the air thick with impending war. Somewhere in the rear a voice was heard in happy song, and Karl knew the Priest was conducting his symphony of the damned, psalms for the wicked, to his waiting cavalry.

Two jeeps rumbled around the bend, machine guns mounted to the beds, and the enemy issued a howling war cry that echoed loud against the hulking rock formation. Two more jeeps came into view, and as they opened fire, Karl yelled, "Artillery!"

Bullet fire erupted from the line, peppering the automobiles in plunks, with splinters and twisted metal spiraling through the air. Mortars rained down as the bulk of the enemy came around the bend. Then their front line saw the mass they were up against and stopped short, trying to turn, but pressed on by the unaware mob in their rear.

If presented the opportunity, Karl and his men did quite well with this tactic of baiting the enemy out of their encampments to charge what they presumed to be a small brigade.

The crackling of bullet fire from behind Karl suggested that the enemy had also emerged from around the other side of bluff, and Mark's men were unleashing their fury.

Some among the line fell as bullets whizzed by, and plumes of dirt shot into the air from the land before them. Shouts yelled out for the medics, and Doctor Freeman and his men arrived, dragging away the injured to makeshift tents in the rear.

The battle itself lasted mere minutes before what was left of the adversaries turned back and beat upon the valley in hastened retreat. The jeeps that preceded their advance sat in ruin. Two caught fire, and as the mob ran, one exploded in a great ball of fire. Dark, almost black, greasy smoke consumed the vehicle. Several fleeing men were rocked to their sides and burned. Some attempted to stand again, while others lay unmoving.

A sniper above shouted, "They're pulling back!"

Karl yelled above the roar of warfare to Liam, who had stationed himself halfway up the hill to relay messages, "Numbers! What are their numbers?"

A moment later Liam yelled back, "No more than fifty!"

Karl got to his feet and turned to the reserve line behind him. He grabbed the reins of his stallion from a rotten-toothed boy. "Advance!" he yelled. "Advance!" Whistles blew and the army stood. Karl thrashed at the bridle, leading the procession with the Priest's mounted brigade, and the men shouted loud into the air at their impending victory, anticipating that fighting would soon be hand-to-hand.

The hooves of the horses beat against the soil, trailing a cloud of dust as the cavalry turned the bend and were quickly at the trailing deserters. A few fleeing enemies looked over their shoulders in horror, their expressions aghast. Some dropped to their knees with trembling arms covering their heads, or hands clasped before their chests in pleading prayer. Some fought on, turning to fire their weapons as the storm of returned munitions shredded their bodies to mists of red.

The cavalry overtook the small retreating numbers and the men on foot were fast to catch up, hundreds upon hundreds, all the reserves running forward to claw their way at the few enemy fighters left alive. Karl rode against a man standing tall, his rifle out before him. The man turned and swung his gun to fire, but Karl struck a heavy boot against the man's skull.

The army was held up in the valley as the enemy soldiers were tied up, stripped of clothing, beaten, and spit on.

"Back in line!" Karl commanded, high atop his stallion. "Back in line!"

The officers repeated his command, shoving and kicking the men into submission, snapping them out of their hypnotic bloodlust. "To the town!" they declared.

The army fanned out in two columns, marching forward into the mountain pass. The cavalry, led by the Priest and Karl, took up the rear, their horses trotting to maintain the speed of the marching men. Mark Rothstein took up the far flank, separate so as to make their procession toward the encampment advance from two angles.

The gates of Odyssey came into view through the towering pines. Shots rang out from behind the walls, and a few dropped from the advancing line, or stopped to hold bleeding limbs. The army quickened its advance, and as bullets continued to pepper the ground and smack at tree limbs, the first explosion was heard inside the town. A plume of smoke erupted into the air like a geyser. A second explosion followed, and a tall guard tower combusted into fiery splinters. The enemy gunfire lessened.

Karl gave the command, "Open fire!" The outer wall of the colony was fractured to shreds of wood and the guards atop the platform evaporated. Karl heeled his mount and the men ran to lay siege, flooding over the villagers like hellfire come alive.

Chapter Twelve
Butchers

Tables and chairs were taken from Odyssey's Masonic lodge and brought outside into the clearing of an adjacent park. A commemorative bronze statue of a World War I soldier stood in the middle. A bonfire was constructed, and the men fed the flames using anything that would burn.

Bushels of produce and pallets of canned goods were brought out from the storeroom and dumped on the tables. A small farm was discovered on the outskirt of town, and before it could be put under guard, three chickens and two lambs were slaughtered, roasted over small flames, and devoured on the spot, half-raw. The guards shooed the men away from the remaining livestock, and Karl sent for the army's butchers to prepare a proper meal.

Alcohol was produced in quantity, and in the early evening the revelry grew to a height. At the center of it all sat Karl Metzger, Liam Briggs, the Priest, Mark Rothstein, and Sultan. The Priest had sustained an injury from the fighting, a burst of shrapnel that came close to taking his eye out. Doctor Freeman set up an emergency triage in a little church, whose decrepit wood and uniquely carved architecture, with peels of white paint, gave evidence to its age. A wooden, handwritten sign outside the structure read:

Historic Church of the Lamb
Preserved

That same church had been used as an office by the prior leadership, and their blood still soaked the dry, thirsty floor.

Earlier, as the Red Hands dealt with the last bit of fighting, Karl and Laurence convened in the church. Seven of Odyssey's former officials lined the wall, including President Clark, all kneeling with their hands on their heads. The rest of the officials were taken as prisoners, but these men and women were the top leaders and advisors. The president's crisp button-down shirt was untucked, and strings of blood stained the front, dripping from his broken nose. Colored light filtered in through strips of stained glass, casting bright hues along the dark woodwork.

"You son of a bitch," the president said in a huff to Laurence. "I trusted you—you were a friend!" Spittle shot from his mouth and trailed down his chin.

Karl rolled his eyes, leveled his pistol, and fired. The president's head jolted and a red mist covered the floor.

The rest of the leadership shrieked, and Laurence and a group of his separatists opened fire. The line of Odyssey's leadership dropped, the wall behind them burst into splinters.

Now outside the Masonic lodge, guards brought out the rest of Odyssey's former officials to stand before Karl, their wrists bound behind their backs, gags stuffed in their mouths. Their eyes screamed at the terror all around them. The drunken Red Hands hollered and threw empty bottles, animal bones, and rocks at their approach. Most were already bloodied, their clothing torn, and two had been stripped naked. They shivered despite the warm evening breeze. They had been thoroughly interrogated, and shared the location of several smaller colonies that were marked down on a map to be saved for leaner times.

Mark got to his feet and raised a glass. "Quiet!" he yelled, and repeated the command until the clamor lessened.

"We're here," he said, and turned to Karl, "because of this man, who devised this strategy and saw it through. We achieved victory because of his leadership, and I see nothing but a long and happy accord between our joined forces. So, it's come time … my men—*line up!*"

The crowd scuffled in something of an orderly fashion, and the men belonging to Mark's brigade formed a line.

Mark unsheathed his long rosewood-handled machete, and held the blade high so the metal dazzled in the firelight. The line of prisoners glanced his way, sputtering into their gags, and as Mark stood behind the man on the end and crashed the blade down upon him, the rest of the prisoners howled and some attempted to stand before being kicked into submission.

Three of Mark's men removed blades of their own, and in a skillful fashion they proceeded up the line. Two prisoners fainted, and were slapped awake before being added to the slaughtered. Sultan stood from his table and joined the massacre, shouting orders for his men to line up. The Priest followed, standing on unsteady legs. The doctor had given him the largest dose of painkillers possible.

Ten more prisoners were brought out, and in quick succession, they too were disposed of. Mark, the Priest, and Sultan wiped the dripping broad sides of their blades over their palms and held their hands out high.

"It's an honor," Mark shouted, his eyes locked with Karl's, "to be joining a brotherhood such as this order. We follow you, General Metzger, leader of this fine band of butchers." He slapped his hand over his chest, and each man in line followed suit, taking an oath to Karl Metzger.

The Priest smiled and proclaimed, "Let it be known that I follow the Lord above all else, but on this mortal earth, my path shall be in congruence with General Metzger as a member of his fierce Red Hands."

Karl sat at the table before them, sipping at a bottle of whiskey.

Dozens, if not over a hundred more prisoners sat shackled, awaiting their fate. Karl whispered to Liam for long poles to be sharpened, crucifixes to be constructed, and ropes to be strung up. These implements were to be mounted on both sides of the entrance leading into Odyssey, and continue down the central lane of the town. Festivities would last all night. Karl would allow his men to celebrate for days to come, but the officers would be needed to begin plans for the next incursion. This victory in Odyssey was nothing more than a step toward the conclusion: invading Alice, and claiming the gardens and reservoir as their own.

Karl found a cigar on the table and lit it, staring over the sea of faces, hundreds of demonic eyes reflecting the leaping flames of the bonfire. This was his army, his legion of horribles, and they would follow him into the depths of hell and massacre all who stood in their way.

Chapter Thirteen
Captain Black

Cold fall nights came early, after an extended duration of late summer rain. It was decided that the army would wait until the spring to travel east to the docks. On the way, they would invade and conquer the town of Masterson, where they had scouted a weak settlement ripe for the taking. Sultan sent a delegate of men to his port city, informing the commander to await their arrival as the seasons changed in the coming months.

Messengers continued to travel back and forth between the settlements, all the way west to Marianna and Haddonfield Maximum Security Prison. However, as fall turned to a cold and bitter winter, long-range scouting trips were halted. Come spring, all settlements were instructed to send the bulk of their soldiers to Odyssey in preparation for the attack on Alice.

The soldiers in Odyssey spent their days indoors, as the bowl-like formation of the land sent shrill winds howling down from the mountaintops. Fires burned around the clock in steel drums, and a large bonfire in the park outside the Masonic lodge warmed the men gathered after being fed the slop-stew from the building's kitchen.

On one warmer than average evening, Karl called his men to gather in the lodge's field, where a makeshift stage had been constructed. An aged bronze statue of a marching soldier with his bayonetted rifle gripped tight adorned the center of the square. To maintain morale, a series of promotions had been planned. Among those being promoted was the elder Sergeant Black, a rightful captain in the Canadian army who had disavowed his rank after society collapsed.

As the men made their slow procession, Karl and Sergeant Black spoke beside the heat of the bonfire.

"It don't mean nothing," Sergeant Black said. "Rank, title. Just words. You want to do it, go ahead. Suppose the men will find something admirable in the motion. As long as you keep me training the troops, I don't give a damn what my stature is."

Karl smiled and said, "Sergeant, no one can keep the men in such combative vigor as yourself. You have a way of directing the human spirit that no other can match. Your new title may be only that, words; but to the men, it means something more. It shows authority and respect. Something to strive for, if nothing else."

Sergeant Black adjusted his wide-brimmed hat. "Speaking of authority, I think there's something you ought to know ... something I've just learned. This may not be the best time to bring it up, seeing as we're about to address the men, but it's imperative. Some of the soldiers, well, they've been talking behind your back—"

Karl whipped his head around to face him. "Talk of what?"

"Mutiny, sir."

"*Mutiny?* Ungrateful bastards ... how many?"

"Just a few that I know of. They think we'd be better off staying put come fall. No more marching. No more fighting. They don't give a damn about the port town and Alice—they want to become sedentary."

"No more fighting?" Karl patted his front pocket and found a cigar. "What kind of a world ..." He paused to light the end with a wooden match, taking in puffs. "What kind of a world do they think we're living in?"

"I don't know, sir."

"Who told you this?"

"Private Pechman, sir. He overheard some men talking, and informed me just this morning."

"Pechman, huh?"

"Yes, sir. It's being orchestrated by Michael Rogers, from Lieutenant Rothstein's division. There's always been something about him ... an unwillingness to march in procession ... an objectionable look."

"I know the man. He was second in command under Mister Rothstein prior to our merger. On my insistence, he was demoted to the fighting ranks before we marched on Odyssey."

"I was gonna wait to tell you until I knew more, but seeing how such things can spread like wildfire, I thought it best you should know right away."

"Indeed. *No more fighting* ... what that idiot doesn't realize is that maintaining the water filtering plant is no easy task, and the reservoir is well below where it should be to support our numbers. Come summer, Odyssey may not be able to house our army. Marching, continuing the fight, is a necessity." Karl patted his soon-to-be captain on his shoulder and began walking toward the platform, where the men were mustered and idling about, rubbing their palms together to keep warm.

Karl stood tall before the podium, and kept his words short. Sergeant Black was promoted to captain, and afterward, Karl looked out over the gathering.

"Private Ryan Pechman," he shouted, scanning the hundreds of faces and clenching his still-burning cigar in his teeth. "Join me onstage, please."

After a moment of uncertainty, the men glancing around, the young private appeared, pushing through the throng of soldiers until he reached the steps and stood before Karl.

"Such valiant effort in battle," Karl said to the young man, "cannot go unnoticed. Pechman here has displayed not only loyalty, but a courageousness that musters his fellow man. I know this, for I have fought beside him and witnessed his fierce determination. It is befitting that you are given the title of sergeant."

As Karl spoke, a bitter wind howled, and the army in the field stood hunched over, noses red and dripping, pulling up the collars of their frayed jackets and stuffing their hands in their pockets. Their thin gloves were full of holes, and those who did not possess woolen hats wore strips of material wrapped around their heads and faces, their eyes peering out like dark slits.

Sergeant Pechman saluted, and Karl noticed how clean the young man kept his uniform. His pants were ironed, his boots polished, and the strip of red cloth tied around his arm was vibrant. With the absence of red paint, the men had taken to using material to differentiate themselves from their enemies in battle, and many wore strips of torn, red cloth over their upper arms, or tied around weapons. This trend began soon after Odyssey fell, and Karl found it so appealing to see his men cast in a red hue, and the material blowing in the wind tied below spear points, that he encouraged every man to adorn himself in such a way.

The ceremony concluded, and the men were dismissed.

"Captain," Karl said, as Captain Black put his battered cavalry hat back on his head. "A moment, please."

"Sir?"

Karl led him to the edge of the podium. "I want the men to begin training tomorrow morning. They need activity, movement."

Captain Black looked up at the overcast sky, the heavens full of dark rolling clouds.

"We're fixin' for a storm, by my perception. It would do them good to sludge through the elements. Harden them up some."

"Look at them," Karl said, turning his gaze to the dispersing crowd. "They're growing weak, soft. Perhaps a foray will sharpen their spirits. We can march on Masterson sooner than planned if need be."

The captain shrugged. "I agree on all accounts about training. Gotta keep them sharp. But by my counsel, if we go marching to Masterson now, I reckon a third will die from exposure before we reach the gates."

Karl nodded. "Not Masterson then. What's that military base twenty miles south? The one we were going to raid come spring, that our colleagues hanging from lampposts on Main Street blabbed about."

"Fort Anderson?"

"Yes, Anderson. Have Pechman muster a squad, and include Michael Rogers and all other malcontents."

"Yes, sir. You aiming to kill them?"

Karl took the last puff of his cigar and flung the end in the bonfire. "Perhaps. I thought about killing them just now, on stage. It would have been good for morale. We'll see."

"Yes, sir. I'll have Pechman assemble a raiding party."

Karl nodded and walked off, spitting a piece of tobacco off his lip.

Chapter Fourteen
BB Guns

Twenty-five men gathered in the stables, including Mark, the Priest, and the scout, Bishop. Michael Rogers was among them, along with the five other mutineers, looking nervous in their saddles. The Priest had recovered from his injuries, but his eyesight in his left eye was partial. He took to wearing an eye patch at all times, and was still struggling to regain his balance.

Karl joined them and saddled his horse, looming tall over the others as he issued, "Move out."

Two pickup trucks met them at the entrances, their engines rumbling loud in the quiet morning. The gates opened, and the men rode out, with Karl and Mark leading the march.

The Priest took up a hymnal tune, but the growl of the trucks kept his singing to a murmur. The mutineers had congregated to themselves, yet Karl never turned to face them. He rode on, his horse clomping the pavement under hoof.

Few automobiles littered the back roads they stuck to, but twice they had to push stalled cars out of the way for the trucks to ride by. They pulled the crusted corpses from the drivers' seats and tossed them to the pavement to put the cars in neutral.

The on-ramp to an interstate was packed with an innumerable number of vehicles, and one large moving truck was stalled among them. Karl led his horse to the back of the truck, eyeing the padlock.

"Open it," he said, and Mark unsaddled his horse. "Not you." Karl glanced behind him. "Mister Rogers. Open it."

Michael paused and licked his lips. All five of his compatriots stared at Karl.

"Is there a problem, Michael? I said to fucking open it."

"No-no, sir." Michael got down from his horse and took the bolt cutters from Mark. He slid the blade under the metal, and after a moment of straining, the handles clamped down, and the lock pieces fell to the pavement in a clatter.

Michael pulled the handle and opened the shutter door.

"What you got in there?" Karl asked.

"Don't know, sir."

"Go on and find out."

The gathering pressed in, and the two truck drivers killed the engines and stepped out of the cabs.

Michael looked over his shoulder, then turned back to the truck and hoisted himself inside the cavernous interior.

"Bunch of boxes," he said, then the sound of cardboard being cut open. He came out holding a soccer ball, still in its sales package. "Bunch of toys."

Karl turned to the group. "You there." He pointed to a man belonging to Michael's rebellion. "Help him out, would ya? And you four. Hurry up."

For a moment the men didn't budge, then one got down from his horse and the others followed. As they passed Karl, he could see the sweat forming on their foreheads despite the frigid afternoon breeze.

Box after box was ripped open and tossed out the back of the truck. Two of the men stood outside, moving the assortment of baseballs, lacrosse sticks, and volleyballs further to the side.

"Hey," echoed a voice from the truck. "Think we got something." The flickering light of a lighter bounced off the cabin walls. "This a gun?"

A man came out holding a rectangular box, opening it as he walked. "It's light."

"It's a BB gun," Mark said.

The man removed a black rifle from the box and a plastic pouch of lead BBs, tossing the cardboard to the ground.

"Give it here," Karl said, and the man handed it over.

"We got a mess of 'em."

"Good. Good. They'll do for birds. And Haddonfield is being overrun with starved rats the size of dogs. The men there can use some fresh meat." Karl played with the pump and action as the men unloaded three boxes full of rifles, and continued going through the truck until it was unloaded.

In the end, they uncovered two boxes of thick woolen socks. They loaded their flatbeds and Michael jumped down from the back of the truck, his entourage beside him.

"Hold on there," Karl said. He looked to Mark and nodded. Mark turned to Sergeant Pechman and gave him a stare. Pechman got down from his horse, along with ten other men.

"Hand me your guns," Ryan Pechman told Michael.

The mutineers stepped back and the soldiers leveled their rifles.

Michael swallowed visibly, and after a moment the men began handing over their rifles. Karl spoke from atop his horse, "Let's cut to the chase, shall we?"

"What are you talking about?" Michael said.

"Oh, for fuck's sake," a man at Michael's side said. "We're sorry, all right? It was all him. All Michael. He's been talking about deserting for months, but then when we got to Odyssey—"

Michael turned sharply to the man. "Shut the fuck up, Frank!"

"He already knows." Frank turned to Karl, his palms together before his chest. "Karl, I'm sorry, for the love of God."

"You all want to leave, huh?" Karl swayed his finger before them, and the men shook their heads, saying, "No, no."

"It's Michael who's been thinking that way. We shoulda told you, Karl. We were only listening—"

Michael swung around with a fast right hook and walloped Frank square in the face. Frank's head jerked back, and he stumbled.

"Jesus!" Frank reached for his knife, but Michael grabbed him and they fell to the ground, arms wrapped around each other's necks.

Ryan Pechman and his men jumped forward to stop them, but Karl motioned for them to halt. "Let 'em at it."

The squad backed up, and the four men next to Michael and Frank moved aside as they rolled on the ground, hands searching for eyes and ears. Michael pulled his arm free and began hammering at Frank's head until Frank had no other choice but to shield his face with his forearms. Michael straddled him and pummeled his fists down, striking arms, face, hits glancing off to grind on the pavement. Yet he continued to wail away.

Frank's arms went slack as Michael continued, then Karl said, "That's enough."

Michael was grabbed and pulled off Frank's unmoving body, his face unrecognizable. The same could be said of Michael's knuckles.

"Disarm them," Karl commanded, and the mutineers were pushed to face the bumper of the truck and forced to put their palms upon it. They were patted down and small arms were pulled from pockets, sheaths, and ankle holsters.

Michael was still huffing and wriggling, and two men had to subdue him. The thick forearm of a soldier wrapped around Michael's neck until his face turned blue and he stopped resisting.

On Karl's instructions, they were stripped naked and their wrists were bound behind their backs. Two of the men struggled with their captors, yet the others somberly obeyed, saying things like, "Karl, we'll follow you. Karl …"

They shivered in the cold as one by one they were hoisted up and tossed inside the open truck like livestock to the slaughter. Karl peered inside, saw them jump to their feet at the shock of their exposed flesh against the cold metal floor.

Michael was lifted, his eyes wide and his jaw clenched. A trickle of blood trailed down his forehead.

"No," Karl said. "Not him."

The door was shuttered with the bound men running to the edge, yelling their apologies, swearing allegiance, and being prodded back by the tips of knives and machetes.

The locking handle was brought down, and a thick stick was worked into the eyehole where the padlock had been. Michael was tied to the tire, the rope around his neck made taut so that he could not lean forward more than half an inch.

He did not speak as the trucks started and the army took its course south.

Karl found a cigar and lit it. "If you're still alive when we get back, we'll bring you back to town for a proper trial. We are, after all, civilized. Are we not?" He tossed the extinguished match at Michael's chest, leaving a trail of smoke as it cascaded to the ground. "That's the last bit of warmth you'll ever feel."

Karl pulled at his horse's reins, and the stallion turned, snorting, the wiry muscles under its thick neck contracting.

***

The march continued until they paused before a tall black-metal fence. Bishop rode beside Karl, reading a map. His finger trailed over the page.

"You sure you know how to read that thing?" Mark said.

Bishop looked up. "Of course I do. We're here."

"No shit." Mark gestured to the fence, the tops arched forward and sharpened to points.

Bishop folded the map into his front pocket.

The locked chain-link doors bent as a pry bar worked its way in, until the lock snapped in half and the gates slid open.

"Hope they left us something," the Priest said, following Karl into the fort.

Karl glanced at the shrunken corpse inside the security booth, and the other slumped over the handle of a mounted machine gun behind a nest of sandbags. Both wore camouflaged hazmat suits, the material like deflated balloons around the bones.

"Why don't you give them a prayer, Mister Dietrich," Karl said.

The Priest opened his mouth, then Karl said, "I was being facetious. I don't think prayer will do much to help them now, do you?"

The Priest laughed. "The power of prayer is a worthy comrade in warfare, General. You'd be wise to heed its ways."

Karl's heart thumped fast. "I'd be wise to tie your naked ass up to a tire and leave you trembling in the wind."

The Priest, Mark, and Bishop chuckled, and the laughter followed down the line of men entering the base.

"I will pray for you then, Sir General, if you will not do so yourself."

"Please do," Karl said. "I need all the prayer I can get. When I was a child, locked away for all those years in a Christian correction institute, do you know how they prayed for my sins? All the priests and saintly teachers—do you know how they prayed for us wayward children?"

"Perhaps I'm better left wondering."

"Indeed."

The trucks rumbled in the rear, followed by the last four riders, and the men stopped before a series of drab, tan-colored buildings, all identical and rectangular in shape. Several of the windows were blackened, with dark soot marks in dancing array around the walls where fires had left their grimy residue.

"They fight here?" Bishop asked.

"No," Karl answered. "There are no bullet shells. No shredded corpses."

Bishop nodded.

There were machine-gun nests constructed at various points, some still manned by the soldiers in hazmat suits.

"Get to it," Karl instructed, and the men took to removing the machine guns and ammunition.

A soldier grabbed the back of a corpse leaning over the handle of a gun, gripped the plastic material of the suit, and dragged it aside. "Good thing these guys come in their own garbage bag," he said.

The men around him laughed, and the tripods and guns were disassembled and loaded on the backs of the truck, then the men divided to scour for what was left in the buildings. Karl rode around the property with Mark, and counted a total of six buildings and one large white dome in the rear, shielding some sort of radar.

"We're not going to find much," Mark said. "Just some ghosts." He looked down to a pile of body bags laid in orderly fashion beside the back fence.

When they'd circled back to the trucks parked out front, the men had piled anything of use on the flatbeds. Karl opened the corner of a cardboard box.

"Shirts," Bishop said. "A whole mess of long-sleeve shirts, and we got a few dozen pants, and some socks too."

Karl pulled a button-up camouflaged shirt from the box, feeling the coarse material between his fingers.

"Shirts, pants, and socks, all brand new. Not a bad haul. Anything else?"

"Some small arms and ammunition." Bishop pointed to a stack of rifles on the back of the truck. "The buildings are untouched. Looks like they were just setting this place up when the virus hit. There are boxes of electronics, mostly still packed."

A few minutes later, the men finished their haul. The trucks were started, and the procession turned back home.

***

It was nearing nightfall when they returned to the cargo truck and Michael Rogers. He remained unmoved, an obelisk of despair in the cold wind, his skin a pale shade of blue.

Karl rode out and studied his face. Clatter from inside the truck increased with his presence, and soon anguished voices began calling out for redemption.

Michael's eyes flickered.

"He's alive," Karl said, and laughed. "Oh, sweetie pie, are you chilly? Mister Rothstein, please, get this man a blanket. He's freezing."

Michael's body convulsed and his eyes faded back shut.

"Cut him down," Karl ordered.

Mark removed his binds, but the man did not collapse when the ropes were cut. They wrapped him in a blanket, and he hollered as his body was touched and moved.

"Oh, come on now. It's just a bit of frostbite. You're fine. Who needs extremities anyway?"

The men locked in the back of the truck banged against the walls, shouting and pleading as the procession moved off.

"Huddle together," Karl shouted over his shoulder. "We'll be back in a jiffy ... or maybe not."

Michael's hands were tied to a rope trailing to a horse's saddle, his fingers like blackened hooks, and a blanket was wrapped around his shoulders. They moved out, and over the miles he slipped and fell, and was forced to stand back up again.

It was night as they entered Odyssey, and a crowd grew at the gates. No one questioned the state of Michael Rogers. Captain Black had made sure that word was spread prior to their return.

On Karl's instructions, two men untied Michael from his binds and led him to the edge of the pond on the outskirts of town. A child's wooden sled was taken from the hardware store on the main street, and Michael was made to lie on it, then tied securely to the wooden planks. He did not protest. He did not utter a word as the ice around the shore was cracked away. He moaned as the sled was pushed, feetfirst, into the freezing waters, and slowly inched over his knees, groin, stomach, and chest, until his face and head were covered. After a moment he was brought back out and dragged, sled and all, to the stage on the commemorative grounds beside the Masonic lodge. A bonfire was lit and extra wood added. Michael rolled in and out of consciousness as Karl stood beside him, the boxes of plundered goods brought before his feet. The men gathered and cheered as the clothing was handed out, first to those whose attire was in dire need. Bottles of alcohol appeared, and a few men who knew how to play acoustic guitar took up impromptu performances, sitting on the podium with legs dangling.

Karl and the Priest stood to the side.

"Are you going to say anything about the popsicle there?" The Priest pointed to Michael, who had most likely expired.

"No need," Karl said. "His words preceded this action, as did the choices he and his associates made. The men understand."

Karl found a cigar and struck a wooden match to light it. Once lit, he flicked the extinguished match, and watched it trail a twisting descent of smoke until it disappeared into the bonfire.

Chapter Fifteen
Target Practice

The onset of spring brought unceasing rain, and in the intervals when the precipitation stopped, a heavy fog rolled in, cascading down the mountains like spilled milk. The air remained so vaporous that after only a few moments outside, Karl's clothing and skin grew damp and he preferred it when the rain returned and beat away at the mist.

On a cool, wet morning, the men marched to a lightly guarded settlement, twenty miles to the north. When the sharpshooters eliminated the handful of watchmen protecting the walls, and the army crashed through the gates, the town they raided was turned to a morgue. The enemies were easy to spot and kill, with nearly all of them donning bright hazmat suits.

"This is like target practice," Liam said to Karl during the melee. "Look at 'em—like giant chickens."

Karl smiled and laughed, taking aim at a fleeing yellow blob.

Over two dozen corpses lined the rear wall, giving evidence to what the winter had done to their numbers prior to the battle. The earth needed to finish thawing and the rain to cease long enough for the townspeople to dig proper graves. But that opportunity would no longer present itself, and the bodies of their comrades would join their numbers, never to be buried or lamented. The more desirable residents were kept alive, stripped out of their hazmat suits, and bound or beaten into submission.

The men swarmed the buildings, finding troves of preserves and a storeroom filled with military-issue fatigues. Karl and Mark remained saddled on their horses during the looting, and ordered a prisoner brought before them. Sergeant

Pechman left and returned after a moment, pulling a frail and skinny man by his arm, and pushed him down to kneel in the mud before the mounted officers.

They interrogated him for many minutes, the man saying, "They all got sick, one after the other. We thought it was the plague again. We thought it was back."

Karl laughed. "Even if it did return, how would those suits help you?"

The man cast his eyes to the ground.

"Don't get me wrong, I do appreciate you wearing them. It made it all the more easy for us to kill you, but they did nothing to stop the disease before— why would they help now? Do you know what the definition of insanity is? You all probably had the flu, a common cold, or something."

"We don't got a doctor. No medicine."

"You all might be the stupidest we've encountered."

Karl looked up to see Sultan appear through the cluster of men.

"General," he said, smiling wide. "Oh, I got something for you, my man."

He handed Karl a full bottle of liquor, the cap still sealed.

"Scotch," Karl said, pulling at the foil wrapper. Sultan held three glasses in his other hand, and Karl and Mark dismounted their horses.

"A toast," Karl said, filling the glasses to the rim. "To victory, yet again."

Mark took back half the glass in a gulp, then said, "Sweet Jesus. Lemme see that bottle."

Karl passed it to him. "It's the earth itself inside that glass. You can taste the wind, the rain, soil, and fire."

"Goddamn." Sultan contorted his face. "Ain't that some shit. I'm more of a vodka man myself, but damn, that's some good stuff right there. We found boxes worth, and not just the brown stuff. Rum, wine, even beer."

The three men began walking off.

"What do you want me to do with him?" Sergeant Pechman called out, standing beside the prisoner.

Karl shrugged. "He's of no use." He paused, and then returned to give what remained of the bottle to his sergeant. "Live a little, Mister Pechman."

The sergeant unscrewed the cap and took a swig. He coughed and spit up the liquor. "Holy hell ... you like this stuff?" He coughed again. "Tastes like dirt." He handed the bottle back to Karl, unsheathed his knife, and walked toward the scowling prisoner.

The man moved back on his knees, saying, "Please. Oh, Christ—"

Karl and the officers walked away, examining the dark hue of their drink in the glow of the overcast sky.

***

They rode back into Odyssey in a misting rain. The guards awaiting their return were tossed bottles of alcohol from the back of flatbed trucks, and the foil caps were quickly removed.

Karl led the procession down the main strip of town toward the storerooms and barracks. The prisoners were stripped naked, and their wrists or necks were leashed to the backs of the trucks. They were prodded forward by the tips of sharpened spears, with red strips of fabric tied below the points. The prisoners stared aghast at the abundance of crucified and executed corpses displayed along the main entrance into Odyssey. The guards took revelry in pointing out some of the more elaborate executions, such as the impalements, saying things like, "Took 'em days to die. Look at them there; we fit three on one pole. Just imagine slidin' down that sharp point, a bloated corpse right below you. We got a pointed stick just for you."

Karl and his officers left the men at the barracks to have their celebratory homecoming, and gathered around a table in a home used as an office of sorts. Bottles of hard alcohol and jars of preserved vegetables were passed out. A sergeant in charge of inventory read them figures and numbers. Their stockpile of weapons and ammunition was more than adequate, as was their immediate supply of food and clothing. It was fuel that would soon become troublesome. Not only was the store running low, but the barrels of gasoline were continuing to go bad. Keeping generators running in the barracks was a necessity—a driving force that gave the men something to fight for. Light. Warmth.

After an hour, when the glasses on the table had been drained and refilled three times, it was decided that the time was right to march east. Sultan ordered an officer from the docks to leave first thing in the morning, along with a squad to precede their advance. Scouts had been sent earlier that week to inspect Masterson, where prior to the winter, evidence of fuel consumption had been seen. Plans were already drawn to attack Masterson, but first they would march to the ports. With the two settlements working together, true dominance would be at hand.

Karl refilled their glasses and called for the kitchen to prepare a proper meal. Something to give them strength. Something dead and cooked over a flame.

Chapter Sixteen
Search Party

A tentative departure date for a company of twenty men to leave was decided for the next week. That being if the unceasing rain would ever stop.

The morning after their fruitful raid, and the celebration that followed, a search party left to find two men who had not returned from their morning duty of checking the fish traps, east of the town. One was discovered a quarter mile downstream, caught up in a thicket of rush, and the other was farther along, at the edge of the bank. One was shot, and the other's neck was so broken that his head faced in the opposite direction.

As an investigation was underway, two sergeants were found dead inside a home on a hilltop, where some of the officers were given housing to keep vigil on the community from above. Both of the men were killed by brute force, and Mark put together a scouting party, along with Captain Black and Bishop, to follow the killers.

Karl was made aware of the murders, but paid it little mind.

"What's the bother?" he asked. "If their tracks are leading away from town, they're long gone. Sending men after them only puts more at risk. We weren't attacked—it was a chance occurrence. And the tracks indicate that it was only two people."

Liam shrugged. "Guess to make an example. Whoever they were, they killed four of our men. One shot, the others mangled. Shit, one of 'em's face was so busted he must have had every bone broken."

"That's still of no consequence," Karl said. "But I trust Mark's opinion;

follow the killers. Just make sure your pursuit is not in folly. We're set to leave in less than a week."

"Yes, sir," Liam said, and stood. "I'll tell them now."

***

One of the guilty men had been found injured in the woods, and brought back unconscious. Mark sent scouts to follow the second man who'd slipped away, as the rest of the company returned. Final preparations were made for their departure to the East, with another few days added to the timeframe, as the weather still had not cleared. The paths outside of Odyssey were thick with mud.

Captain Black spent much time with the captive man, claiming to Karl that he was the largest man among all the soldiers, except perhaps in comparison to Karl himself. Among the man's possessions was a weather-beaten map. A clear line of travel was marked, but most of the eastern section had been marred beyond readability. The officers studied the path, and Captain Black claimed it was the best possible route for them to take to the docks, before it appeared to veer south by a number of miles. The final location was lost to pulp. Karl met the captive and asked him about his travels, but the man had been put on strong sedatives by Doctor Freeman, and could not offer much of a response.

The following days saw torrential rains that battered the soil in thick droplets, and floods sprung up throughout town, water sweeping across the roadways and pooling in soil depressions to form small ponds. Then finally, on a cool morning, the clouds broke to a pale shade of gray, and no rain fell. The next day saw the same conditions, and Karl ordered the advance party to ready for departure. Captain Black was left in charge of Odyssey, and before they left, he showed Karl the area on a map where the captive man had claimed he was heading to a settlement of unknown size. It was north of Alice by several miles, in a municipality called Hightown.

Karl took the map and they left to witness the man's inauguration into the brotherhood of the Red Hands. The squadron was waiting to depart in the stables, and Karl joined them after the man affirmed his ritualistic oath. The officers and scouts mounted their horses and pulled the reins. The gates opened, and the delegates left for the East.

Chapter Seventeen
Convoy

After the second night sleeping in the woods, the group encountered a highway, and continued to follow roads for the majority of the trip.

The worldwide destruction became more apparent as the wilderness of the South and West gave way to increased towns and cities. Civilization was nothing more than rubble heaps and vacant, dusty shells of buildings. The Priest hummed tunes during the long afternoons, and conversation was subdued. Sultan rode lead with Karl, Liam, and Mark, telling them all the things they already knew about the port town, and some things they did not.

"Commander Sergei Ivanov is the leader, and his two lieutenants, Ivan Volkov and Viktor Petrov, are second in command. Ivanov, Volkov, and Petrov."

"I been trying for months, and I still can't get 'em right," Mark said. "Iva-Ivana?"

"Ivanov," Sultan continued. "All three are genuine Russian military, and the main battle cruiser is theirs. They came on it, and it houses most of the men. A few live dockside around the guard towers, and the rest live in the other warships. Their main defenses are the ships themselves. Some aren't docked at the pier, but can only be accessed by boat or raft. They're like little islands out there, able to shoot at anything on land."

"How many ships comprise their fleet?" Karl asked.

"About a dozen. Some destroyers, some anti-submarine. These are big ships, General. Fully armed."

"Are all of the men military?"

"Only a few. The commander's crew got the disease and died off on their way to the US, all except the lieutenants and maybe a dozen more. Some are from other armies, a few Chinese, but most are homegrown survivors."

"And they can navigate those vessels?"

"The commander can, and his lieutenants know enough. The others have been taught how to man the guns and run some of the equipment, but actually steering those things—especially the battle cruiser—isn't an easy task. The main one's broken down, the reactor's not working right, which scares the shit out of me, being that it's a nuclear vessel and all. But the commander says it's safe, so I trust him. If anyone knows how to work one of those things, it's him. Them ships, even the smaller cruisers, are like floating cities."

"I could steer 'em," Liam said. "No problem. Russian, US, whatever. There's not a vessel I can't navigate."

"All right," Karl said. "Commander Ivanov, Lieutenant Volkov, and Lieutenant Petrov. Easy enough."

"You got it, my man."

Karl found a cigar and lit it, then riffled through his saddlebag for a bottle of dark liquor. "Rum," he said. "Seems appropriate." He took a drink, then handed the bottle to Sultan.

***

Days passed, and with them, no evidence of human life. At times, they identified extinguished campfires that could have been days old, but they saw nothing to suggest recent activity. Not even any large game. No deer, and few rabbits and squirrels.

Dead soldiers of unknown nationality littered the land in such numbers that it was impossible to decipher their values. There were plenty of small arms to sort through, and some of the men swapped out what they carried or added to their inventory.

Bishop made a hobby of collecting patches from uniforms, and he stopped every now and again, knife in hand. He took to sewing the national flag patches on the arms of his jacket, and he now had five. Three on his left shoulder and two on his right.

In the collapsed form of a building, they discovered four boxes containing military rations, still vacuum sealed, and the eating was plentiful. They found themselves nearing the East Coast with renewed strength and vigor.

At little more than a crawl, Karl led Bishop, Mark, and Liam near the area where the prisoner had told of a settlement, leaving the rest of the party behind in a wooded field. Before they came upon the town, they heard movement in the woods. Rustling. Voices. They slowed their advance. Bishop was in the lead, and when he raised his fist, Karl froze.

There was an irregular dark shape through the thicket of trees. Movement. A helmeted head. Two, and then three. They backtracked until they were far enough away to speak, and it was decided that Bishop would scout alone. Karl took out a map and selected a location to meet in several hours. The rest of the officers went back to the waiting party, and led the squad to the prearranged area.

As evening approached and the men were settling down, one of the horsekeepers ran into the clearing.

"Karl," the man said, rubbing his dirty palms together. "You gotta see this."

Karl followed the man, with Liam and Mark at his heels. About a quarter mile into the woods, they heard rumbling.

"I was looking for a grain field for the horses, and I heard it coming. I ran back as soon as I saw them."

The men squatted in the brush, their elevation sufficient so that they could see the road ahead. Karl took out his binoculars and steadied himself against the side of a tree. A procession of five vehicles were driving down the road. The lead car and the one in the rear were pickup trucks, and the flatbeds on each were lined with armed men. The vehicles in-between were cargo vans, military issued, and the one in the middle was long, cylindrical, and shiny.

"What the hell you suppose they're carting?" Mark whispered.

"No clue. Liquid. Fuel or water."

"I'll round up the men. We can overtake them." Mark began to stand.

Karl counted the armed soldiers on the back of the trucks as the vehicles passed.

"No," he said. "We'd never catch up. Plus, those men look clean, well-fed. Genuine military. We might outnumber them, but they'd kill at least half of us."

"We could catch up. I'll lead ten men now, fast through the woods. We'll intersect them a half mile down, cut them off. You can take up the rear, and we'd have them all dead as a doornail before they knew what was coming."

"Sometimes, Mister Rothstein, it's better to wait and watch. They're heading from Hightown, due south." Karl found his map in his pocket, and trailed his finger over the page. "If they keep course, veer a few miles to the west ... here, on this road, the convoy leads straight to Alice. Hightown and Alice ... they're allies, I presume. Send a scout to follow them, and leave someone watching the road. Make sure they stay far away. Let's go back and wait for Bishop."

Chapter Eighteen
Sergeant Marcus

Bishop returned at dawn. They compared notes, inspected a map, and then he was allowed four hours of sleep before leading the officers to a vantage point overlooking Hightown. The climb up the hill was tough, but once at the peak, the scene was incredible.

The walls were metal and cement, with hardened bunkers lining the tops in perfect intervals. Bishop had spent the night tracing the perimeter. The town was partially bordered with water, an immense bay to the northeast that fed into the ocean.

"We'd never overtake them," Mark whispered. He removed a small backpack and passed out high-calorie survival bars, followed by a canteen.

"Patience, Mister Rothstein. Patience." Karl unwrapped the silver foil and took a bite of the rock-hard bar. He soured his face and said, "Is this thing wood?" He tapped it against a rock and continued. "We know nothing about them; who these people are, what their ambitions may be."

"Look like army to me."

"Yes." Karl peered through binoculars. "Look there, east of the wall ... are those hummers? And ... a tank?"

"Appears so," Liam said. "What's the plan?"

"Plan? No plan. Not yet. We sure as hell can't attack them head-on. We might break through down in Alice, if the defenses are what we've been led to believe. But up here? Not a chance. And if these two colonies are connected, if they're allies, our efforts will require something outside of a direct assault. What we need is more information. For now, we continue to the docks."

***

Back at camp, Karl and the officers met with Sultan and the Priest and explained what they could see of Hightown. A soldier sitting on the broad side of a fallen tree interjected in their conversation. "You say they're military?"

Karl looked to Sergeant Iain Marcus.

"It appears so."

Iain played with a thin stick against the ground. The tip of his pointer finger was missing below where the nail would be.

"If they're military, a direct assault would be the hardest battle we've fought, and victory isn't certain. Overtaking them like how we took the bunker is the best plan. We were lucky then, because the people were ripe for revolt, and they were stupid enough to let us walk right in. Judging from what you've explained of this colony, and what we know of Alice, there's nothing to suggest these settlements are on the verge of an uprising. They won't be kind to strays. Getting in will require a degree of tactical know-how that we have not yet employed."

Karl stared at the man for a moment, and then said, "Quite a knowledgeable observation. By my own experience, the hearts of men can always be turned. There are regularly a few with dark ambitions. The key is to find them, strengthen their resolve, and make the rest of them whither from within. Tell me, how do you know any of what you've said?"

The man shrugged, and looked up from the random designs he was carving in the dirt. He scratched at an old scar running the length of his cheek, leading to his gray and dusty hair. "If the men are military, they'll be under order," Iain said, "and if anything, the military knows how to follow orders. They've survived this long because they have strong leadership. It's safe to assume they keep to their own, are dedicated to the civilization they have created, and are fiercely loyal to their command."

"Mister Marcus," Karl said, "you were in the military yourself, am I correct?"

"Sir. Yes, sir. I think I could be of help."

"How so?"

"If they're military, genuine US military, there's a chance they'll talk to another soldier. If I can get an encounter with a few of them alone, I might be able to strike an accord."

They were silent for a moment. Then Karl said, "Come closer. Take a seat. Let me hear what you got."

Chapter Nineteen
Harbor

Camp was broken down at dawn the following morning, and the men mounted their horses.

As the scouting party began to disappear in the thick woods, Iain Marcus and three soldiers stayed behind.

The last thing Karl said to him was, "Don't fail me," and he pulled on his reins.

A few yards away, Liam asked, "You think he'll get in?"

"I think he has a logical plan. Whether he gets himself behind the gates as a friend or as a prisoner is yet to be seen."

Liam spat tobacco juice to his side. "True enough. Might do us well to have a backup plan."

"We'll cross that bridge when we get there, Mister Briggs."

As their journey progressed, the wilderness diminished, and soon they were in an urban terrain. The body count here was impressive, with whole town squares and parks turned into scenes of macabre fascination. At noon, they stopped in the shade of a department store, the shattered glass before the skeleton doorframe covered in a layer of dust. Two men went inside as the rest of the party filled buckets of water for their horses.

The great majority of the parking lot was cordoned off, with strips of bright yellow caution tape stretching from one telephone pole to the next, and torn strips fluttering in the breeze. Larger neon signs read:

CAUTION POTENTIAL BIOHAZARD PRESENT

A geometric design indicating a biohazard was underneath the lettering.

An orderly operation had been underway in that parking lot, with hundreds of decayed corpses in body bags, wrapped in sheets, dressed in full clothing, robes, nightgowns, underwear, business suits, military camouflage, and hazmat suits, arranged in perfect rows. Hives of winged insects floated over the blacktop in dark clouds. Whatever association had started this cleanup was no longer present, the disease unsparing to even the most careful, and many of the bodies in protective gear could have belonged to the same people responsible for this organized mess.

Several white tents were erected in various places, and a few of the men went to inspect the ones on the outskirts, but nothing was left behind except old biohazard suits and barrels of chemicals.

In a second section of the parking lot were four massive incinerators. A metal conveyor belt preceded each, and a line of bodies remained on the tracks. Industrial trucks, backhoes, and small cranes sat cold and idle, along with a line of dump trucks with their cargo in various stages of fill. It appeared that at some stage this operation was augmented by the addition of two massive pyres, both left half burned.

Resting at a fair distance, Doctor Freeman removed his leather-bound binder and a cloth containing an assortment of charcoals, and began sketching the scene before him.

Karl watched him for a few strokes, then leaned his head against the side of the building and closed his eyes.

The rest of the men took to lighting cigarettes and cigars, and a few meandered inside the department store, but came back empty-handed.

Twenty minutes later, Karl opened his eyes. "Saddle up," he said, and the men left.

***

The docks were on the outskirts of a residential area, the once manicured lawns now shin-high grasses and weeds. Sultan took lead, and he turned to Karl with a smile. "Almost there, my man. Right this way."

A few blocks further they passed under an overpass, and on the other side they came to the fenced entrance of a proper US military naval base. Two ceremonial cannons were displayed, one on each side of the gate. Sultan walked his horse to the guard post, and a man stood from behind the glass-enclosed booth.

"Sultan," he said, strapping a rifle over his shoulder. "That you?"

"In the flesh."

The guard stepped out from the booth. "Welcome home."

"Ha!" Sultan said, shining down a mouthful of white teeth. "Home ... the world is my home, my man. I never left it."

Another guard appeared and exchanged pleasantries, and the two men began sliding back the tall chain-link fence. More soldiers appeared, five or six, all dressed in full military fatigues and armed with rifles and side arms. Sultan introduced a few to Karl and the officers, and the congregation continued through the gates.

The guard stepped into his booth to speak into a microphone, and when he returned, he said, "I sent word. The commander will be expecting you by the boats."

Beyond the checkpoint, they followed a wide lane lined with row after row of military housing and facilities. They were all painted the same drab color of tan, and other than some having more windows than others, they were identical.

They continued riding down the road for many minutes, and the size of the base became apparent. A city of its own, complete with a park and baseball diamond, a boarded-up convenience store, and even a once working gas station.

They came around a turn, and before them the sea overtook the horizon. The dock extending out from the mainland was more of a bridge, with two vehicle lanes going down the center, protruding for what looked like a half mile out. Ships of assorted sizes were moored in intervals, and at the end, the jetty split into three lanes like a trident. The ships anchored there were like floating metropolises.

Along their march through the base, only a handful of the dock's men were visible, but now at the harbor, dozens were walking about. Tables lined the waterfront, and more were being brought out from a nearby building. Soldiers followed, carrying pitchers of water, bottles of wine, and a rack of glasses.

Karl and his men unsaddled their horses, and the horsekeepers were led away by the dockworkers to an area of grassland for the animals to graze.

Just as Sultan led Karl and the men to the tables, the faint sound of an engine could be heard. The men turned to watch two jeeps advance from the far stretch of the dock. They parked at the entrance to the mainland, and the engines were turned off, filling the air with silence.

The doors opened and six men stepped out, dressed the same as the others: olive drab pants and shirts, black boots, and holstered sidearms. One man walked quicker than the others, and smiled at Sultan.

"Finally," he said in a whispered purr of a Russian accent, and shook Sultan's hand.

"Commander," Sultan said returning the smile. "Here's the man of the hour. Meet General Karl Metzger."

The man, standing a full head shorter, turned to Karl. He first saluted, then reached out to shake. "General," he said. "Welcome."

Karl shook his hand and smiled his mouth full of gravestone teeth.

"Sir Commander, the pleasure is all mine. Let me introduce you to my officers."

Karl turned to his men, and full and proper introductions were made. The commander slicked back his dark hair with a palm and introduced his lieutenants, Viktor and Ivan. All three men were of similar stature, yet the lieutenants both had blond hair in contrast to the commander's. Ivan walked with an obvious limp, and his right ear was chewed up with scars.

"I can say for myself and for my men," Karl said, raising a wineglass from the table, "the journey was well worth the effort to be received with such a considerable welcoming."

The men all found and raised their glasses.

They stood lingering for a time as the commander spoke to Sultan about his travels. Then at his instruction, they took their seats. A small table was set away from the long one, and Karl sat with the commander alone. Soldiers came out from the nearest building, carrying large plates of breads, dried meat, and grilled fish, and placed them on the table before the men, who tore into the food with their dirty fingers and combat knives, largely ignoring the present cutlery. Talk and laughter rose from the table as the wineglasses were drained and replenished. Separate plates were brought to Karl's table, the steam from the fresh-baked bread lingering in the air like something that could be felt, seen, and touched.

Karl and the commander spoke of trivial matters, of travel, survival, and of the disease, as the first bottles of wine drained. The eternal question of *why* was pondered, much to Karl's dismay. *Why* did the disease happen? *Why* did humanity have to perish? Rubbish questions, which Karl found both infuriating and overthought. The answer was simple: it happened. Case closed.

The commander refilled their glasses and said, "Sultan informed me that you discovered a settlement south of here."

"That's correct," Karl said, and took a tear of dried meat.

"That settlement is known to me. It goes by Hightown, and the men behind those walls are fierce."

"I gathered as much. Military, I presume."

"That's right." The commander stopped to sip at his wine. "Our own scouts discovered it last fall."

"I have to say, your English is impressive. Your accent is barely a whisper."

"I spent several years in the US when I was younger." He put his glass down. "Now, this town, Hightown, we've been watching them for months. They not only maintain a strong number of fighting men, they have something else at their disposal even more valuable than all their vehicles and equipment combined." He paused and took another sip of wine.

Karl patted his pocket for a cigar and said, "You can spare me the dramatic delay, Sir Commander. Go on."

The commander gave him an amused look and said, "Please, General, have one of mine." He motioned to a soldier at his side and the man arrived carrying a box of cigars. "Hightown," he continued, "controls the import of fuel. It arrives by ship on a regular basis. The ship travels from the south, from where, I do not know."

Karl's eyebrow rose. "You don't say?"

"I do. Not only that, but they trade their fuel for a steady supply of clean water and fresh food from our friends in the south, Alice."

"Hmm," Karl mumbled, and struck a match to light a cigar. "We saw one of their cargo transports during our march here. But tell me, why haven't you intercepted the fuel boats?"

"Several reasons. One is that they travel escorted by two warships."

"Warships?" Karl waved across the horizon. "That shouldn't be a problem for you."

"It wouldn't be if we had sufficient fuel ourselves, but we only have enough to power two ships for a short duration. We could run out before the battle is won. Do you know how much fuel these ships burn?"

Karl didn't answer.

"The other reason is this; if we attack, if we capture the cargo vessel and steal their fuel, we would eliminate what appears to be a steady supply. We could perhaps track them back to wherever they're coming from, but for all we know, they're arriving from an even more heavily fortified city than Hightown."

"Surely the cargo ships would have enough to power some of these vessels, and keep your people happy for a long stretch."

"But not enough for what we need."

Karl took a deep inhale and let the smoke out slowly.

"And how much, roughly, do you need? Is your goal to establish a running navy?"

The commander shook his head.

"No, General."

"It's Karl. Call me Karl."

"It is not my intention to start a navy. However, if you would like to start one, by all means, you are welcome to do so." The man met Karl's eyes and took a cigar from the box.

"You're stepping down?"

"No," the commander said. "Not stepping down. Leaving."

Karl smiled. "Leaving? Ha! Have you been out there, in the world? You have it pretty good here."

"Home, General—"

"Karl."

"Home, Karl. I'm going home. Myself along with Ivan and Viktor—we were still traveling to the US when the sickness hit and spread. It was decided mid-trip to continue to America instead of turning back, since we were closer by a margin. By the time we docked, over three-fourths of our men were dead, thrown overboard. Two days later, the radio stopped working and the phone lines wouldn't connect to Russia. We were stranded here with no crew and not enough fuel for a return trip."

"What do you expect to see when you get home? It won't be any better, I assure you."

"Perhaps. But this is the way we see it: we can die on foreign land or we can die at home. Perhaps we have some family that was spared."

"And your men, they are willing to go with you?"

"Some, but not all."

Karl looked at the scene around him, the table of his soldiers and the soldiers of the docks. A dozen or so stood nearby with platters of food, alcohol, and cigars. He looked to the boats, sitting idle.

"How many men do you have?"

"You'll have to ask Viktor for the exact number, but it's about eleven hundred."

"Out there?" Karl pointed. "In the boats?"

"Yes. Mostly. There is no need to keep the men on land. A revolving guard watches the perimeter, and if anything other than a few wanderers comes to our fences, the men fall back, and the boats act as our fortress."

Karl nodded. "Like I said, you have it pretty good here. How many men want to leave with you?"

"Out of the group, only five are Russian. Another hundred or so are eager to follow me, to see if the rest of the world is as broken as it is here. I've spent months teaching them how to operate the ships. The rest would like to stay. I made it clear that they are not being abandoned; they will be provided with adequate leadership. Before finding Hightown, seeing the fuel come in, we had every intention of merging our groups and attacking Alice for our mutual benefit. Plans have changed."

"I think I see where this is going."

The commander exhaled a cloud of smoke and finished his glass of wine. A man promptly came to his side with the bottle. The commander put his hand over the glass. "I believe something harder is in order. Karl, do you have a preference?"

"Whiskey. Any kind."

The soldier turned and left.

"The men can all be yours," the commander continued. "Along with the fleet." He motioned to the docks. "All of the boats are in working order. With fuel, you can scour the seas, sail to Florida, Bermuda, or Cuba in no time at all. You would have a floating city with the best protection available—the ocean."

Karl took a puff of his cigar as the soldier returned with a bottle of bourbon and two glasses. He poured a shallow drink in each and stepped back.

"Come here," Karl said, and took the bottle from the soldier's hand. He filled their glasses to the rim and put the bottle on the table.

The commander laughed and picked up his glass.

Karl drained half in a gulp, then said, "So tell me, Sir Commander, you are presenting me with both an army and a fleet of ships … what's your price? What do you want from me?"

"I think it's obvious," he said. "Fuel. I need fuel, and plenty of it. I want you, Karl Metzger, to get it."

"Why not get it yourself?"

"You've seen the walls of Hightown. You know it would be a hard battle."

"And you want me to fight it for you?"

"Not exactly. From what I've been told, you are crafty, to say the least. You've gotten inside of other settlements, destroyed them from within without heavy losses. What I have for you is a proposition. You get me the fuel supply and you will have the largest known army in the world. A navy. Renegotiate whatever the trade deal is that they have going on with the fuel ships. You can have unrestricted access to the seas. Your officer, Captain Liam, is it?"

"Yes. Liam Briggs."

"Captain Briggs. I've been told that he can operate a vessel. I will catch him up to speed with our fleet and train some of your men on how to operate them. We can start tomorrow if we make a deal tonight."

Karl finished his glass and remained silent. After a pause, he poured another drink and said, "Hightown is powerful, but I think we could win a fight if we use one of your warships, use what fuel you've got. We could attack from the water and the front at the same time. From what we know of Alice, they're not as capable as Hightown, and they're not genuine military. They may not counterattack, but if they do, we can defend the town with our vessels."

"No," the commander said. "I can't risk burning what fuel we have. If it weren't to succeed, the docks would be left with little defenses."

"And if I attack the front alone, I will be left with nothing."

"That is why this is a proposition. We are not joining forces quite yet; we are coming to terms. However, if you agree, I will supply you with incentives. A bonus, if you will." He stopped to sip from the glass.

"And that being...? What did I say about pausing for dramatic effect? Just fucking talk."

"Ha! That's what I like about you. An upfront man. All right, here it is. I will supply five hundred men toward the initiative, along with a number of ground vehicles. We don't have any tanks, but there are dozens of jeeps and hummers in storage. I will provide what fuel I can spare for those vehicles, but you will have to supply the rest. I'm under the impression that you have some yourself, and I believe you aim to attack Masterson in the foreseeable future. Our scouts have reported the same as yours: an indication of fuel consumption, power, and electricity, albeit they seem to be small in number."

Karl leaned back and put his boots up on the table, a slab of dirt falling to the wooden top.

"And what's to stop me from taking what you offer and disappearing?"

"Well, for starters, the five hundred men are loyal to me. They will follow you to war without so much as a pause, but they will not accept treason and deception. Secondly—and I believe this is the stronger case—you, Karl, *want* this. You need this. The world can only get bigger for you through force and war, and once yours, you can inflict upon it whatever you desire. I've been told something about you. The other men—*all* other men—they take treasure from their forays. Some collect objects of sexual desire, others seek narcotics, and there are the more twisted who amass physical objects, such as teeth, or cut away the ears of their slain. From what I understand, you are something of a frugal man, despite the riches your army encounters. You could have whatever you want, yet you sleep alone, and desire only cigars, whiskey, and a solid meal. But you don't stop moving forward; your feet continue marching. I believe your true ambition, the treasure that you receive, is the battles themselves. You're addicted to warfare, deceiving your enemy, and the thrill of victory. Am I reading you correctly?"

Karl flicked an ash from his cigar. "Perhaps," he said, amused. "Or perhaps I'm content to see the world come to its knees, one inch at a time. As far as how to attack Hightown, I again must implore you to reconsider using one of your warships. They're sitting idle, a tremendous waste of firepower: floating death machines. But if an attack on foot is the only recourse, I believe the key to bringing them down is through Alice. Make them fall first. Cut off Hightown's supply of water and food, or use Alice's own people to attack Hightown's gates if their minds are pliable enough to be led in this manner. It still won't be an easy fight, not by any means. Our numbers will be high, but against tanks and hardened defenses?" Karl puffed at his cigar and took a swig from the glass. "I'm starting to see this all come together."

"I believe you are, General. You're an observant man, to say the least." The captain took a drink from his glass, and was silent in contemplation. Then he said, "Perhaps ... perhaps, if Alice falls—"

"*When* Alice falls," Karl corrected him.

"When Alice falls, I will lend more of my men to the ground assault ... and maybe we can work out sending a ship or two into the bay. At that point, without the risk of a counterattack from Alice, we will be better suited to throw our full strength against the might of Hightown."

"Captain," Karl said, turning to the man. "Attacking from the land and sea, we would be unstoppable."

"Karl, I do believe that we have a promising future. Working together, we will both prosper. Tell you what, how about we stop talking about such things for a while? How about we drink more, hmm? Let me give you a proper tour, show you the fleet up close. I have a fine selection of prisoners locked in the rooms for you and your men to enjoy. We can discuss plans later, tomorrow." The commander leaned back in his chair and put his feet on the table.

Karl took a last inhale of his cigar and flicked the nub into the water, where it trailed a cascade of smoke. He tapped the half-empty bottle of bourbon with the toe of his boot. "Hope you got more of this," he said, putting his hands behind his head, feeling the sun spread warmth on his face.

"Plenty more." The commander motioned to the soldier beside him and took another two cigars from the box. "Later tonight," he said, "we will discuss our future."

Chapter Twenty

Turncoat

For three days and two nights, the four scouts remained in the woods outside Hightown, observing from afar the recurring pattern of the guards, who walked in squads of three down a well-worn path, less than a quarter mile from Hightown's front gate. They would begin in the easternmost section, first thing in the morning, and then pass again in the early evening, peering from side to side for the slightest indication of a disturbance.

From deep in the brush, with binoculars pressed to their eyes, the scouts examined the soldier's clean, dark green camouflage army fatigues, tactical helmets, and bulletproof vests. They were armed with automatic machine guns, holstered pistols, and full ammunition pouches on their belts and vests. The crackling of their handheld radios could sometimes be heard, faint across their distance, yet in startling contrast to the calm wilderness.

On the third morning the plan was set in motion. A half hour before the guards were expected, three of the scouts took up position behind an earthen mound, directly on the path of the oncoming soldiers. They'd been instructed to begin shooting once the guards passed a sycamore tree that had been marked with a notch. Sergeant Iain Marcus crouched several yards to the south, so that the path was right before him, and his three men behind the mound were far to his left.

The scouts waited as instructed, one of them peering out at the sycamore tree. They were ordered to fire precise, clean shots, and not spray the guards with bullet fire, so as to not ruin their uniforms with an abundance of holes and blood.

The seconds ticked away in the quiet. The slightest chirp of birds or scurrying of small woodland animals sent Iain's senses darting through the thicket. A small black tick with a fat torso and a head like a poppy seed scurried across his hand and down his forearm. He flicked it away ... and then he heard it. The crunching of boots. The low murmuring of whispering. He peered out, saw through the vertical slats of trees the three guards make their lazy round as the sun rose up from behind them.

Each step they took seemed an eternity as Iain clicked the safety off his machine gun and pressed the butt of the stock against his shoulder, ready to spring to his feet.

The guards passed before him, three distant drifts of dark camouflage, and continued toward the awaiting scouts. He saw the sycamore tree ... saw the three men step up to it ...

One pop cut through the air and the branches above fluttered with the sudden evacuation of birds. One of the guards fell backwards, making a half spin to land facedown. The two other soldiers instinctually dropped to their stomachs and scurried off the path. They grabbed their fallen comrade by the collar and dragged him behind the side of a fallen tree.

Bullet shots rang out from both sides. Iain watched the leaves and branches between the two fighting sides quiver, and chunks of wood and bark shot out from where the bullets struck. The guards shouted, but whatever they were saying was lost to him.

Staying low, Iain closed his eyes. He sharpened his hearing as the nearby bullets whizzed back and forth, and took a deep breath ... then he snapped his eyes open and jumped to his feet, running, weaving through the trees.

He was behind the guards, and beyond them, the helmets of his three scouts stuck up from the mound, their rifles aimed. At sight of their sergeant, they peered further out, waiting for Iain to finish off the soldiers, as was the plan.

One of Hightown's guards caught sight of Iain standing behind them, and his eyes flashed in terror. The remaining two soldiers lay in pools of blood, one unmoving and his eyes unfocused, the other clenching a wound on his thigh, his free hand holding a pistol. The uninjured soldier swung his rifle in Iain's direction just as the sergeant released a volley of bullets in three methodical pulls of the trigger.

But the shots were not intended for Hightown's soldiers.

Two red mists popped into the air from behind the mound hiding Iain's scouts. Iain took off in a sprint toward the mound, and swung out to the side. Two of his men lay on their backs, their heads like squished grapes inside their helmets. The third man wobbled up to his knees, a dramatic dent on the side of his helmet and a trail of blood from an unseen wound.

The scout looked up at him, his eyes blinking, not focusing. He seemed to register who was standing before him and opened his mouth. "Ia—" was all he got out as Sergeant Marcus pulled the trigger and killed the last of his own men.

Hightown's uninjured guard ran up to Iain's side, his rifle up, swinging between the dead scouts and Iain.

"Who—who the hell are you?"

Iain didn't answer, just looked down.

"Who are they? Where did you come from?"

The soldier was young—clean-shaven, chiseled chin. Iain bet his hair was cut down to a buzz under his helmet. One hundred percent prime American soldier.

"Where—"

"Get that damn gun out of my face, private," he said, turning to the soldier. "Your men okay back there?"

Iain slung his rifle over his shoulder and began walking fast toward Hightown's injured guard and the presumably dead one. The young soldier followed, his rifle still aimed.

The injured man squeezed at his thigh, the blood seeping out.

"It's not that bad," Iain said.

The man gritted his teeth. "Who-who the fuck are you?"

"Iain," he said. "Iain Marcus. Those fuckers back there killed a man I was traveling with. I escaped, but they took all of our water and food. Left my friend dead. I tracked them here, watched them from a distance. When I heard bullet fire, I made my move."

Iain's hands danced over the injured man's leg in well-practiced fashion, cutting back the material of his pants, pulling gauze from a medical kit. The injured man gritted his teeth and said, "Call-called in reinforcements." He was pale, on the verge of passing out. "They-they're on-on the way. Oh-oh, Christ ... I'm b-bleeding o-out."

"It's all right, Derrick," the young soldier said, and kneeled at Iain's side. "You're not bleeding out."

"Your name's Derrick?" Iain asked.

The man nodded.

"Derrick, you'll be fine. You got a bullet stuck in your thigh, but it's right here. I can practically see it. It's far from the artery."

The young soldier kept an eye on the perimeter, and glanced over as Iain finished wrapping Derrick's wound. When Iain finished, he sat back on his heels, his hands covered in blood.

"Here." The young soldier passed Iain a camouflage bandana and unscrewed his canteen, pouring water over Iain's hands. "Where'd you learn to shoot like that?"

"Same place as you."

"You a Marine?"

Iain shook his head. "Special Forces, eighteen Z—operations sergeant. *Was* Special Forces, a long, long time ago. My friend, Michael, the one those repugnant pieces of shit killed, he was Special Forces too. We traveled far together, survived a lot … only to be killed for a few sips of water." Iain spat in the brush.

"Where you headed?"

Iain shrugged. "Here is as far as I know."

A voice called out from deep in the woods, "Derrick! Derrick!"

Derrick opened his mouth, but the young soldier called back first, "Here! We're here!"

Iain turned to the young soldier. "What's your name, private?"

"Turner, sir. John Turner."

"You got a cigarette there, John Turner?"

The soldier opened a pouch on his vest. "These are hard to come by," he said.

"Then you know how much I'll appreciate it."

The private pulled out three cigarettes, handed one to Iain, and put one between Derrick's trembling lips. "They're here," he told his comrade.

Derrick sucked at the cigarette.

A dozen men crashed through the brush, rifles up, scouting the perimeter while medics swarmed over Derrick and the dead soldier. Rifles were pointed at Iain.

A man wearing sergeant insignia walked up to John.

"Who is he?" He pointed to Iain.

"My name's Iain Marcus," Iain said before John could reply.

"He saved us," Private Turner said. "He's special forces. Killed those three in a bat of the eye."

The sergeant scratched his chin. He looked between Iain and Private Turner. "So he did. Tell me what happened."

Iain finished his cigarette and ground it out in the dirt, listening to his new friend tell the tale of his heroic endeavors.

Chapter Twenty-one
Jacob

Jacob chose to be exiled from Alice rather than face imprisonment. The choice was given to him through the bars of a holding cell as he sat on a cot, his head held in his palms. The blood on his fingers had dried, yet they were sticky against his forehead.

Before discovering the town of Alice, Jacob survived for six months on his own. General Tom Byrnes, Alice's beloved leader, had a soft spot for service men, and allowed him to become a member of the community. He was issued quarters in the barracks, an apartment complex with running water, and he shared a room with a soldier named Barry Reed. The first night that Jacob arrived in his new home he stripped out of his ragged clothing, stiff with filth, and stood under the jets of his shower for a half an hour. A shower. Hot water. Tears streamed down his face, flowing with the grime that washed off his skin. Even more, his new accommodation had electricity. It was rationed to several hours in the early morning and the evenings going into the night, but he was told that soon enough they would have a steady stream of fuel, and the electricity would operate all night long. Nothing more was mentioned about where the fuel came from, since the project of getting it was still in its infancy. Jacob didn't care. He could read a book in the evening by lamplight, comfortable on a couch with a throw blanket over his legs. He had unrestricted use of filtered water, a clean uniform, fresh food from the gardens ... and all he had to do in return was keep lookout in shifts like a regular job.

For many months, Jacob stood guard atop a lookout tower, observing the tree line in the distance, past the zigzagging trenches that encircled the bottom portion of Alice Springs Park. He was allotted time in the garden, as was every member of Alice, and although he was not particularly skilled at gardening, the task was easy enough. Pull weeds. Go up and down the rows, hunched over, and pick at the little green sprouts protruding between the vegetable stalks. Easy. And sneaking the occasional tomato off the vine, or a crisp cucumber, was generally overlooked.

The middle-aged Tom Byrnes was responsible for the town's founding, and his son, Nick Byrnes, was second in command, and responsible for leading a small group of soldiers to clear out the vagabonds who had infested the area before Alice was established. It was Nick who offered Jacob the ultimatum from the other side of the jail cell. His father was unaware of Nick's offer, and would have been at odds to let Jacob go. Once a member of Alice, and privy to information only given to the citizens, turning someone loose was unacceptable.

The need for fuel was in constant debate, with Tom giving speeches from a stage behind Alice's volunteer fire station, saying, "Soon—any day, fuel is coming!" The soldiers, men, women, and children were told that an agreement was in the works with a neighboring colony. Only the soldiers involved in transporting the fuel were privy to more information. In the meantime, the gardens were doubled, with enough crops to feed three times their population. For what purpose, Jacob did not know. He was taken off of guard duty and moved to labor. All those hours spent digging seemed to be a huge waste of effort. His hands blistered and burst, but still, he turned the soil over, one shovelful at a time. The plan was to convert an existing soccer field in Alice Springs into a cornfield. Day after day, he tore away the earth— held firmly in place by the roots of the knee-high grass.

But he didn't complain. Not at first.

He accepted the work. He endured the ache in his arms and back, the scrapes on his fingers, and the constant bug bites. This was not the life he envisioned for himself, apocalypse or not. He was a soldier, a fighter, and had managed to survive on his strength and skill alone. During a small melee one morning, when the whistles blew and the townspeople fled to their predetermined location along the trench line, he himself shot and killed three hostiles. He saw them drop from behind the scope of his hunting rifle, as a dozen more were decimated in a hail of gunfire from the trench line.

Jacob made Tom aware of his exploits one morning, when he had an opportunity to approach the man while breakfast was served from the buffet line. Tom dismissed him when Jacob insisted he'd be of better service as a permanent member of the guard. They needed workers, Tom told him. It was only temporary. They'd talk later. And that was that. Tom walked to a table with his food tray in hand. Nick was standing in line behind his father, and as he was served a scoop of scrambled eggs, he told Jacob that he agreed with him wholeheartedly. He looked over his shoulder, making sure his dad was out of earshot, and said that using able-bodied men to tend to the gardens was a waste of manpower. Skilled people like Jacob should continue training, be made into better warriors, and join the elite in Alice's hierarchy.

It was no secret that Nick was at odds with his father when it came to governing Alice. It was evident in his demeanor, in the way that he spoke. Nick promised a stronger army, an influx of fuel, and better defenses. Tom talked about solar power, and the need to maintain gardens much larger than the population needed.

The fight happened a few weeks later. Every night Jacob would return home, his dirty hands and fingers cramped into hooks from holding the shovels, picks, and rakes. He had splinters, blistered feet, and the occasional bee sting. His roommate, Barry, would be home before him, his crisp fatigues folded on the couch, and his rifle leaning by the door. Jacob rarely spoke to him anymore. He preferred to spend his time in his room, alone, letting his sore muscles melt on his mattress.

Barry was a member of Alice's Ranger division, and allowed outside of the perimeter on hunting and scouting patrols. He shared with Jacob the occasional prized goods that he found, like cigarettes, which were in constant demand. Jacob endlessly complained that he could hunt—that his talents were being wasted out in the fields. Barry would say that it was temporary, and once the gardens were finished, he could ask to be reassigned. This angered Jacob even more. Having spent the entire summer out in the fields, it seemed like an eternal endeavor. Having someone with the freedom to leave the town regularly tell him that everything was fine was insulting.

Once a week, Barry hosted a poker game in their apartment. In the past, these games had been fruitful for Jacob. The Rangers had enough to bargain with. After sharing half a bottle of whiskey, Barry would start making stupid bets. He'd throw in a bottle of wine and a pocketknife for a few working ballpoint pens.

But during the last few weeks, the late-night card games weren't going well for Jacob. He blamed it on being exhausted. On coming home aching, tired, his head throbbing. He was playing poorly, and on one particular evening, with the whiskey flowing, he did something stupid. He took off his watch, the battery long dead, and tossed it on the pile of cigarettes, match packets, and batteries. Barry paused, and said that he didn't think it was a good idea. Jacob watched the glare from the candles reflect off the inscription from his mother and father on the back of the watch.

Barry again told Jacob to reconsider, and Jacob felt heat rise in his chest. He took back the glass of whiskey before him, and said, "Hit me."

Jacob lost the hand. Barry didn't move to take the pile. Two other members of the Rangers were at the game, and they remained silent as Jacob stood, the waver in his legs giving evidence to the alcohol he'd consumed, and Barry said to him that he didn't want his watch. But Jacob turned and left, closing his bedroom door behind him. Barry once more yelled that he wasn't going to take the watch, but Jacob had already collapsed on his bed and let his mind swirl to a drunken stupor.

The sun was up when he awoke, and his eyelids felt like sandpaper against his eyes. Once the room stopped spinning, he drank a full glass of water, holding the glass with a shaking hand. The poker game from the night before had been cleaned up, and Barry had already left for his daily routine. He was late for work, but if no one had knocked at the door yet, it had not become an issue. The thought of standing exposed beneath the blazing sun for the next seven hours was cruel. But he had to. Moderate drinking was permitted, but being too hungover to function was not. Everyone in Alice had to work, all of the time. It was part of the deal.

He dressed, and then sped to the toilet as his stomach lurched. Christ, he needed some aspirin.

After a few dry heaves, he spit away the tangle of drool from his lips and made himself stand. He grabbed his hat, put on his boots, and stepped out into the blinding sun. It was so bright his eyes teared, and he walked to the fields squinting and shielding the rays with his hands.

And so, his day began in abject misery. Each push of the shovel against the knotted earth was arduous; each swing of the pick had no strength behind it. He couldn't speak to any of the workers, and managed to avoid the supervisor, old Pat O'Hern.

Since he was late, lunch was served only two hours after he'd arrived, and he couldn't yet think of eating. But as the hours went by, he grew hungry, and his exhaustion conspired with the sun's strong glare to hasten the onset of a migraine.

It was an hour until dinner—an hour until quitting time. His name was called out, and when he looked up, with sweat blurring his vision, his head throbbing in pain, he saw Barry walking toward him, his heavy boots clomping in the soil. He said, "Jacob, my God, man, you don't look good." He smiled, made some joke about being hungover too, and then held out his hand, showing the watch. "I don't want it," he said.

Barry's uniform was neat, new, his hands mildly dirty. No calluses, no blisters. His hair was parted, his face shaven that morning. He was smiling.

Jacob stood, shovel gripped tight, his vision throbbing red. He swung like he was batting at the moon, and Barry's body twisted around and fell.

Nobody saw the swing, but a few workers heard the terrible whack of metal against skull and came running over. They stopped short of Jacob, who stood tall over Barry's body. He was a thing of dread, a monster of rage, huffing up strings of drool, his red eyes bright, his body filthy, his muscles taut, his hands clenching the splintering handle. He would later recall that he barely remembered swinging the shovel. It was more like a dream, like he watched himself do it from above. But he did it. He killed Barry, and then he pointed at all the people standing around him, the crowd gathering and armed men approaching. He yelled and shouted, accusing them all of doing this to him, of turning him into a beast. Three men pounced on him, put him in cuffs, and locked him away.

He slept that night on a cot in a holding cell in the basement of Alice's police department. A few times during the night he awoke in pure darkness, no candle burning for him in that dungeon. But the darkness felt good, comforting, cool on his sun-beaten skin.

The next morning a soldier came and gave him a piece of toast and a glass of water. He said that he'd be put on trial for murder, and perhaps executed by firing squad. More likely, he'd spend an eternity behind bars, each day snuffed out to be replaced by total darkness. Jacob protested that he was defending himself. The soldier just shrugged, and said that it didn't seem that way. But it would be up to the jury to decide.

Hours passed into evening, and then into night. He had been relieving himself in a bucket, which nobody came to empty, and it had passed the halfway mark.

Two more days passed with no human interaction other than a guard in the morning and evening. The darkness of night was no longer reassuring. It was so pitch-black that nothing seemed able to exist during those hours. He tried to sleep, but woke up in a panic, and spent most of the nights curled up on the cot, blanket over his body and head, trying to hide from the demons that terrorized his thoughts. These people thought they were civil. They thought they had the right to keep him imprisoned just as much as they thought they had a right to keep him laboring in the gardens. The world had almost ended, humankind practically wiped from the face of existence, and yet, here he was, awaiting trial.

No.

Right and wrong no longer existed. They were notions, and nothing more. He was being tortured, after having already faced the hurdles of surviving the plague and enduring the near-destruction of the world.

Days passed, and it was in the afternoon when Nick arrived at the cell and offered Jacob a way out. He told him that although he had killed one of their own, Nick understood that such things can happen, and that Jacob had an almost justifiable grievance. The people in Alice didn't treat him right. He shouldn't have been out in the fields. But nevertheless, he was no longer welcome in Alice. The trial was planned for the following day ... but he could leave that night if he wished. Nick would set him free and deal with the fallout from his father.

It didn't take much consideration on Jacob's part. He wanted to be far away from Alice. So late that night, before the darkness panicked his thoughts, he heard footfalls down the hall, and soon saw the bouncing glow of a flashlight. His eyes took a minute to adjust to the intense beam. The lock rumbled as the key turned, and the hinges creaked. He stood on aching legs, his clothing stiff from the sweat and dirt soaked into the fabric, which he had not changed since that fateful day.

The voice of Nick's assistant, Will Holbrook, said to follow him, and turned back toward the stairs. Jacob followed. At the top of the staircase, Will gave him a backpack containing clothing, water, survival bars, a sleeping bag, and a pistol. He was led through the quiet streets, down toward checkpoint Z in the wooded western section. The escort stopped at the guard post, and Will told Jacob that he should never return.

Jacob didn't turn around or acknowledge what Will had told him.

***

Jacob traveled for weeks on foot. The freedom of living outdoors, away from the drudgery of Alice, was exhilarating at first. He often thought of the people there, and his anger would flare. If he were ever to return, it would be to see the town burn.

Food was becoming scarce, and although he could identify a few edible plants, it was not enough to keep him alive. Out of necessity he ate bugs: big plump earthworms, and some crickets that he roasted over a fire.

He didn't know where he was heading; he simply started walking west and didn't stop. There was nowhere to go. Not once did he see any people.

It was in Kadoka, South Dakota that he met Mark Rothstein and his group of survivors. At first, he had no desire to join them. But being alone for so long had made him yearn for human companionship. He was also starving, and the offer of food was attractive.

He saw with his own eyes the difference in Mark's way of governing compared to how they did things in Alice. Mark's people were all fighters first and foremost, and although they sometimes had to do the unsavory tasks of building and fixing things, they often conducted scouting missions and raids, which all took a part in. Mark allowed Jacob to mingle with his colony as he pondered whether to join them permanently. Ten days later, Jacob was told that they were leaving, heading south with the coming of fall. Jacob joined them, and became a member of the group. He was a great shot, and loved the thrill of warfare. It was in his blood, his DNA, as it was in all of humankind.

During their travels, he told Mark all about Alice and the people there. He drew maps, showing the Ridgeline River bordering the northern section, and the half-moon formation of trenches. He told Mark about Tom and Nick, and their plans to get fuel. He told them of Nick's Dragoons, his fierce special forces of sorts, and of the Rangers and the Guards that made up their army. The people of Alice were the police officers, the judges, politicians, and prison guards of the world. They were the people who kept the likes of Mark Rothstein locked up and labeled a danger to society.

Jacob annotated the maps with lists of the people who worked behind the walls. He shared everything with Karl Metzger, who examined them all and let the story that Jacob shared roll around in his thoughts during the long march from Odyssey to the docks.

A plan was made prior to arriving at the shipyard, and readjusted with the Russian officers. Liam led the bulk of the military to Masterson, where the resistance was expected to be light. The town was in close proximity to Alice, and would serve as a suitable staging ground for the army to muster until Karl gave the order for them to advance.

Karl, along with a smaller force, made his way to Alice's border. He told Mark as they marched, "I was right in my assumption that the hearts of men can be easily corrupted, for I see it now. The desires of one man in particular are different from the others. The key to getting into Alice will be thorough Nick Byrnes."

Karl left his brigade in the woods, and heeled his stallion toward Alice's gates, alone.

Chapter Twenty-two
Partners

The day Karl rode to Alice's perimeter, wearing a crisp uniform and smiling down to the armed guards, he knew these people were of simple minds. "A dumb lot of peasants," he later told Mark. It took a little persuasion, a bit of charm, and above all, a high degree of articulation indicating authority and confidence, for them to radio Tom and Nick Byrnes.

He spoke to the old, stout, and round-bellied man, and his tall, lean son. He offered them his army on a contractual basis, for them to command as they saw fit. He told them all the things that he knew Nick would want to hear: the army that Nick desired, hundreds of soldiers that would do his bidding without hesitation. These things were proposed with a degree of flattery, an indication that Nick's rank and title were thoroughly respected. The young second in command scratched at his chin as Karl spoke, standing tall in a pressed uniform that seemed tailor-made to fit his frame.

After his speech, when his presentation had ended, Karl saddled his horse and rode off. The look in Tom's eyes said it all: that Karl would never be allowed to enter. But Nick ... he wanted more from this world ... he wanted the power that Karl was offering.

Before Karl rode away, he told them that he would return in two nights so they could digest the information he had presented. It was no surprise that Tom did not show up two nights later, but after Karl had waited only five minutes, Nick appeared, and they met outside the gates.

A young soldier named Will was present, Nick's personal guard of sorts, but he remained a few steps behind. Karl had brought the Priest along, and after a brief introduction, with the Priest issuing all sorts of praise, he fell back to let them speak. It was funny, Karl noticed then, how he had grown so accustomed to hearing the Priest ramble on about prayer that it no longer bothered him as it used to. The jabs of hot anger had lessened to something of a manageable glimmer of firelight.

Nick and Karl stood beside a tree.

"Sir Nicholas," Karl began, "I hope my proposition excited you."

Showered in moonlight, Nick's slick-backed hair appeared dramatically black.

"It's something to consider," he said. "It would be useful to bolster our fighting force, and we have the resources to support your numbers."

Karl smiled. "Indeed," he said.

"It will be difficult convincing my father."

"That can all be worked out, in due time. You come off as a strong leader. Please, do tell me a bit about your exploits?"

Nick told a fast tale of Alice's establishment, and Karl acted surprised and enthralled. He produced two cigars and handed one to Nick. From a saddlebag, he found a bottle of whiskey and took a swig, then handed the bottle across.

"It isn't easy commanding men, am I right?" he said.

"Commanding them is the easy part," Nick replied. "For me, it's getting past the bureaucracy that's the challenge."

They spoke at length about the struggles of leadership, of battles waged, of mishaps and narrow escapes. They spoke about war and disease, the *whys* of the world, and when they finished, over an hour had passed, and with it a good portion of the bottle.

"They need the whip sometimes more than anything else," Nick said, in reference to his men. "They're liable to grow lazy otherwise."

"I couldn't agree more. To be frank with you, sometimes losing a few in battle is essential to strengthen the resolve of the rest. It reminds them that they are fragile, and this world is an inhospitable place. A bit of blood spilled on your own side is encouraging."

Nick nodded. "Never thought about it that way, but you're right. I think"—he paused to take another swig—"we'll be able to work something out."

"Mister Byrnes, I do wholeheartedly agree. It is no coincidence that we have met. Fate has put us together. I knew it when I stumbled upon your town and saw the majesty of your defenses. We are destined to be partners."

They shook hands and went their separate ways.

***

It was during their second meeting that Nick confessed his dissatisfaction with Hightown, and how they were demanding more than their fair share of Alice's water and food in trade for only a trickle of their abundance of fuel. This was something Nick was passionate about, and Karl assured him that with a larger army, Hightown would have to supply more fuel or face the might of their forces. It became apparent that Nick was keen on the second choice—he wanted Hightown to face his wrath. Especially the elder general of the town, Albert Driscoll, who held his soldiers in higher regard than Nick's Dragoons.

During their third meeting, Nick secretly brought Karl into town. The guards on the line were commanded to another sector as Karl was led over the threshold in the darkness of night, and brought closer to the center of the community. They sat alone at a folding table in a massive storage warehouse, with a lantern between them. They shared a bottle of whiskey and smoked cigars as Karl explained his plan.

"No, it won't work," Nick said.

"Please, Sir Nicholas, I beg you to reconsider. My army works like a well-lubricated machine. No mistakes will be made, I assure you."

"I'm sure that it does, and to be honest, I would like to see your men in action to get a feel for their potential. However, sending a small brigade against the walls of Alice, with you swooping in to offer assistance, is not enough to sway my father's decision. There needs to be more."

Karl nodded. "Go on."

Nick took a drink of whiskey, breaking off eye contact and speaking more to the floor than to Karl. "We need to scare him—scare them all. Make them feel that they *need* you and your army to enter Alice. Like you've said, a bit of spilled blood on your own side does wonders at motivating the masses."

"Indeed," Karl said, a bit surprised and happy to hear Nick speak so frankly.

"I think ... I have an idea. Every day like clockwork my father makes his rounds, checking on the line, the trade grounds, the various posts, and the water filtering plant. One of the communication centers is set far away from the center of town, and could be sacrificed, with an attack occurring a few minutes after my father would be leaving. I will supply the coordinates, and you could lob off a few mortars to coincide with his departure. The explosion will have to be close enough to my father so that he knows he was targeted—but he must be at a safe distance. At the same time, you could unleash the small attack on Alice—the prisoners you have to sacrifice. Then you and your men would swoop in and flank the enemy, helping our defenses. My father would surely open the doors for you then."

"Interesting," Karl said, and brought his glass to his lips. In the end, when this was all said and done, Nick might make a worthy lieutenant. But that was yet to be seen.

"To pull this off, we'll have to be exact. The attack has to be precise, and the timing must be perfect."

"It will be. Sir Nicholas, I assure you. Has anyone ever told you that you would make a capable general to this town?"

Nick huffed out a chuckle. "Well, one day perhaps."

"Your strategy is well devised. We will work out the details in full over the coming days, and the plan will be set in motion."

They shook hands. Partners at last.

Chapter Twenty-three
Alice Betrayed

Karl marched into Alice sitting tall on his buckskin stallion. To his left and right were his lieutenants, Mark Rothstein and Sultan. The Priest rode one over, adjusting his eye patch and humming a light tune. Behind the riders marched two columns of the Red Hands, all in clean uniforms, with their weapons oiled and glistening. In between the columns were the prisoners: the five men left alive after they had stormed Alice's gates and were apprehended by Karl's brigade.

The whole entourage was led to the police department to drop off the captives, who were bleeding and battered, and had gags tied tight in their mouths. The people of Alice gathered, boiling with rage. These men were responsible for killing Tom Byrnes, or so they were led to believe. And Karl was responsible for bringing them in to face punishment. The group that had attacked Alice were all prisoners taken from past forays, selected out of the cells in Odyssey, and told that any who survived the battle would be offered their freedom.

Earlier that morning, before the sun rose, Karl met with Nick, and once again snuck in—for the last time. After today, he would become a most beloved member of Alice. They met in the warehouse, and Nick was just as angry as Karl had predicted.

"You were five minutes early!" Nick shouted again and again.

It took some analysis, along with a gentle touch of aggression, to explain to Nick that this was the best way for them to achieve their directive. If Nick wanted to attack Hightown, Tom needed to be eliminated. It was impossible with him still alive. "With your father in charge, we would never be able to achieve our goals. This is something you know—something you have always known," he told Nick.

Their relationship would be strained for a while, but it was not lost. Despite his protests and anger, Nick's eyes gave away his true feelings. He wanted power. He wanted control of Hightown. And he needed Karl to see his objectives met. Nick was led to believe he now shared command of the Red Hand army, and yes, the army was told to obey Nick's orders, but Karl could supersede those orders at any time. For the plans to work, Karl needed Nick. He needed Nick's men, the Dragoons, who were capable soldiers. Combined with his army soon arriving from Masterson, they could attack Hightown before they became aware of the scope of their presence.

The day the prisoners arrived, Nick addressed the people of Alice on a stage behind Alice's volunteer fire department, offering condolence over the loss of his father and their beloved leader, Tom Byrnes. Karl was soon introduced, and he took the stage and spoke to the assemblage. He praised Nick and referred to him by his new title: "General." Nick retook the stage and finished off by driving home the most important point, that someone in Alice—one of them—a traitor—gave the exact coordinate of the recon office and the time when Tom would be present. Keeping the population apprehensive was part of the plan, and the people looked from one to the other, formulating guilty parties in their minds.

Nick told them that it was Tom's plan for Karl and his men to join their own, to take over the soldiering so that the people of Alice could focus on constructing the defenses. From there, as the people became comfortable with their new position in Alice, they would take away their weapons, and trick or force them into imprisonment inside the school gymnasium before the attack on Hightown. It would be much easier to simply kill the majority of them now rather than later, but Nick would never agree to such terms. He actually thought that he was doing all of this—attacking Hightown, even participating in the death of his father—for the advancement of Alice as a society. Pure rubbish.

The prisoners were brought onto the same stage the following morning and executed before the townspeople. They received no proper trial, and yet the people cheered as the five corpses swung.

It was after the executions that Karl became aware of his predicament. A forward detachment of the Red Hands entered Alice—all in clean uniforms, combed hair, beards trimmed—and a scout came running forward, explaining to Karl in private that the fighting in Masterson was fiercer than anticipated. Several miles to the west of the town was an unknown settlement, which had an alliance with the people of Masterson. They counterattacked in the dead of night.

Karl took the Priest aside. "Go now with a few men. Ride to Masterson, and help Liam. Win this goddamn fight, and get yer ass back here with the army. Send Liam to the docks, and have him ready the ships. We attack Hightown as soon as the men are mustered."

The Priest turned away, and was soon seen riding out of Alice in haste. Karl wore a smile as he doled out shiny new pistols to Nick's Dragoons, along with brown leather chest holsters. It was time to differentiate the men deemed worthy, and let the peasants of Alice see who was really in charge.

The festivities went on into the night. His forwarding men brought crates of hard liquor, bales of marijuana, and a variety of narcotics. Karl drank his fill, mingling with the men, issuing praise to the people of Alice, and sympathy over their lost leader. Above all, he commended Nick on his ability to lead, and the virtues that Alice would soon attain under his guidance.

After dinner was served, which consisted of freshly slaughtered livestock that the Red Hands brought with them on the back of a pickup truck, Karl took Mark aside and passed him a cigar.

"We may be in," he said, passing a lighter, "but victory is far from certain." He told him of the fighting in Masterson.

Mark lit his cigar and scratched at his beard. "'Ya think we should fall back, help the efforts in Masterson? The men never fought without you by their side."

Karl raised an eyebrow. "Fall back? You're smarter than that, Mister Rothstein. Captain Briggs is a capable leader. This is only a delay, nothing more. Soon—days, not weeks—we will lock these idiots away, or slaughter them all. Alice will fall; I swear it. I don't care if it takes a year, this town will be crushed under my heels. Do you remember our conversation, all those months ago when we first met? Do you remember what you said to me?"

"I ... umm—"

"It's the world that I want, Mister Rothstein. The world. And it all starts here, in Alice. We'll have enough food and water to last a lifetime, and best of all, we won't have to lift a finger. Their people we let live will do all the labor for us."

Karl gazed at his lieutenant, his eyes holding on to Mark as if he were gripping him tight. He could see Mark quiver, could feel his tension. Then he smiled and slapped him on the shoulder. "Ha!" he said, holding his cigar between his teeth. "Lighten up—this is a party, after all!"

"It's a mourning, sir."

"Same difference."

Karl grabbed a bottle of whiskey off a nearby table and took a swig. He handed Mark the bottle, and looked to the sky. "Beautiful evening, is it not?" he asked.

Mark looked up and scratched at his beard. "I guess."

Chapter Twenty-four
Unravel

The fighting in Masterson was about over. The resistance dwindled down to a fraction and fell back to their settlement, five miles to the west. The Priest led the bulk of the men to finish them off for good, while Liam and a contingency traveled to the docks. A forwarding detachment arrived in Alice in the shroud of night, and marched straight to the lawn of Nick Byrnes's mansion—a home that Karl ordered his men to clean up, and install massive generators. Nick and his girlfriend of sorts, a strange girl who didn't venture outdoors often, were allotted a private wing, and the rest of the house would be used to lodge the ranking officers.

By all accounts, the plan was back on track.

The fuel ransacked from Masterson would prove beneficial for their supply of jeeps and trucks. Alice had a large supply of fuel as well, which Karl planned to dwindle down. In the days following Tom's death, order had been maintained, but the veil of the Red Hand's friendliness was beginning to wear thin. However, the days were counting down, and with them, many of the town's more vocal proponents of Karl's occupation started to disappear. Some were brought in for questioning, while others were driven out of Alice to a field of rolling grass, and executed.

It came to light that a small group of rebels were meeting at night to discuss these disappearances, and offering ways to try and overthrow Nick's leadership. The group was discovered with the help of a man named Chris Lockton, who had been a member of Alice's round table—the men responsible for governing the people. The other members all proved to be incompetent, and subsequently executed—all except for an urban developer named Douglas Banks. He designed a variety of arcane defenses, catapults, and the like. Nick found them appealing in a trivial sort of way, and some were constructed. Karl had to admit that he liked the idea of rocks raining down on his enemies. Or perhaps severed heads. It was delightfully medieval.

Chris Lockton joined the group of malcontents under the guise of friendship, and turned them all over to Karl. Among them was the head gardener, an old man who couldn't walk faster than a crawl. A girl was also mentioned, who had arrived recently from Hightown to work on the trade route. Three men were leading the group: Simon Kalispell, Jeremy Winters, and Frank Morrow. These men were high-ranking members of Alice's Ranger and Guard divisions, although both divisions were now defunct. Nick told the people to let the Red Hands do the fighting; it was a way for the town to progress. Nick was good, Karl gave him that. His words were a delicious poison, and the people yearned for more. Under the same guise of safety, Nick told the people that firearms were no longer permitted inside of Alice, and that all weapons were to be turned over. The people were wary about this decree, but with a bit of oppression from the Red Hands, weapons were being turned in.

The resistance group was rounded up early in the morning, and the gardener, the girl named Beth from Hightown, and Will Holbrook—Nick's old personal guard, turned traitor—were brought in for questioning. The rest of the dissenters were brought to the field to be executed.

Karl delighted in seeing what Doctor Freeman did to make Will Holbrook talk. The boy was strong, but the doctor had his methods.

"It ... it's in a p-park," Will said, the light in his eyes fading.

"Please go on, and your suffering will end," the doctor told him.

Will lay on a stainless-steel table, his arms stretched out overhead, and his ankles tied tight. Pieces of him were missing, sitting on another stainless-steel table. Tears had rolled down his face in nonstop trickles, but he no longer cried. After his genitalia was removed and placed on a weight scale, the boy stopped crying. The doctor took notes during the entire ordeal, keeping track of various weights and sketching hasty diagrams of the organs' inner workings.

"S-Sullivan ... Park ..." With those words, Doctor Freeman kept his promise, and gave a final incision with his scalpel to end Will's life and suffering. Brahms was playing on the portable stereo. A light sonata that Karl didn't recognize.

After hearing the name Sullivan Park, Karl left to address a guard stationed outside the door. "Find me a map," he said. "And a scout brigade—now."

"Yes, sir." The soldier took off fast.

They were in the basement of Nick's mansion, using the top of a pool table in the game room section to study a map. Karl sent scouts to inspect Sullivan Park to see if it contained the amount of armaments, tanks, helicopters, and transports that Will Holbrook claimed. The scouts were then ordered to intercept the Priest and the main army of the Red Hands. They could arrive with enough firepower to make the war in Hightown a fast victory.

Karl turned back to the rear hallway, toward the unfinished laundry room where they questioned Will Holbrook. He caught Doctor Freeman exiting the room.

"Doctor," he said, "are you ready to begin on the gardener?"

The doctor nodded. "I'll have the men bring him in now."

Karl walked past him, following the hallway to a rear bedroom, once used for the staff of the mansion. The young girl, Bethany Rose, had been brought down while they were questioning Will. They took a break in their procedure as she was strapped to a bed and given tranquilizers on Karl's insistence. She had a fierce determination, and fought her captors until the last moment.

"I'll kill the fucking lot of you," she said, twisting in the arms of a soldier. "All of you—all dead!"

In another world, she would have made a good addition to the Red Hands. Perhaps even an officer.

Karl stared at her tied to the mattress, her hair fanned out, her cheeks red against her fair complexion. "Put her to sleep," he ordered.

Doctor Freeman didn't question the order. He gave her an IV line. She resisted and had to be held down. As she was given tranquilizers, her eyes grew heavy, and then closed. The doctor left. He knew about Karl's disorder. It was part of their unspoken agreement. Karl allowed Doctor Freeman freedom to do as he wished to prisoners in exchange for his assistance fixing up their own men, and the doctor gave Karl drugs so that he could satisfy his desires. Unfortunately, parts of him just didn't work otherwise.

Karl was staring down at the beautiful girl when someone knocked at the door.

"What is it?" he said in a huff.

The door creaked open, and a soldier entered. "Sir, he's awake."

"What?"

"Nick. He's awake."

The soldier was doing his duty, but still, Karl was tempted to shoot him right then and there. He'd ordered one of his men to wait in the bedroom beside Nick's—where the man had fallen into a drunken stupor from the previous night's party. He was instructed to let him know at once when Nick was awake.

"All right," Karl said, and turned from the room. He spoke to a guard outside Bethany's door as he passed, "I will be doing her interrogation myself. Make sure the doctor is aware. Keep her alive and untouched."

"Yes, sir."

***

The scouts returned with good news: the armament in Sullivan Park was beyond what they imagined. There were dozens of vehicles and thousands of rounds of ammunition. But, then came the bad news.

While giving the extremely hungover and sick Nicholas Byrnes a tour of what they'd accomplished in the basement overnight, Mark, Sultan, and Ryan Pechman appeared. They were filthy and injured.

Karl sent Nick on his way and spoke to his officers in private. "What the hell happened?" he asked.

They looked at one another, frightened to speak. "It was … Hightown, sir."

They'd botched the execution of Frank Morrow, Jeremy Winters, Simon Kalispell, and Martin Howard. A supply convoy from Hightown spotted them out on the plain, and there was an exchange of gunfire. Ryan Pechman clutched a wound on his stomach, the rags stained red.

"We sent an envoy to the cargo team, said it was all a mistake," the young sergeant said.

"Oh?" Karl's eyebrows rose. "Well, maybe we got off lucky then."

"Um, yes, sir, I think—"

Karl stepped toward him, bumping into Sergeant Pechman's chest, making the injured man wince. He loomed tall over the young sergeant, casting his face in shadow. "Who ... the fuck ... asked for your opinion?"

"I-I, um," he swallowed, "sir—"

Karl grabbed Ryan Pechman by the throat. Ryan's eyes seemed to bulge as Karl's grip tightened, and he dropped the bloody rags clutched to his wound. His feet lifted off the ground for the last conscious moment of his life as something audibly snapped. When Karl let go, Sergeant Pechman fell to the ground, his eyes staring up at the ceiling. In a practiced motion, Karl unholstered his pistol, fired into Ryan's head, and re-holstered his gun.

"Send men back to the grave, and bury the dead. Cover our tracks. There's no possible way that Hightown believes it was all an accident, but we need to buy a little more time before we attack."

Karl patted his pockets for a cigar. His officers were standing at attention.

"What the fuck are you waiting for?"

"Sir," they said in unison, and left fast up the stairs.

***

"You found this on who?"

"Frank Morrow, sir. What was left of him," a soldier told Karl.

"He's dead, you're sure of it? What about the others?"

"Found them all bludgeoned beyond comprehension, or shot up."

"But was it them?"

"They had their IDs on them, and were wearing uniforms from Alice."

Karl looked back to the papers, but remained skeptical. However, if what was outlined on the blueprints was correct, it wouldn't matter anyway.

"Get a team assembled," he said, and shooed his officers away.

He coiled the papers, marked *Operation Blue Rapture* on the top, and proceeded up the basement stairs toward Nick's wing of the house. He found the man slumped in a plush leather couch in his office, a glass of whiskey in his hand.

"Sir General," Karl said, snapping Nick out of a daydream. He went on to explain that he had an errand to run, but not to worry, he would return shortly.

"Wh-where you going?" Nick said in a drunken slur.

"It's of no concern."

He left before Nick could ask any more questions, and met with the team assembled to extract the B83 nuclear bomb that the blueprints said was hidden in a nearby house. Operation Blue Rapture called for all of Alice to be destroyed in the event of an emergency. Hightown had set up this failsafe without anyone in Alice becoming the wiser, and it appeared that Frank Morrow, Jeremy, and Simon had been planning to act on these plans.

At dawn, they drove down Ridgeline Road and parked in front of the house. The directions led them to a glass greenhouse in the rear, and to a storage shed inside. Karl lifted a paver and saw the metal of a trapdoor beneath.

"Open it," he said, barely able to contain his excitement.

They removed the pavers and cut the lock. An engineer proceeded down the steps along with Sultan. Mark stayed by Karl's side, along with a few soldiers.

"We see it," the engineer said.

Mark walked to the stairway, Karl behind him. He was just saying, "Don't touch a thing," when all at once a flash enveloped his eyesight, and he felt the force of the world crash against his chest as the explosion blasted a gale of torrent up the stairway. Mark disappeared. Before Karl hit the ground his vision turned black, and reality was extinguished.

Chapter Twenty-five
Awake

His eyes twitched and then cracked open. Whatever dark crevice of his mind first became conscious was trying to rationalize his sudden reentry into the world, as he stared into an unknown void.

I'm home, under the covers, and I'm a child, his mind substantiated, then jumped, *I'm staring at the cement ceiling in my cell in Huntsville—or maybe Atlanta ... No, I'm staring at the ceiling of the train car, and any minute now the door will slide open and the conductor will find me lying here using my stained orange jumpsuit as a blanket.*

But ...

... wait ...

I'm staring at the sky ...

It was the smoke billowing out from the house that woke him from the depths of unconsciousness, causing him to cough himself awake. With each convulsion of his body, he remembered where he was and how much pain he was in.

Karl attempted to move, but the rushes of agony forced him to stop.

He lifted his right hand, flexing his fingers one at a time, and then he moved to his toes and began contracting each and every muscle in turn, seeing what was there and what was not.

A fire raged in the house, and the flames bellowed out through the doorway. The heat was so intense that he felt the hairs on his body singe. Drifting cinders floated through the air, some searing his skin where they landed. The room was collapsed, with flames emerging from the ground, and he saw the outline of a decapitated head mixed in with a pile of wreckage.

Smoke poured out like rapids on a river, escaping through the shattered glass frame of the greenhouse. Asphyxiation was close at hand if the flames did not cook him first. His arms reached out and his body twisted and turned over, shedding the blanket of thick dust, rocks, and glass shards off his chest. Gritting his teeth against the pain, Karl peeled his body off the ground, where dried blood had kept him stuck to the floor like glue.

As he crawled, his wounds reopened; yet onward he went, ignoring his suffering and the pangs of bright light and dark spots that at times consumed his vision.

Outside on the lawn, as the intense heat dissipated, he turned on his back, panting, to see the flaming house that had almost become his pyre.

Karl stared in fascination, and then a funny feeling overtook him.

He began laughing. "You cannot kill me—no one can kill Karl Metzger, although they try!"

He laughed uncontrollably, but any movement caused sharp pains in his abdomen and back.

He pushed himself up on his elbows and then his forearms. Dizziness gave him pause. A length of splintered wood lay on the lawn, mixed with other debris propelled from the house. Karl grabbed it and used it to pull himself to his feet. It was a slow and deliberate process, and twice he nearly passed out.

Where the hell are my men?

Before he could finish asking his own question, he knew the answer. He knew it as the early morning sky turned a paler form of black. The horizon was filled with a burning orange tinge and clouds of gray smoke rose high. Karl saw at that moment the blades of helicopters—one, two, maybe more—moving up and down along the front line, far off in the distance like malicious flies.

I've been defeated.

He stared a moment longer, and soon he laughed again despite his body's painful protests. "Burn it all down, then. Ha! Let it turn to ash! There is always another fire to start, another town to ignite! The inferno of the world, it will never be extinguished! The horizons will forever burn, and I will hold the torch!"

Karl Metzger turned to where a narrow gate led to a path down a steep embankment and to the Ridgeline River below. Moving was hard, and the blood streaming from his open wounds was made worse with each step. But Karl Metzger made it to the gate, and to the steep staircase and ramp beyond, where a small dock bobbed up and down on the water.

On the platform beside the dock was a tall wooden rack, the pegs constructed to hold canoes and rafts. Two rowboats were tied there, and it took a considerable amount of strength to pull one down. Blood made his grip slippery, and before he dropped the boat in the water, he had to sit and catch his breath. He tied a tourniquet made from a scrap of his tattered shirt around his kneecap, and then he pushed the boat into the water. He slid his ragged body into the hull and let the boat drift over the bounding swells.

After some time, Karl found a single oar bungeed to the side and paddled his way toward the opposite shore.

You cannot kill me ...

His vision was grainy, with swells of pixilated lights. His strength was fading. The oar almost fell from his numb fingers.

"Easy does it, old man. Stay with it."

The opposite bank was steep, just as in the towns of Fairview and Alice, but Karl could see a natural, earthen ramp where several small docks jutted out among old half-sunken and lopsided yachts.

As Karl rowed closer to shore, he saw a fishing boat pulled up on the embankment, identical to his own. He followed the course, rowing until the bow of his small boat hit land. A man wearing a black trench coat stood watching him the entire time, not moving from his perch atop the hill. The man shifted his briefcase to the other hand and pushed his glasses up the bridge of his nose. Karl stood on shaking legs, careful not to slip on the blood smeared inside the hull. He swallowed, staring at the only man who could put fear in his heart.

"Hey!" Karl shouted. "Arthur, ol' pal. Be a sport, would you? Give me a hand here."

The beady eyes of Doctor Arthur Freeman stared down at Karl Metzger.

Chapter Twenty-six
Rise

His eyes blinked open, staring unsteadily down the embankment to the rowboat he'd left bobbing against the shore. Judging by the dark blue shade of the morning, Karl judged that he had been unconscious for only a moment.

Doctor Freeman knelt in front of him, tightly wrapping his thigh with duct tape. Karl clenched his eyes shut against the pain. He'd passed out twice already since making his way up the embankment, and he wanted to remain conscious. The doctor roughly jostled his leg, pressing fingers to the wounds to stem the flow of blood. Karl leaned his head against the back of a tree as lacerations on his face and neck were explored. He gazed at the rowboat moving with each gentle wave; saw blood streaked on the seat and walls, and wondered how much blood he'd lost ... how much he was still losing ...

... how much could he lose and survive ...

stand ...

... walk ...

... to leave this godforsaken land.

"You need stitches, but we got to move. That's all I can do for now." The doctor's words brought Karl out of his reverie, and he noticed just how still and quiet the world was outside of his thoughts.

The war is over ... I've lost.

Doctor Freeman packed up his supplies, wiping the blood off his tools and hands with a cloth, and tossed everything in his leather briefcase. He stood and found his trench coat, and was putting it on as he asked, "Can you stand?"

Karl wasn't sure. His outstretched legs might have been logs.

"Find me that oar there," he said, pointing to where he dropped it.

The doctor handed him the oar and helped pull him to his feet. The blood seemed to rush from his head in a whoosh, and Karl's vision was a sea of dull pixilation. Everything became numb: his limbs, his ears, his nose. His upper lip tingled, and his knees quaked.

But he did not fall.

Using the oar as a crutch, and Doctor Freeman putting his arm under his opposite shoulder, Karl stepped forward, feeling the pull of the duct tape with each step. A warm wetness spread from many of the wounds, and his vision throbbed with dazed pain. His ankles, at least, felt sturdy, supported by the stiff tape wrapped around his torn boots to keep them on his feet.

As they neared the street ahead, he took one last look behind him. He saw the maple tree he had leaned against, the embankment where he had collapsed by the rowboat, and all the way to Alice on the distant shore, where his men had been slain. Trails of smoke still rose high into the air.

His soldiers would now be getting interrogated, hung from the streetlights, or shot in the backs of their heads. That's what he would be doing if he had won the battle, and he would have won the battle if not for whatever trickery had befallen him.

What had exploded down in that cellar? Definitely not the atom bomb. He'd be nothing more than a whisper of smoke if that device had detonated. Was there even an atomic weapon down there at all? Was it a trick?

"Are any of the officers alive?" Karl asked.

"What's that?" the doctor said, laboring under Karl's weight.

"Who's alive? Did you see Captain Black, maybe Mister Rothstein? What about Nick?"

"Didn't see anybody. I was in the basement when the fighting started. The explosions from the front line rattled the house, and when I got upstairs and looked out the window, the horizon was on fire. The men were running around like dimwits, looking for you and Nick, or someone to tell them what to do. Then the front yard blew up all over and I heard a noise, something I hadn't heard in ages: a helicopter. It came swooping down, blowing the trenches to rubble."

"How did you manage to get out?"

Karl felt him shrug under his shoulder. "I turned and left out the back door. I was lucky enough to find a boat on the dock. There are more who left—I saw them jumping in the dark water, swimming away. A few boats trailed far behind me, and I expected to see them pull up to the same embankment. I waited, but they must have moored somewhere else. I was just turning to leave when your rowboat cut through the mist."

Karl suppressed his first emotion, which was anger at his men fleeing from a fight, no matter how hopeless. But he needed every available soldier he could muster, all that survived. "How many ..." He paused as a wave of nausea passed. "How many do you think escaped?"

"No idea. Don't know if any survived the swim. And I couldn't guess if any escaped the trenches at all."

They were silent as they took to a wooded trail. The morning was bright and warm, and the sun made Karl's burnt clothing reek of charcoal, smoke, and sweat.

"How did they break our line?"

"I don't know. Something happened to the men during the night—they were getting sick. I tended to some in the house when the fighting began. They were vomiting, had substantial diarrhea, and were exhibiting severe hallucinations and abdominal cramping. Food poisoning is my guess, or a norovirus."

"How many?"

"In the house, only a dozen or so. But reports coming in from the line suggested it was widespread, an epidemic. The men in the house though, they were developing blistering rashes all over their bodies, from head to toe."

Karl shook his head.

"This was a diversion—all of it. The explosion in the cellar, the men being poisoned. I don't know how they did it, but they did."

"It would appear so."

After an hour, Karl became severely lightheaded, and they had to take a break to rest.

"You think they're going to follow us?" the doctor asked.

"Yes. They're going to round up every last one of us they can find. They'll send scouting parties for miles around, if they haven't already, and they'll see our boats—"

The branches nearby crackled, and they heard distinct voices. Doctor

Freeman helped Karl stand, and they got ready to run.

"*Don't move*," Karl whispered and unholstered his pistol, aiming it toward the brush. The voices grew louder; the leaves underfoot crunched. Karl's finger tensed over the trigger, his blurred eyesight peering down the sights.

Three men came out from the thicket, one semiconscious and being dragged by the others. They froze when they saw Karl and the doctor, and the lead man swung a machine gun from its shoulder sling. His eyes went large and he said, "Karl? General ... sir, is that you?"

Karl lowered his pistol and sighed.

"You know," he said, "I should shoot the lot of you for desertion. Come 'ere and give me a hand, would ya?"

Chapter Twenty-seven
Thirst

At sundown, the men tried the handles of homes in a residential section, not wanting to make noise kicking down a door, until they found one unlocked. Doctor Freeman helped Karl to a couch in the small living room as the two soldiers closed all the blinds.

"I hate sleeping indoors," Karl said, waving his hand at a shaft of illuminated dust motes.

The other injured man had been dragged into the living room beside the couch, and blankets were found to make him comfortable.

Doctor Freeman inspected the wounds to the man's abdomen and chest, his delicate fingers dancing over various lacerations. He then pulled the blanket up to the man's chin.

One of the soldiers watching, a young, tall boy named Greg, said, "Aren't you going to do something?"

"Nothing to be done," he said, and turned his attention to Karl. "Lie back, please."

Karl did as instructed, issuing a reluctant groan.

"Don't any of you got a bottle?"

The two men shook their heads. The other soldier, Reed, was a few years older than Greg. Both were unharmed by the battle, but the same could not be said of the third soldier, who was unconscious for most of their journey. Karl wanted to leave him behind, miles back, and had even told the two privates to do so. But upon their pleading that they had the strength to carry him, Karl relented.

"What happened to him?" Karl asked as Doctor Freeman snapped on a pair of latex gloves.

The two soldiers moved chairs close to the windows, peeking out from time to time.

"The three of us were in the trenches," Greg said, "when almost everyone started acting funny. Aubrey here was sick, grabbing at his stomach, all twisted in pain."

"Yes, yes, he was poisoned," Karl said, then gritted his teeth as the duct tape was cut from his thigh and the rancid layer of clothing near the wound was peeled back. "Jesus Christ … you all sure you don't have some whiskey? Vodka? Check the cabinets."

Greg stood, leaving his rifle leaning against the windowsill, and started going through the cabinets in the kitchen. Karl focused on the pictures on the wall to take his mind off the pain. Happy faces, people in nice clothing posing: a gray-haired man and his wife, smiling, over and over again behind dusty frames. Their unbridled happiness angered him, and Doctor Freeman paused to say, "Karl, relax. Please."

He looked away.

"So, he was shot?" Karl asked Reed.

"Yes, sir. In the stomach. Something also hit him on the head, shrapnel, or a rock, or something. The whole line was blown to pieces. I got hit in the leg here." The soldier lifted his pants leg, showing a discolored welt on his calf. "Don't know what it was, but it knocked me off my feet. Thought for a minute it took my leg clear off."

Greg came back in the room. "Sir, I found this." He displayed a half bottle of cooking brandy.

Karl's eyes lit up and he reached out. "Give it here."

The room became dark as Doctor Freeman continued to work by flashlight, splashing disinfectant over the wounds and slipping the pointed end of a sewing needle back and forth into his flesh. The pain was beyond comprehension. Karl hoped he would pass out and awaken all patched up and made right again. But he remained conscious for the duration, each stab of the needle causing daggers of electric distress.

He took a long swig from the bottle.

"Doctor, you're going to have to finish soon for the night," he said. "We can't have the flashlight shining through the blinds."

The doctor turned to Greg. "Go outside and see if the light is coming through the blinds." He turned back to Karl as the soldier stood to leave. "I'm nearly done. You need water. A lot of it. You're dehydrated, and I don't have an IV."

Karl was aware of how profusely he was sweating. His mangy shirt and pants were soaked through to the couch cushions. Back on the riverbank, the doctor had packed a canteen of water in his briefcase, but that water didn't last half the day's march, and none of the men had a drop since.

The front door opened and Greg returned. "Can't see much. A little light through the corner of the blinds."

"I'll finish fast," Doctor Freeman said. "You'll need to go scouting," he told the soldiers. "We need water. Food, maybe."

"Now?" Greg asked.

"Yes, now. Get to it. And be quiet."

In the stillness, all Karl could hear was the gentle rustling movements of the doctor at work and the occasional moaning from the man on the ground.

"How long has he got?" Karl asked.

Doctor Freeman shrugged. "Can't say for sure. Surprised he's still alive after being pulled around while bleeding out. But then again, I could say the same for you. Back at the riverside, I didn't think you'd make it for more than a mile. God only knows how much blood you lost."

Karl huffed a laugh. "Oh, doctor. Your bedside manners are impeccable."

With the soldiers still away, the last stitch was sewn, and gauze was placed over the wounds, held in place with strips of duct tape. The pulling of Karl's skin as the tape clung to his flesh was about as painful as getting the stiches, and at times it was worse. When the doctor finished, he took off his bloody gloves and rummaged through his bag, examining the labels of pill bottles.

"Here," he said, opening the cap of one and putting the bottle on the table. "You need one three times a day." He handed Karl a large white pill, and Karl took it down with a swig of brandy.

There was an inch of liquor left, and Karl offered Doctor Freeman the bottle.

"For your nerves," he said.

"My nerves are fine." But he took the bottle anyway, and searched through his bag, finding a small cylindrical device in a leather case. He unclasped a small lock on the side and removed a paper-thin glass tumbler.

"You keep a glass in there?"

The doctor poured a drink. "It's a traveling cup," he said. "Over a hundred years old." He held the delicate rim to his lips and drank.

Karl took the last swig from the bottle and placed it on the coffee table. In the dark room, Karl could just make out the shape of Doctor Freeman sitting on a chair beside the couch. They talked for a while about where they were going, and decided on a new plan now that they'd found Reed and Greg.

Talking was becoming difficult. Pain was everywhere, emanating from deep within his more serious wounds, and spreading to every inch of his body. His eyelids were closing when the front door creaked open and two shadowy figures emerged. Karl reached for his pistol on the arm of the couch before realizing they were his men.

"This is all we got," one of the shadows said, and placed a can of iced tea down on the coffee table.

"That's it?" Doctor Freeman asked, snatching the can.

"We checked a few houses; they're all wiped clean, and even with a flashlight it's hard to see. We can go further down the side streets."

"No," Karl said, fighting to keep his eyes open. "No more venturing. We're not far from Alice and Hightown. Their scouts will be everywhere."

The can opened with a pop and a hiss, and a moment later the doctor held the rim to Karl's lips. He took a sip and the sweet fluid burst in his mouth and coated his raw throat. He drank it greedily, pulling in over half the tea in two gulps. The doctor took the can away and drank a sip himself before handing it to the two soldiers.

One of the soldiers asked about where they were going, what they were going to do, and how they were going to survive. Doctor Freeman explained what he and Karl had discussed on their first leg of the venture, and then again just moments before the soldiers returned. There were two places any of their fellow fleeing soldiers would go. One was north, to the docks, in the same direction they were heading. The second was Masterson, their closest conquered town. Karl's guess had been most would head to the second, and Alice's and Hightown's fleet would be fast at their heels. So what was needed was a full-scale departure from Masterson, with every available man fleeing to the docks, where they would be safe in the boats.

Doctor Freeman instructed that one of them had to immediately leave to Masterson, to deliver Karl's orders to evacuate. More importantly, he had to dispel any rumors of Karl's death. In the meantime, they needed a place where Karl could rest, heal, and hide from enemy patrols. They knew a safe location several miles away, much closer than both Masterson and the docks.

The men did not sound happy at the proposition of one of them leaving in the dark to travel through the night, with enemy scouts all about. The last thing Karl heard before sleep overtook him was each man presenting his case for why he should not go, and offering why the other was a stronger candidate. The doctor was listening to them in silence, the glass tumbler making a slight clang as he placed it on the coffee table. Before he could make his verdict, Karl was fast asleep.

**

Sunlight stabbed at his eyes like razors. A hand was on him, shaking him.

"*Wake up. Wake up*," a voice said in a hiss.

He might have been in the bed of his youth, or a prison cell, or a cot, or out on some scavenging foray. Karl blinked, and after seeing the doctor above him, reality came rushing back.

"What—what is it, what's wrong?" He attempted to sit up, but the wound to his abdomen forced him back down. He looked across the room and saw Greg standing by the window, rifle in hand, peering out between two thin slats in the blind.

"They're here," Doctor Freeman said. "Scouts from Alice—they're right outside."

Chapter Twenty-eight
Boots

Karl blinked, attempting to return some degree of moisture to his eyes. A fly droned over his face, tickling his nose. He swatted it away and rolled to his side to press himself up to sitting. The blood seemed to plummet from his head, and for a moment his vision faded.

Easy, old man. Take it easy. Breathe.

He grabbed his pistol and listened for engines or voices, but heard nothing. Once the dizziness passed, he pulled himself to standing.

Stumbling forward, he nearly tripped over Aubrey on the ground, who was still clinging to life. His sweat-covered face was white, bordering blue, yet his chest moved under the blanket with shallow breaths.

Karl moved toward the window with Doctor Freeman holding his elbow. Things in his body were crunching and popping, grinding together. Greg moved aside and Karl peeked out.

The front yard gave way to the road ahead, the morning sunlight blindingly bright. Karl forced his eyes to stay open. He watched two men on the opposite side of the road walk from one house to the next. They wore matching olive drab uniforms and small backpacks, armed with machine guns on slings, and tactical pouches attached to their belts. One held a black metal pry bar over his shoulder, about three feet long.

Seeing these soldiers—these victorious men—made Karl's blood beat fast.

It was mine—Alice was mine!

His vision throbbed with his anger. Flash images of these men, all of

Alice's people, disemboweled, strung up from lampposts, danced around in his thoughts in delight.

"What are they doing?" Greg asked.

"Searching," Karl said. "House to house."

"They're following us?"

"If they had any degree of scout in them they would have seen our tracks and kicked in the front door before daybreak."

The two soldiers were at the door of the house across from them, guns up. One tried the handle, then maneuvered his pry bar into the grove beside the doorframe. The other man was ready to storm inside.

"There must be more in the area. They're checking in pairs."

"What—what do we do?"

Karl didn't answer. He peered at the house across the way, at the dark void of the open door where the men had disappeared, and then he looked at what he could see of the road ahead. They were on a dead end, just a few houses from the circling roundabout. If the men continued their path, they would be at their front door after inspecting four additional homes. Twenty minutes, half an hour tops.

"We got to move," he said.

"W-where?"

Karl turned and looked at Greg. The man's eyes were huge, bloodshot, and he clutched his rifle to his chest.

"You know how to use that thing? You know how to fight?"

"Y-yes, sir."

"Well, you're going to have to prove it."

Greg nodded.

"You have a choice—you can man up now, or you can die. It's as simple as that. Do as I say and you will live. Or stay here quivering like a child and let those mongrel peasants hang you from the nearest tree. When this is all over, and we're back at the docks, a promotion might be in store for you. But that will be decided based on how you handle yourself at this juncture. Understand?"

"Yes, sir."

"Yes, sir, what?"

"I understand. Yes, sir. General. I understand."

"Good." Karl turned back to the window, watching the two scouts appear from the doorway and proceed to the next house.

Stepping back from the blinds, he looked at the filthy rags he was wearing: burnt, stiff with blood. Duct-taped bandages emerged from beneath the rips. His feet were black with filth. He looked to his boots beside the couch. The duct tape that had kept them closed was sliced open, and the raw, torn leather resembled something dead.

The doctor stood beside the couch, briefcase in hand. Karl limped over and sat, picking up the pillow he had slept on.

"Greg," Karl said. "Go to the back door. Wait for us, we'll be there in a moment."

Greg didn't move.

"That's an order. Go *now*. Doctor, I need your assistance."

Greg turned and left.

Each second that passed was filled with an anxious dread, thinking that at any moment the door would be kicked in.

When Karl and Doctor Freeman joined Greg, Karl was dressed in Aubrey's cleaner pants and boots. He limped even more with his toes cramped together, but the boots were in reasonably good shape.

"They're two houses away," Karl said, and began explaining what they needed to do. Greg swallowed visibly and wiped the sweat from his eyes.

"Why don't we just leave, hightail it away?" Greg asked.

"For one thing," Karl said, "once they come in here, see Aubrey on the ground, the bloodstains on the couch, the ruffled blankets, they'll call in reinforcements. And, in case you've forgotten, I'm not in the position to *hightail* it anywhere. Does that make sense to you?"

Greg nodded.

"Is this going to be a problem?"

"No. No, sir," Greg said.

Karl explained the plan, and when he was done, he said, "Ready?"

They nodded and opened the back door.

Chapter Twenty-nine
Scouts

Karl clutched at the wound on his chest with his left hand, his right gripping his pistol as he led the men to the side of the neighboring house, closer to the oncoming patrol. Twice his feet gave way, and the doctor grabbed on to his elbow, but it did little to keep him from stumbling.

The enemy scouts were two houses away, and they would be exiting at any moment. Karl led his men behind a large, rectangular central air conditioner with a puff of hedgerow that blocked it from view of the road, and then he collapsed to sitting with his back against the house siding. Doctor Freeman and Greg stayed crouched low, not daring to look out over the top of the brush.

The gentle sound of footfalls came from down the pathway leading to the neighboring house, growing louder as the scouts neared. Hinges creaked. A quiet voice said, "Ready?" and then there was a crack and a thud as the door was broken and pushed open.

Karl looked up and over his shoulder, to a window several feet above him. He held his pistol in his right hand and unsheathed his knife with his left.

A flutter of birds flew overhead, landing on power lines connecting the properties. Their melodic chirping drifted over the breeze.

Karl closed his eyes and leaned his head back. His mind was swirling, like he was on a roller coaster with the scenery soaring by.

Hinges creaked ... footfalls from down the steps ... ruffling grass.

Karl opened his eyes. Greg was trembling, yet ready to pounce, the long blade in his hand wavering. The doctor remained motionless, yet ready to leap forward. He too held a combat knife, the blade long and thin.

Greg inched to jump forward, but Karl reached out and put an arm in front of him, shaking his head back and forth.

They heard the footfalls of the two men before they came into view from the front of the house, cutting straight across the yard to the next property, where inside lay the deceased Aubrey. Their heads appeared over the brushy hedge, then after a few more steps their backs were to them. Tall men. Wide shouldered, and covered with instruments of warfare.

The man to the right held the pry bar over his shoulder. One of them was whistling a quiet tune.

Karl removed his arm from Greg and displayed three fingers in the air ...

... two fingers ...

... one ...

... a fist.

Greg and Doctor Freeman sprung to their feet, and Karl aimed their only rifle upward from his sitting position.

The two scouts were a few feet away and jolted at the sudden activity. The one on the right half turned before the doctor reached out, his left forearm going over the man's face, pulling up, all the while hammering down on his neck and collar with the knife. Each stab was as meticulous as his skill would allow. The man grabbed at the doctor, trying to reach for his head, face, anything to hold on to.

Greg attacked the other man before he could turn, jabbing the knife forward at the base of the soldier's head and his back, but the soldier turned around, the pry bar swinging before him, his mouth making noises like, "Don't-don't ..."

Karl had the man dead in his sights, watched him grab at his rifle in the sling, but he was unable to do so while swinging the pry bar and stumbling backwards. The rifle slid down the man's arm, and when he tried to grab the handle, the gun fell from his grip.

Greg surged forward, slashing with the knife, hitting the pry bar with the clangs and scraping of metal on metal. Blood appeared on the scout's neck and forearm as Greg lurched and leaped, his mouth set in a growl.

The pry bar caught Greg in the arm, sending him reeling. The soldier backpedaled and turned, his free hand grappling for a pistol or maybe a radio, when Doctor Freeman swooped in to his side, ducking low. The other soldier lay unmoving in a pool of blood. As the guard turned and swung, the doctor rushed in, ramming his blade into the soldier's armpit.

The man howled and dropped the metal bar. Greg was fast to grab it, and commenced to beat hell down on him.

"Enough," Karl said, then louder, "Enough! I need his clothes."

Greg stopped, hunched over and panting. He dropped the pry bar and looked at his bloody hands, then beat his palms against his pant legs.

A rush of satisfaction enveloped Karl's senses at seeing the nearly decapitated man on the ground. *You'll all suffer … by my own hands; I'll kill the lot of you.*

The doctor bent and grabbed his knife handle, the blade still planted deep. It took a few yanks until the knife came free, and he stood wiping it with a cloth and licking at his fingers.

"Come on, bring 'em over here," Karl said.

Greg stared down at what was left of the scout's head and face, rubbing his left arm where he'd been struck. Then he turned and doubled over, vomiting up strings of bile while falling to his knees.

"Oh, for fuck's sake …"

"W-why didn't you shoot?" Greg asked between heaves.

"You want more of them coming this way? Pull yourself together, and help Doctor Freeman."

The doctor grabbed the ankles of the first soldier and pulled the dead man behind the small hedge and air conditioner, then went back for the second.

Karl began removing his own frayed and battered shirt, his face set in agony as he attempted to pull the sleeves down his arms.

"Hold on." Doctor Freeman rummaged through his briefcase for a pair of scissors and began cutting away Karl's rags. As the doctor undressed one of the scouts, he pulled a canteen from the soldier's belt and took a long drink before passing it to Karl.

Karl drank long gulps. He sighed, water trailing down his face, and he tossed the canteen to the grass next to Greg, who was still hunched over.

"Drink," Karl said, and reached for the dead scout's feet, examining the larger boots. "Then come over here and help us gather what we can. We have to move out."

It took a moment for Greg to stand, and when he did, Karl and the doctor had already stripped off the weapons, ammunition, and backpack—containing some smoked meats, apples, and stale bread—and had outfitted themselves with whatever they needed. Karl turned to Greg. "Here," he said and tossed him his rifle, then inspected the slide and mechanisms of the slain scout's machine gun.

The naked torso of one of the guards shined pale in the tall grass, and Karl caught Doctor Freeman staring down.

"No time," he told him. "We got to move."

The doctor didn't budge.

Karl rolled his eyes.

"No time."

The doctor nodded and reached down for his briefcase. "I'm aware," he said.

Greg finished drinking from the canteen and wiped his mouth with a sleeve.

"Come on," Karl said.

As they neared the edge of the house, with Doctor Freeman several paces behind, Greg whispered to Karl, "What did the doc want to do back there?"

Karl shook his head. "An arrangement we have," he said. "It doesn't concern you."

Chapter Thirty
Landsville

Twice they had to stop and hide in the brush when they heard engines far off on the highway. Now, they stopped once more after hearing voices, and saw through the thicket a group of maybe a dozen armed men marching on the shoulder of the road.

After the soldiers passed, Greg said, "We're never going to make it." He clutched at his shoulder where the pry bar hit him. Doctor Freeman had examined him earlier, and the bone wasn't broken; but the bruise grew so large it was difficult for Greg to mobilize his arm. He shook his head. "They're spread everywhere."

Karl didn't answer. He was fairly certain the stitches on his leg had burst open, and the wound on his chest caused his breathing to become labored.

"They'll find us sooner or later," the doctor said. "More than likely, they're following our tracks now, after seeing what we did to their men back there. It's only a matter of time until they catch up."

Karl turned to him. "Would you rather we give ourselves up?"

"No."

"We're going as fast as we can, given the situation." He glanced at his legs.

"Do you know what they'll do if they find us?" Greg said. "They'll skin us alive, crucify us ... leave us at the mercy of the wild."

Karl huffed a slight laugh. "Skin us? No, no. Greg, these men are bleeding hearts. They'll either shoot you in the back of the head or hang you from a lamppost. No torture. Doctor Freeman and I, we'll be brought in for questioning. Probably endure a bit of torture."

Greg gulped, his Adam's apple going up and down. "What exactly is this safe place in Landsville? Are more of our people there?"

"No," the doctor answered. "The place … it's sacred to me."

"Sacred? Like a church?" Greg asked.

Greg was becoming bold with his questioning, causing the heat in Karl's chest to rise. If it weren't for the circumstances, Karl would reprimand him.

"In a manner of speaking," the doctor said, and patted his pocket for his folded map. He traced the paper with a finger and said, "Here. We're getting close."

Greg leaned in, despite already having been shown the location.

"What's so special about the place?" he asked again.

"History," Karl said, and patted Greg on the back, a bit hard. Greg flinched and grabbed at his arm. "The good doctor has invited us to his home."

Greg opened his mouth to speak, but Karl hushed him down. They remained quiet, squatting in a bramble of vines, listening to the wind rustle the leaves overhead, and then Karl said, "All right. Let's move."

***

Karl tripped and stumbled many times, and after several hours of walking, Greg told him, "We got to take a break," but Karl replied, "Life before comfort. No break."

Five miles outside of Landsville, another procession of Alice or Hightown's men were seen going door to door in the town of Ashland, and the men had to hide in a wooded section.

Karl sat with his back against a tree and closed his eyes. Doctor Freeman and Greg peered out through the brush, watching the scouts fan through the street. They were far enough away that the din of the enemy's conversation was barely audible, and Karl rested his head back against the rough bark. He thought that when they would have to stand again, he would not be able to do so.

He listened to the low murmurs of voices and the rattling of far-off engines. He listened to the gentle trickling of a nearby stream that cut through the narrow strip of littered woods they were hiding in.

Then he felt hands on his shoulders, movement, and his eyelids snapped open, blinking raw against his eyes.

"Karl. Karl, wake up." It was Doctor Freeman.

"How …" He swallowed against the dryness of his throat and looked up to the sky for an indication of how long he had slept, but was offered no clues from the gray overcast.

"Move," the doctor said. "We got to move. They're sweeping the area."

Karl scanned the brush and could see blurs of movement. The enemy patrol was heading off the road, toward their position.

Greg grabbed his hand and pulled him to his feet.

Karl attempted not to groan as he stood, and looked around for the boat oar he'd used as a crutch, then realized he hadn't used it since they'd left the house. Greg and Doctor Freeman moved to either side of him and grabbed his arms, helping him maneuver through the woods.

The trees offered little protection, being that the area was residential and developed, and before too long the thicket ended abruptly at the side of a road. Across from them was a large, open field, with the horizon stretching on for miles.

A rumble caused the three men to turn to the right, and although they couldn't see it from around a bend in the road, the sound was undeniably an engine.

"Christ," Karl said. "Left—go left."

He didn't dare turn to see how close the enemy was behind them, but by the absence of troops shouting and firing at them, it was safe to say they had not yet been spotted.

Karl was pulled and pushed faster than his legs would allow, and at times his feet swept over the pavement as Greg and the doctor lifted him in haste.

"Where, where do we go?" Greg said.

No one responded, and yet he continued, "Where, where—"

Then the solution presented itself as they reached a turn in the road, and the wooded section that they had been hiding in moments ago ceased, replaced by a long iron fence, extending over a block in length. Flowers had once been tied all along the posts, and some dry stalks and twigs could still be seen. Photographs, cards with written words, and hundreds of mourning candles were scattered all over the sidewalk and road. The papers were half-decomposed and bleached by the sun, and many of the candles had melted to dry blobs.

Behind the black fence, the tops of tombstones could be seen in various places, with the majority of the grave markers buried under the thousands of corpses that had been brought to the cemetery and piled in heaps and mounds. Some orderly, placed with care and affection, and others dumped in haste from the backs of trucks, to form jumbled piles of intertwined limbs.

The men stopped short at the sight, and Karl said, "Go—*let's go.*"

They followed the fence until they came to the entrance, and passed under the ornate arched gateway. Karl tripped as the bones beneath his feet moved and buckled, making crunching and crackling sounds. He looked over his shoulder, and could just see the front of an approaching truck from down the road.

"Down," he said in a whisper, and fell to his stomach, fighting through the pain to crawl over the decomposed wretchedness.

Despite the majority of the bodies being nothing more than bones and dried skin, the stench was still thick, and swarms of flies engulfed them as the men pulled themselves across a narrow channel. The sound of the engine neared the front of the cemetery, and Karl turned and rolled the last few feet to hide behind a wall of bodies. He lay panting, Greg and Doctor Freeman beside him. Greg was trembling, holding his knees tight to his chest, his eyes squeezed shut. He appeared on the verge of a breakdown, and if he made any noise at all, if he began to cry and moan, or shout out in anguish, Karl would surely kill him.

But Greg didn't utter a sound as the rumble grew louder. Karl nudged his way to the top of the mound, his shoulder slipping under bones and sinew. A contorted face stuck out from the mass, its voided eyes staring back at him, its mouth stretched open in a silent, dramatic scream.

On the road, over two dozen armed men followed behind the pickup truck, their assault rifles attached to tactical slings. Most faces looked to see the spectacle of the graveyard, but a few turned away, indifferent.

Karl stared up at the overcast sky. The clouds were foreboding rolls of gray, and sections looked dark enough to unleash rain at any given moment. A sharp bit of ribcage poked his side, and the smooth roundness of a skull matched the nape of his neck. The near-blinding sky forced his eyes closed, and when they did his mind felt as if it was tumbling over and over. He listened as the engine grew quieter, and let his mind blink out of consciousness.

***

An undetermined amount of time had passed, when again he felt a hand on his shoulder.

"Karl," Doctor Freeman said, shaking him awake. "Wake up. They're gone."

The doctor put a canteen in Karl's hand.

"We got to get on. Only a few more miles." He placed the back of his hand against Karl's clammy forehead. "You're burning up."

Karl turned to see Greg already moving fast over the crunching bones. Doctor Freeman took Karl's hand and helped him to his feet, then held his elbow as they maneuvered over the sea of bodies.

Once outside of the cemetery, the doctor found a thick branch to use as a crutch, and they made their way over the memorial sidewalk, trampling on bundles of dried flowers and photographs of happy, smiling people. Whole families, children, and the elderly stared upwards from the pictures. The happiness in their faces, the backdrops of beautiful homes and flowered gardens, days spent at a picnic ... those things seemed to never have existed at all.

Karl's boots trampled the smiling faces, and after the first block, his legs loosened up a bit. The smell of death lingered heavy from his clothing, soaked into every pore on his body. He was one of them already, he thought. He belonged to the departed.

A mile went by, and then another. They reached the outskirt of Landsville near sunset. As they cut through the tall grasses of a Vietnam memorial park, they spied a row of dark figures ahead. Corpses, no doubt, and as they neared, it became apparent they had recently died.

There were five of them, facedown, hands tied behind their backs, wearing an assortment of dark military fatigues of no particular origin. The grasses that enveloped their bodies swayed rhythmically in the breeze, the blades near their heads stained red.

Greg stepped beside one and nudged the man over with the heel of his boot. When the red handprint on the man's chest became visible, he released him back down.

"Let's get out of here," Karl said.

The doctor led them forward, down narrow streets with driveways every few hundred feet that disappeared behind walls of overgrowth, or twisted away over the ample terrain to unseen houses.

"One more block," Doctor Freeman said.

The sun blazed a reflection against the street signs at the intersection, but the letters were just a jumble of bright nonsense.

They turned, and Karl's shoulder rubbed against the side of a car left crashed into the bumper of a minivan. A dark face stared at him through the window as he passed.

Greg put his arm under Karl's shoulder and pulled him away from leaning on the car. The doctor's pace quickened, and he said, "This is it."

Chapter Thirty-one
Holy Relics

They turned on a pebble driveway. The weeds poking through had grown to shin height. After a long and slow leftward turn, the property opened up to a grass field, still wooded with tall oak and maple trees. A magnificent three-story home stood far off, muted by the overgrowth, with a red brick façade half-succumbed to creeping vines. An opulent veranda with arched doorways and intricate carvings around the windows extended from the side.

"Is that a guard tower?" Greg asked, pointing to a tall and narrow spire attached to the left of the house, emerging a half story taller than the roof.

"It's a bell tower," the doctor said without turning.

"This place is a mansion. You lived here?"

Karl laughed. "Among other estates, yes. This is Doctor Freeman's home. The man was, after all, a highly respected surgeon. He was caught in his Texas property and sentenced there, where we had the pleasure of meeting. Do you not recall the news, back when he was making headlines?"

Greg didn't answer.

"You're young; perhaps it was before your time."

"I remember. Just not so much."

"The estate is a wonder to be seen, is it not? A brilliant display of Victorian craftsmanship."

"Italiante," Doctor Freeman said, walking off from the driveway and toward the side of the house. "It's not Victorian, it's Italiante."

"And this is where we're staying?" Greg asked.

"No." Karl shook his head. "In the back."

They turned around the property, and followed a brick-lined path into a wooded section.

"Here," the doctor said. "We're here."

The woods opened up to a clearing with the gentle rustling of a nearby creek. An ancient-looking structure stood before them, not much larger than a shed. The sides were made of round river stone, with arched stained-glass windows, and a domed roof. A crucifix extended from the top. To the side of this strange building in the woods were two bright-yellow excavators. Yellow caution tape fluttered from nearby trees, the connections long broken.

"By my own eyes," Karl said. "I never thought I'd lay witness to this marvel."

"Marvel? It looks like some old church," Greg said.

"It is precisely that. But not just any old church—this is the doctor's sanctuary. The place that earned him the monikers Demon Doctor and Hell's Surgeon, among others."

They arrived at a thick, uniquely carved slab of wood used as the front door, covered in tacked-up papers, noting the date the building was set for demolition. As Doctor Freeman pushed the door open, the bright sealant tape ripped in two. A rush of dust kicked up from the ancient tiles and woodwork.

Inside, narrow stained-glass windows cast varying dark, yet colorful hues against the walls and floor. The doctor stopped before a pew, petting the wood in ritualistic form, as if it were a delicate animal. "This building," he said, walking toward the altar place, past the golden iconostasis with the portraits of saints in brightly colored robes, "was brought over from Greece, piece by piece. It is not a reproduction. During the construction of some high-rise, this tiny church was to move to a new location closer to Athens. But with enough money, enough palms greased, it wound up in a shipping container, bound for America."

Greg brought Karl to the front and sat him in the first of the four pews.

The doctor passed an arched opening in the middle of the iconostasis and walked down a narrow path behind, following the back wall. Karl pulled himself back to his feet. "Come on," he told Greg, who was sitting heavy beside him.

On the opposite side of the ornate façade of paintings, at the end of the passageway, Doctor Freeman delicately removed a strip of police tape that secured two pieces of stone in the wall. A marble holy water font sat beside him. He peeled back the tape, careful not to leave any glue on the stones. "Those arrogant monsters," he said. "This whole place is a work of art. To think the police were going to destroy it." He felt along the crevices of the stone.

"And now," Karl said, "we will witness the genius that kept the good doctor undiscovered by the authorities during his two-decade-long killing spree."

Greg didn't say anything, but his sudden influx of breath could be heard as the doctor pressed against the wall, and interlocking rocks cracked open at the seams, displaying a doorway.

Doctor Freeman disappeared inside the passageway and Karl stepped forward, to a steep, circling stone staircase with a thick rope attached to the side as a railing. He paused there until a glow emanated from the unseen base, and then he laboriously proceeded into the cellar.

Chapter Thirty-two
Labyrinth

The hallway was long and straight with doorways on either side, and then turned a sharp left at the end. Doctor Freeman was in the first room, and Karl stood looking in as the doctor flipped switches inside a circuit breaker.

"How in God's name is there power down here?"

"Solar, back at the house. The wires are underground. This place is designed to be self-sufficient."

Greg appeared at the entrance to the winding stairs, wide-eyed at his surroundings. He wiped his forehead with a sleeve. "This really it?" he asked.

Doctor Freeman closed the circuit breaker door and left the room.

"Follow me," he said, and proceeded down the hall.

Karl peered in the doorways that were open as they walked, at the dark outlines of tables and furniture.

The doctor paused. "Through here is the kitchen." He opened the door and flipped a switch, brightening a room paneled in dark woods, with a round mahogany table in the center. The room was small, yet sophisticated, with aged framed paintings on the walls, and a marvelous granite countertop. A metal water hand pump rose from the counter to a bowl underneath.

"My God," Karl said. "So this is the famed kitchen, huh?" He stared at the blank space on the wall, where the forensic teams had removed the refrigerator and freestanding freezer. He remembered the photos in the newspaper, men wearing coveralls and face masks carting a stainless-steel, French-door refrigerator and bulky rectangular freezer out through the doorway of the church. Bright biohazard stickers had been stuck to the sides.

Doctor Freeman went over to the water pump, pushing and pulling the handle. A deep gurgling noise gave way to a sputter of brown liquid, which began flowing more freely, and a little more clear.

"The pipe needs to be drained, but we have well water."

Karl leaned against the doorframe; sweat was rolling down his face, dripping from his nose. A rush of air came from a vent on the ground, and he reached down to feel the cool breeze against his palm.

The doctor turned to him and said, "You need to rest, now. I'll give you the tour later."

They continued walking around the bend in the hallway. Karl looked into an open room, where the light from the hallway illuminated a surgical table mounted to the floor. Neon yellow crime scene markers were placed here and there.

"How-how'd you get away with this?" Greg asked. "I mean … I remember hearing about this place, thought it was torn down."

"If the disease didn't come when it had," Doctor Freeman said, "it would have been. The destruction of the church was held up in court, since the building is, after all, a Greek artifact, and smuggled here illegally. Down here, though, was set for destruction nonetheless."

"How did you build it?"

"I didn't. I hired three separate companies to each built a section of what they presumed to be a survival shelter. I even went so far as to have them install an incinerator at the end, for what I told them was human waste, garbage, with a vented flue poking out in the woods. They believed me … and in a sense, that was what it was for."

Karl was going to add to the story, fill in some of the blanks for Greg, but his throat was overwhelmingly dry, and it was becoming hard to keep his eyes open.

The doctor opened a door, flipped a switch, and said, "Here we are."

The room was a perfect square, bare except for a twin bed and a side table and lamp. Karl sat on the mattress and slowly laid himself out, using a rolled-up spare jacket taken from one of the soldiers they'd killed as a pillow. His eyes closed, and the pounding in his forehead was subdued by being off his feet.

"We need medicine, more antibiotics, food, and maybe some blankets."

Karl didn't respond.

"You rest. Greg and I will make a foray into town later, see what we can muster."

Karl grunted as the lights were turned off and the door was closed.

***

His eyes opened at the sound of movement, the feeling of fingers on his shoulder, arms, and chest. He looked up at a man wearing doctor scrubs, complete with a cloth hat and face guard. A portable light with a flexible neck had been brought into the room, shining down on his torso.

"Doc ..." He opened and closed his mouth, trying to lubricate his raw throat. "Thirsty."

"Here." Doctor Freeman picked up a glass of water from the side table, and helped Karl sit up enough to sip from the rim. His arm and chest muscles strained at holding his weight up. "We were able to round up a supply of IV bags and medicine. Thank God the local population died off before they could use up the stores of medical equipment. You'll be back on your feet in no time."

Karl drained the cloudy water and lay back down, feeling a drip trail down his cheek. Doctor Freeman returned to undress him and cut away his old bandages. He squirted liquid onto gauze to clean the wounds, and sprayed other liquids directly onto the lacerations. The stinging was bad, but mild in contrast to the terrible march he'd endured and the stitches performed by moonlight. There was a pillow under his head and he could smell the starch of new blankets still folded at the foot of his bed. Even the heat emanating from the small spotlight felt like a warm embrace.

He remained with eyes closed as new bandages were applied and a needle was inserted into the crook of his arm. After a moment, a cool rushing sensation spread down his arm as the IV solution flowed into his vein.

"Doctor ... back in Alice, whatever happened to that girl in the basement, Bethany?"

"Nothing happened to her that I'm aware. I was told to wait for your arrival to begin interrogations, and that's what I did."

Karl nodded, and didn't add anything further to the conversation. He was surprised that the image of her on the bed, her hair fanned out, her cheeks flushed, had stayed in his mind. Even along their journey here, with his consciousness fading, the thought of her danced inside his head. Perhaps it was coming so perilously close to death that was inspiring new life inside him, but he thought that if given the opportunity again, he would be able to perform on her sexually without her being unconscious, and him on medication. She would still be at odds with him, of course, and would have to be subdued, beaten. The thought stoked a fantasy where he imagined himself on top of her high atop a perch, overlooking Alice as it burned in a torrent of flames … or perhaps with her at his side, riding a horse into combat, a worthy lieutenant of the Red Hands …

The doctor pulled a blanket up to his chin.

"We found enough medicine to help you along. But food is going to be an issue."

At the mention of food, Karl became aware of just how hungry he was, and the fantasies with Bethany were erased from his thoughts. The pain of being poked and prodded combined with the relief of lying on an actual bed had dulled his sense of hunger.

His eyes cracked open, watching Doctor Freeman stuff the soiled bandages and clothing into a plastic garbage bag, and then remove his latex gloves with a snap.

"We have a few chews of dried meat left over from those soldiers. That's it. I'll get you some before it's all gone. Greg's going to go hunting, gather what he can. I don't like him out there, but we don't have a choice. The best thing we can do is lay low; stay underground as Alice and Hightown scour the area. They'll fall back after a few days, or a week or two. In the meantime, you recover, and we will leave here strong." The doctor rummaged through a tray he'd set down on the nightstand, picking up two small vials of fluid and a syringe. "I'm going to give you antibiotics, and a little something to help you sleep." He pierced the needle into the injection port on the vial, and then inserted the needle into the receiving port on the IV line.

"I don't think I need any help with that," Karl said, his eyes already closed. "Give me a full report of our resources after Greg returns from the hunt, along with a list of our firearms and ammunition."

"Yes, sir."

Doctor Freeman picked up the tray, flipped the light switch, and backed out of the room.

Chapter Thirty-three

Hunger

Karl had just enough time to twist over the side of the bed and aim for the pail before the heaving began. After many minutes, he spit at the trail of saliva, and a wave of dizziness forced him back on the soaked mattress and pillows.

Again, he closed his eyes.

When they reopened, music was drifting in from the hallway through the cracked-open door. Each note produced dancing colors in his ears: swirls of violins, piano, flutes, and deep, guttural drums. Karl's mind was lost somewhere, and although he attempted to rein reality back, the pleasantness of his chemically and biologically altered state of mind made his thoughts slip away.

Then came the darkness. Darkness so black it enveloped the absence of time. Out of the black came hallucinations: dirty faces, broken limbs, blistered skin, crushed bones, and torn sinew. Bodies in dramatic states of decomposition, twisted in wreckage, gnawed at by packs of rats, wild dogs, wolves, and dark swarming masses of insects. All the insects, thousands and thousands of buzzing wings, tiny black legs, their entire composition like one living consciousness, hell-bent on consuming flesh, rotten or fresh.

Karl saw them in his room, the endless crawling horde a giant shadow by his feet.

A spike of fear shot his eyes open. The images his fevered imagination produced still played out over his vision as he focused on a ceiling tile above, his breaths coming as rapidly as his drumming heart.

"Doc ..." His meager words fell dead in the air.

He placed a trembling palm over his eyes, felt heat emanating from his forehead, and reached for a glass of water sitting on his bedside table. He blindly hit the cup, and sent it to the ground in a shatter.

Footsteps from down the hall. Louder, and then the door squeaked open. He felt the doctor's presence.

"Doc ..." he said. "I-I'm dying."

The portable examination light clicked on, the brightness overwhelming. Clatter from the medicine bag, and the cap of a vial popping off. A pinch on his arm, and then a rushing warm embrace. His insides calmed and radiated a pleasant, glowing sensation.

Doctor Freeman helped him sip a glass of water mixed with protein powder, and explained in jumbled words that Karl needed food to regain his strength. The doctor detailed the meager supplies found by Greg in the nearest town. Hightown's soldiers were still nearby: scouting, scrounging, and killing deserters.

Greg appeared at the doorway, talking to both Karl and the doctor, but his words were lost in Karl's fevered brain.

Karl closed his eyes, the taste of artificial vanilla lingering on his tongue from the drink, and he fell back down to the depths of sleep. But this time, there were no rancid faces to disturb his dreams.

***

He awoke again in pure darkness. No light came from the hallway, and no music came from the distant room. The fevered swelling of his thoughts had subsided, and with effort, he swung his legs off the side of the bed, and waited a moment for a wave of dizziness to pass. He placed one foot on the cement floor and then the other. The cold from the ground felt good against the underside of his feet.

Holding the rolling IV stand, he pulled himself to stand upright, and once steady, he clicked on the room light and cracked open the door.

Thirst and hunger motivated him forward. A hunger like he'd never experienced before. An all-consuming need for fuel.

He made it down the hallway with the rolling IV stand creaking. At an open doorway, he leaned in and squinted. It was the room he'd seen on his way in, something of a doctor's office, but with a stainless-steel surgical table mounted to the ground instead of a padded examination bed. A host of surgical tools and medicine bottles were set on the counter. Doctor Freeman had been fast to restock his inventory.

Karl stepped away and walked around the bend in the hall, where he found the kitchen. With the light clicked on, he saw a small refrigerator that wasn't there before. He opened the door and vapors billowed out, filling his lungs with pleasant, cool air. The interior was empty. He turned to the cabinets, opening one after the other, and found the bottle of protein powder. The powder had a slight sharp smell to it, and Karl could only guess the drink was expired. Still, he scooped a portion and dumped it into a glass of water.

Pockets of unstirred powder exploded in his mouth as he drank, and the liquid filled his stomach. Nausea hit him, but he scooped more powder, spilling it over the counter, and filled the glass again.

There was a muffled sound behind him, and Karl turned to see Doctor Freeman standing at the doorway, wearing nothing but his underwear, his hair matted with sleep.

"Karl," he said, "what are you doing out of bed? It's the middle of the night."

"I'm starving."

Karl drained the glass.

Doctor Freeman walked up beside him and opened a cabinet. He pulled down a half sack of white flour and said, "Sit."

Karl sat at the round table as the doctor mixed a portion of the flour with water, making a thin porridge. He heated a pan over a butane camping stove that Greg must have found, and poured the batter. After a moment it started to sizzle, and he flipped the patty, and after another minute, he placed the steaming pancake before Karl.

The dough was hot, singeing his tongue, but still Karl devoured every crumb.

"There's nothing out there," Doctor Freeman said.

"What's that?"

"Food. There's no food. The town's been wiped clean."

"Are there no rabbits or squirrels?"

The doctor nodded toward the hallway. "Not that Greg can find."

"Plants then. Grass. Whatever."

"The boy wouldn't know the difference between cabbage and poison ivy. I'll go out tomorrow, see what I can find."

Karl swallowed and said, "Where'd you get the fridge, and the music I heard earlier?"

"My home. The police took most everything down here, but my home is largely intact."

"Are there still soldiers around?"

"Greg saw another group of our men, executed."

"How many?"

"Maybe a dozen. Don't know." The doctor chuckled. "If they weren't too ripe, we'd have a proper meal."

The thought of Doctor Freeman hunched over a rotten corpse, his lips and mouth bloody red, caused bile to rise up in his throat. The rush of food and water in his stomach, which had been empty for days, began to cause too much pressure.

"I gotta lie down."

Doctor Freeman helped him back to his room and put him into bed.

"I'll be back in the morning, after Greg and I return from scouting."

Karl gripped at his stomach.

"I think I'm going to be sick, Doc."

"Be right back." The doctor turned and left. A minute later he returned with a loaded syringe, and inserted it into the injection port of the IV. A rush of pleasure invaded Karl's bloodstream.

He closed his eyes and embraced the warmth.

Chapter Thirty-four
Mutiny

Keeping track of time, down in that windowless bunker, was hard to do. There were no clocks, no indication of the sun's position, and it might have been the morning when Karl awoke to see Doctor Freeman standing above him, tending to his bandages.

"Stitches look good," he said after seeing Karl awake.

"I'm feeling better."

If anything, lying in bed for so long was now causing more discomfort than any of his injuries. Every muscle ached. What he needed was to get back on his feet. Move around. Wake his body up.

"We were lucky today; managed to snare a rabbit."

Karl's eyes went large.

"You don't say?"

"Got it stewing in the kitchen with some dandelion greens, wild sage, oyster mushrooms, and a bottle of red wine. It's funny, the liquor store in town was one of the few places not fully ransacked. It'll be ready in an hour."

The doctor took a syringe from the counter and inserted it in the medicine port.

"I don't think I need that," Karl said. "I feel good. I need to get back on my feet."

"It's antibiotics. You still have a fever and your wounds are infected."

The familiar wave of pleasantness tingled at his mind as the medicine absorbed in his bloodstream.

"Sleepiness is a side effect," the doctor said. "I'll be back with the food when it's ready."

Doctor Freeman stood, and left Karl alone in the dark room.

***

Steam wafted over his face, filling his lungs with the earthy aroma of simmered meat and wild foraged herbs. Karl placed the first spoonful in his mouth, and a deep range of flavors burst on his tongue and filled his throat with warmth.

He closed his eyes, savoring the sensation of food—real food—in his stomach.

Doctor Freeman sat beside him holding a bowl, blowing steam off a spoonful.

"My God," Karl said. "This is the best meal I've ever eaten." His mind was still numb from the medicine, veiled in a sleep-induced fog. He ate another spoonful, and said between bites, "Where's Greg?"

"In his room." The doctor paused to take a bite, and then said, "Sleeping, I think. He wants to go back out on a hunt later. Thinks he saw larger tracks, maybe a deer."

"Deer?" Karl looked at him, amazed.

The doctor shrugged. "He's probably wrong."

Karl ate with abandon. "Just be careful," he said, nearing the bottom of the bowl. "Don't let him go out for long. The whole point of us being down here is to hide."

"I'll tell him." Doctor Freeman placed his empty bowl on the tray and then took Karl's. Before leaving, he gave Karl another dose of medicine.

"Doc, I think we got to change up whatever you're giving me."

"I know it's strong, but we don't have a choice. I can scout the neighboring town, see if the pharmacy there has any other options."

Karl's eyes began to involuntarily close.

"Tell Greg …" He paused to yawn. "Tell him good job."

Doctor Freeman nodded, took the tray, and left the room.

***

A day, two days, maybe a week went by. Karl squinted at the light above him, and tried to decipher his place in reality.

He'd eaten quite a bit recently, and he should have his strength back. But if anything, he was getting worse. Time breezed by when he was awake, his head throbbing a dull ache, and all he wanted to do was sleep. The doctor told him the wound on his leg was infected, and with it came a strong fever. He was pumped with more and more medicine, and twice a day, his injuries were examined with that insanely bright lamp.

Greg had been out on the hunt incessantly after he'd caught the first deer, despite Karl telling the Doctor to order him to stay in. There was no need to further expose himself if it wasn't crucial; the deer carcass would supply them with enough meat to last for days, and by all accounts, they had to leave soon.

But Greg wasn't listening. Every time Karl ordered Doctor Freeman to go get him, the doctor would return with palms open. "He's gone out." His own relentless sleeping didn't help. Twice, the doctor said Greg came to see him, but he himself couldn't be awoken.

But Karl knew what was going on. With him bedridden, Greg was attempting to step up, take over leadership. Or perhaps he was out scouting a path to flee; maybe he no longer believed in Karl's ability to get them to the docks. Maybe Greg was gathering supplies, waiting until the time was right to leave them behind. It wouldn't be surprising.

Karl finished the last bite of the roasted venison loin, the meat a bit tough and with a tang of lemon. Apparently, the doctor and Greg had brought down a working hot plate and a small oven from the main house.

Karl put his plate down and Doctor Freeman cleaned up.

"Where-where'd you get the lemon ..." His eyes began to close.

"What?"

"The meat. It tasted like lemon."

Doctor Freeman shook his head. "There's no lemon. That's fear you taste. Greg botched the kill. He shot the animal in the torso, and it lived for hours. He had to stalk it while it slowly bled out. All the while the animal was stressed, the adrenaline using up glycogen, which then can't be turned to lactic acid. After death, it's lactic acid that keeps meat tender. The result is an acidic pH level, not lemon."

"We have to talk about Greg. He's going to flee."

There was a pause. Then, "I think you're right. He's going out incessantly, and not listening to orders. I was going to mention it to you when your fever passed."

The medication was kicking in, and Karl said, "We'll talk … talk later."

After a moment, he heard the clatter of his plate and silverware being picked up, and Doctor Freeman took his leave.

***

It was dark when his eyes snapped open, and he turned quickly to his side and heaved in the bucket. Classical music came in from the open door as he continued to heave.

The retching continued long after his stomach was empty, and for many minutes he remained leaning over the side of his bed, half-asleep, listening to the trumpets blaze as a trail of drool dripped from his lips.

When … will this pass?

It was thirst that got him to sit up, and his shaking hands felt for the familiar smooth side of a glass on the table, but in the darkness he could see that there was no glass.

He swung his feet off the side of the bed and remained sitting there, eyes closed, for a long duration. A thought hit him: *Brahms's first symphony* … then he realized the music he was hearing was exactly that. The fast progression of the strings and horns indicated the finale was close.

He stood on wavering legs, then fell back to sitting. After a deep breath, he stood again, and let his feet and legs regain some stability before stepping forward. The rolling IV stand helped, and when he was out in the hallway he leaned his shoulder against the wall, and dragged himself forward.

His wounds didn't throb in pain like they had. It was his entire body that was fighting each step, and his mind more than anything else.

Get ahold of yourself, old man … you're tougher than this. You're Karl Metzger, for Christ's sake.

Karl passed the doorway to the examination room, and light was visible from under the closed door. The music came echoing out as he continued around the bend in the hallway, and he arrived at the kitchen.

His trembling hand filled a glass with water. The cool liquid soothed his raw throat, and offered a degree of comfort to his body and mind.

The muffled music was reaching a ferocious peak, and all at once it ended.

Karl put the glass down faster than anticipated, and it fell into the sink, making a clatter. He found that moving had become easier as he headed back to his room. With each step his muscles tightened and flexed, and despite the waves of dizziness, the movement felt good.

As he neared the bend in the hallway, he heard the creaking hinges of a door open, and Doctor Freeman stepped out from his office.

"Karl!" he shouted, wiping his hands with a rag. "What are you doing out of bed?"

"Thirsty, Doc."

"No, no, no." The doctor shook his head. "You're liable to burst a stitch."

"I got to move. I can't stay in that bed any longer."

"All right, all right. I understand. We'll work on that, tomorrow."

Doctor Freeman took his elbow and led him to his room.

"Doctor," Karl said, being put into bed. "I want to walk more."

"Tomorrow, I promise. You have to be monitored, and it's late now."

Doctor Freeman patted his pocket and removed a medicine vial. He placed it down, then continued patting his pockets.

"Stay here," he said, and left the room.

Karl glanced at the vial of antibiotics. The small glass container was brown, with a green cap and sticker. The writing was small, and he was too far away to see clearly, but he squinted nonetheless.

Benzo ... Benzodiaz ...

He couldn't read the whole word.

Underneath the name was a description. He leaned in closer.

Multidose Vial ... Slow IV Injection ... Sedative ...

Sedative?

The doctor returned with a clean hypodermic in a sterile wrapper. In swift movements he popped the cap off the syringe, plunged it in the bottle, and injected it in the port. Karl said nothing as his eyes closed. But as sleep overtook him, his thoughts grew dark.

Chapter Thirty-five
Empty Chambers

"We need to get moving," Karl said. "It's safe now, it has to be."

"Agreed." Doctor Freeman pulled the syringe out of the port and recapped the needle. "You've healed up well. As soon as your fever breaks, we'll head out."

Karl's eyes closed and the door hinges creaked shut. The doctor's footsteps grew faint down the hallway. Soon, music became audible—shrill violins and cellos.

For a moment, Karl listened to his pulse beat heavy in his chest. He breathed in and out, steadying his heart rate, focusing his thoughts. Then he pushed back his covers and sat up straight, letting the blood in his body adjust to his sudden movements.

It had been two days since he'd seen the medicine vial. Once he'd awakened from his chemical-induced fog, he pulled the needle out of his arm and inserted it in the mattress between his bicep and his torso. It took a while for the drugs to dissipate from his bloodstream enough for him to regain some strength, but once he was up, he walked around the room in a circle, letting his muscles flex. He reinserted the needle in the intervals between his medicine doses, and took it back out again when the doctor showed up with the hypodermic, hiding his arm under the covers.

Now, he waited on his bed for many minutes, until he was reasonably sure the doctor would not be returning. He reached out and clicked on the examination light. All his injuries were healing up fast. Whatever concoction of medicine he'd been receiving, antibiotics might have been one of them.

There was still some redness, and the skin was puffy through the stitches, but by all appearances, the wounds had clasped together. There was little to no pain, but the itchiness was becoming maddening.

It felt good to be on his feet, great even. This was the second night in a row of being able to walk around, stretch, feel the strength return to his hands. It was time to leave. Find Greg in this underground maze, and get the hell out.

But first, he'd have to deal with the doctor.

And to be honest, he wasn't sure what the best course of action would be. The man deserved a chance, an opportunity to explain himself, to see if there was some reason that he'd been dispensing sedatives and God knows what else, keeping Karl solitary and idle, locked away deep underground.

After all their time together, the cities they'd sacked, plundered, consumed, Karl hoped this wasn't going to be the end of their journey. But deep down he knew the man was an addict of the worst kind. This labyrinth bunker was proof positive of his nightmare cravings. Over a dozen rooms, each designed for a purpose. Torture in some, medical experiments in others. In the back, in the oven, what remained of the victims was burned to ash, then scooped up and dumped in the pond.

What was the death toll under the doctor? Before the war, the news said something around twenty confirmed, another few dozen speculated. In Texas alone, there were at least twelve, killed in a bunker much like this one. Karl read all about it, locked up in the cell next to the man back in Haddonfield Penitentiary. The librarian had snuck him all sorts of current affairs magazines.

And once the doors of the doctor's cell were opened, when he came blinking out of the darkness, reborn into a world of death, decay, and insanity, he fell right back to old behaviors. The neighboring cells had become similar to this underground bunker, each designed for brutal execution, torture, and consumption.

In many ways, the room Karl was in now was much like his cell in Haddonfield. Only this time his door was unlocked. A pile of clothing, washed in the sink, sat folded on a chair in the corner. Karl went to it now, and reached for his pistol belt that hung by the strap. The dark grips felt cool in his palm, and the bulk of the weapon offered a familiar reassurance. He clicked the cylinder open.

That monster ...

The bullets were gone.

He rummaged through his belongings, feeling the pockets. Nothing. Even his knife was absent.

For a moment, he paused, gathering his thoughts.

The classical music—Brahms, by Karl's reckoning—still trickled in from behind the closed door. Slowly, he dressed himself, trying not to make too much noise. Then he clicked off the light, and waited in the darkness.

Chapter Thirty-six
Brahms

Footsteps fell from down the hallway, growing louder. The door opened, emitting a sliver of light that quickly grew, and then the doctor walked into the room. He reached for the examination lamp, but then paused, his gaze fixed on the empty bed illuminated by the outside light.

Karl stepped out from behind him and swung his arms around Doctor Freeman's head, his hands clamped around the plastic IV cord that he'd doubled up and stretched taut. The doctor moved just as Karl sprung forward, and the makeshift garrote wrapped around his chin, but still Karl tugged, leaning back, using his height to pull Doctor Freeman against his chest. The cord slipped to his neck, and Karl heard the gasp of his old friend attempting to inhale against the plastic tubing.

The doctor bucked and flailed his arms, and the men spun. Karl's back hit the wall, and then they spiraled again. The doctor's glasses fell off, and he reached back, grabbing at Karl's face, head, and ears with a sinewy strength. Karl yanked to his side. Doctor Freeman let out sickening gurgling noise, and then the first, then the second plastic tubes snapped in half. The doctor fell forward, grasping at his throat, and quickly turned to face Karl.

The ends of the tubing were still wrapped up in Karl's hands, his knuckles and fingers white. Karl was panting, his bed-sore muscles at the limit of their strength. But without hesitation he leapt at the doctor, whose red face was set into a scowl.

"K-Kar—" he began to shout in a rough voice, before Karl's giant hands were grabbing and punching him.

Doctor Freeman got off a few blows before he fell, his nose exploded open, and began scrambling on his hands and knees for the door. His foot kicked a small, cylindrical vial as he fled, and the item rolled fast under the bed. Karl reached out and grabbed the doctor's foot, yanking him back into the room. The wound on his side screamed in pain, but he held on, battling a man who was fighting for his life.

Karl kicked the door closed and drew his sidearm.

They paused for a moment, both men breathing heavy. Doctor Freeman lay on the ground, looking up at the pistol. A smile broke out on his face, a trail of blood and drool dripping down his cheek. "Go on," he said. "Pull the trigger."

Karl grabbed the gun by the barrel with his right hand, and with his left he moved in, grasping at the doctor's flailing arms while he brought the pistol hammering down. After about a dozen whacks, Doctor Freeman's thrashing subsided. Karl stood up tall, his pistol hand warm from the splatters of blood.

He was so out of breath that his vision pulsed dark circles in his periphery. But before he could relax, he knelt by the bed and felt underneath until his fingers grazed the slick side of the medicine vial. The doctor was making deep grumbling noises, and his limbs twitched sporadically. Karl patted Doctor Freeman's pockets and felt a long, skinny object, like a thick pen. He pulled out the syringe, tore open the sterile wrapper, inserted it in the vial stopper, and pushed the needle into the crook of the man's arm.

The doctor stared up at him and his mouth opened to speak, but then his eyes rolled up in his head as his eyelids shut.

Karl knew nothing about the medicine, but judging from his own experience, he had several hours before the doctor would come around. After a lengthy time spent sitting on the chair, exhaustion making the smallest movements difficult, he stood back up and grabbed Doctor Freeman under his armpits. He hoisted the man onto the bed and patted down all his pockets, before using the two split pieces of the IV cord to tie his wrists to the bedframe.

He opened the door and stepped out into the hallway. Brahms was still playing, and he called out, "Greg! Greg!" through the music, but there was no response.

Going down the hallway in a direction he had not yet ventured, he opened each door in turn, finding nothing but empty rooms with drain holes in the center. One room still had two crime scene markers on the ground, small yellow B and C photo tents. At the far end of the hallway was the famed incinerator. The cast-iron behemoth sat cold and sinister. Karl turned and continued, opening doors on the opposite side, going closer to the room bellowing the orchestral music.

The next room had a large queen-sized mattress. The sheets had been smoothed over, and on a dresser sat Doctor Freeman's briefcase. His leather binder was open on the nightstand, a piece of charcoal in the crook of the opening. Detailed sketches of a leg being dissected were shown in various poses throughout the page. The flesh ended below the groin in a neat, round stump, and beyond was the skeletal kneecap, shin, and foot. Various sections of veins and muscle were separated, displayed, and labeled.

Karl left. The next bedroom was identical to his own. The sheets there were unkempt, and Greg's jacket and rifle hung from the back of the chair.

Karl took the rifle and walked up the hallway, until he arrived at the doorway to the doctor's office. He closed his eyes, sighed, and turned the handle.

The light was on, bright, and inside the music was much louder. He knew what he was going to witness before seeing it, but still, the sight was horrific.

"Jesus," Karl said, shaking his head. "You'll never change, Doctor."

Greg lay on the stainless-steel gurney in the center of the room, stripped naked and tied around the chest, arms, wrists, and one leg. The other leg was an exact duplicate of what he'd seen on the pages of the sketchpad. Various bags of medicine hung from stands, and tubes snaked to each of his arms. Greg's face was white, nearly blue, and a ball gag was stuffed in his mouth.

Karl walked past him, trying not to look at the leg. He tried not to think of Greg's torture, of Doctor Freeman using the tools he saw glistening and polished on trays beside the table. Tried not to think of Greg being eaten alive …

… of his own meals …

… the deer …

His stomach twisted, but still he pressed on, finding a satchel bag in a cupboard, and began swiping handfuls of the medicine and supplies. He searched the depths of his drug-induced subconscious from the past several days, and found that somewhere deep down he had known all along what was happening to Greg—what he was eating. But hunger is strong, and denial is even stronger. As he turned to leave, he heard a noise. He froze, and then turned, making eye contact with a barely conscious man. Greg stared at him through unfocused eyes, as if he were drunk, and attempted to speak through his gag.

Karl shook his head.

"Greg, ol' sport. You've seen better days." He picked up a slender scalpel from the examination tray. "Doctor Freeman's a tricky one. I don't blame you for getting caught." Greg's head was shaking back and forth.

Karl swiped the blade and tossed the knife back onto the tray. He turned and left.

***

When the doctor regained consciousness and his stare searched around the ceiling, Karl was there, sitting beside him. It seemed to take a moment for the man to realize where he was and what had happened. Then all at once his body tensed, pulling against his restraints, which Karl had reknotted, using rope he'd found in the examination room.

"Doctor Freeman," he said.

The doctor licked his lips. "Water," he said.

Karl took a glass from the nightstand and fed him sips.

Once the glass was drained, Doctor Freeman lay back down, his eyes closing.

"Jesus, what have you done to me? My face ..."

Karl sighed. "We've walked a long trail together, have we not?"

The doctor didn't answer.

"Hell, our friendship has lasted longer than most marriages ... back when there were such things."

The doctor swallowed, and asked, "What are you going to do to me?"

Karl sighed and rubbed the bridge of his nose. "I ... don't know. I found Greg, down the hall. I regret to inform you that he's on the way to becoming spoiled. I have a few questions, and please tell me the truth. I've thought over every conceivable answer and lie in my head, so don't explain that you were just keeping me sedated so you could feed me human flesh unaware to get my strength back. Tell me; were you planning on offering me the same treatment as you gave to Greg?"

The doctor stared at the ceiling, and after a pause, he said, "I don't know."

"No?"

"No. Before I was apprehended in Texas, I was careful, meticulous in my abductions. But now, with death an everyday occurrence, I've learned to follow whatever avenue will offer me the best chance for survival and reward. When you came to see me in the recesses of Haddonfield, I had no inclination of joining your band of mercenaries. I'm not a fighting man. But then I went over my options, and the choices you presented. In the basement, my food would have run dry, and I'd have been forced to face the dismal world alone. With you, I could live how I always wanted—free, and encouraged to do as I pleased. All I had to do was fix the occasional soldier, and fixing people brings me almost as much pleasure as taking them apart. In exchange, you gave me the liberty to keep any prisoner I wanted. With you, I had a better chance for survival and happiness."

"But now, you've turned your back on me?"

"No. I don't know. This is circumstantial."

"But you might have killed me, stripped me of flesh like ol' peg leg?"

The doctor shook his head. "Maybe. I can't control it. This thing that I do, it commands my life. I've given it my soul."

"It *is* you, Doctor. Don't kid yourself. If I let you go, would you still try to kill me?"

"I ... no. I'd want to join you for the rest of the journey. Whatever I was doing to you, to Greg, it's over. I'm a calculating man, and judging by my current position, my chances for survival are greater obeying you rather than fighting you."

They were silent for many minutes, then Doctor Freeman said, "I'm not afraid of dying. To be honest, a part of me yearns for it. I want to feel my blood flow. I want to see my reflection, my own eyes stare back at me as my life fades. So if you're going to do it, get on with it."

Karl sighed, and stood. He picked up a backpack and swung it over his shoulder. The rest of the rifles and ammunition were near the stairway. He reached into his pocket and removed a syringe, then dug in for three small vials that clanged in his palm. He drained the fluid from all three into the one needle, and put the hypodermic in Doctor Freeman's hand.

"I believe everything that you've said. If I set you free to join me once again, I believe you wouldn't do anything to harm me … as long as I kept you happy and fed. But one day, a month from now, a year, things could change. You are indeed a calculating man, and I cannot foresee what the future will hold. Unfortunately, I can't trust you to not repeat this episode. So, I am leaving now, and your binds will be kept in place. In that vial is enough morphine to kill five men. You hold your own destiny."

Karl turned to the door and flipped the light switch. He looked back at his old friend on the bed, cast aglow in the hallway light.

"I'll turn the music on for you. You'll have a few hours before it's quiet. Goodbye, Doctor Freeman."

He turned and left. In the examination room, he found the stereo and hit play. Blood still dripped in long, lazy trickles from Greg's gurney to the floor. Karl turned off the light and went down the hall, flipping switches as he went. When he passed the kitchen, he reached in for the light, not wanting to look at the refrigerator.

At the end of the hallway, he gathered the rest of his belongings, shouldered the rifles, and kept his finger hovering over the last light switch as he peered up the stairway, imagining the great open world beyond.

Chapter Thirty-seven
Fire Blind

Two full days after leaving the bunker, the fresh, warm breeze felt miraculous. Sitting at the bank of a small pond, Karl vowed that he'd die before ever sleeping below ground again. Humans required sunlight and fresh air, much the same as plants.

There had been no sign of Alice's or Hightown's soldiers, and after the progress he'd made going it alone with his strength renewed, he felt confident that the enemy patrols had ceased. He put himself in their position, in their heads, and could see no reasonable benefit in continuing to send large patrols so far from their settlements. By now, all of his own fleeing men were either long gone, captured, or murdered ...

... oh, those smug peasants down south, controlling the fuel and water. They probably held a huge victory celebration, the men sharing battle stories, drinking the night away as the officers gave speeches, and his own fierce Red Hands were brought before them, wrists bound, and executed to the crowd's jubilation ...

Since leaving the bunker, the past days offered him the first opportunity to dwell on his defeat with a clear mind, unhindered by injury or clouded by drugs.

The loss of his men's lives was something he could deal with. He'd lost many before. In war, nothing was certain, and the lives of even the most experienced and valiant soldiers were gambled upon. Bullets held no deference.

What bothered him was that the sheer number of his lost men meant his efforts would have to be doubled to see his force rise again. But they *would* rise again ...

What about Dietrich and his army?

He knew the answer.

Dead ... all dead ...

Sitting beside a pond to fish, Karl picked up a twig and tossed it in the still water, watching the circular ripples as the twig floated off. The bobber on his fishing line rebounded over the disturbance, then settled back to floating. He'd wait another ten minutes before continuing on.

To pass the time, he'd been flipping through Doctor Freeman's journal, being careful of the crisp leaves and tree specimens that were pressed between pages, and scanning the intricate sketches and descriptions. He put the journal back in the bag, and unfolded his battered map and inspected the terrain he'd soon encounter. If his pace stayed the same, he would be at the docks in a little over a day. And aside from the gnawing hunger, he felt better than he had in days. Since ... the explosion in the basement in Alice. The wounds had all closed up, and he was planning to remove most of the stiches before arriving at the docks.

All the medicine vials from Doctor Freeman's laboratory were stuffed in a pouch in his bag. Four of them were powerful amphetamines. If he took one at nightfall, he could march straight through to dawn; and if he stuck to the roads, he could be reasonably sure he wouldn't trip and break a leg in the darkness.

But maybe he'd hold back on taking the amphetamines. If he wanted to enter the docks with any degree of sensibility and strength, he'd need to take the journey slow, and rest when possible.

The bobber still floated idly on the water, making gentle quavers in the heavier gusts of wind. Karl reached for the stick planted in the dirt and pulled in his line. The hook caught a ray of sun as he coiled the string, and a drop of water fell from the looped end.

Ol' Greg's not sounding so unappetizing now, is he?

Karl laughed out loud at his own remark, packed his bag, and continued into the brush.

***

I'll be damned ...

He stopped short, and knelt to touch the soil.

Footprints ... two ... three ...

They were barely recognizable, on a portion of soft ground exposed from fallen leaves. If he'd not stopped to drink from his canteen he wouldn't have seen them at all. Not boot prints, but definitely human. Like rounded half moons.

They trailed to his right, roughly in the same direction he was trekking.

He squatted low and pondered, listening to the rhythm of the woods, the birds and wind. There was no indication of a disturbance.

I need to get away. Continue due north.

Maybe they have food.

They'll kill you.

I need to eat.

There were plenty of squirrels and small game all over. A family of raccoons had scurried near his camp the previous night. Karl walked holding a long, sharpened stick, so that maybe he could get close enough to one of the critters to spear it. But the chances were low, and shooting his rifle was still risky. He spent an hour scavenging a town he passed through earlier that day for a pellet gun, but the shelves of the small-town sporting goods store were wiped clean.

At some point in his travels, he'd been told that wild clover was edible, so he'd pinched and grabbed at the little three-leaved plants that littered the woods and lawns for two days, along with some of the tiny bright-yellow flowers that grew along with them. They offered nothing to satisfy his deep craving for nourishment, and after he ate his fill, his stomach cramped and he felt feverish for a short spell.

He was still processing his various choices when his fingers felt the next footprint over. Another smooth half moon. Then he lurched forward, squatting low, examining the ground for the trail of the prints. They were difficult to spot, but a scattering of leaves a few yards away told a telltale path straight across. The crisp groundcover had been broken, cracked into pieces.

In this manner he continued, and all the while his mind said things such as, *You're fucking crazy ... No one can kill Karl Metzger ... Turn back ... I'm starving ...*

As the light dimmed into early evening, it was becoming difficult to see the tracks. He had another hour, maybe less, until they would be impossible to decipher.

The warm breeze disappeared, replaced with a chilling evening, and Karl's grime-covered fingers were absorbing the cold.

Then he smelled it, and stopped moving.

Smoke ...

It was faint, yet unmistakable.

Using his nose as much as his fingers and eyes, he continued, each step slow and precise, making as little noise as possible. Soon, it would be too dark to walk without making a disturbance, and he'd have to stop and curl up in his sleeping bag. But there was light on the horizon, cutting through the thick bramble. Firelight. Warmth. People ... *food*.

He stalked closer, hearing voices and laughter. The last rays of light helped guide him to take small steps past twigs and clutters of dead leaves. He removed his backpack and assortment of arms, taking one small assault rifle and a pouch of spare magazines that he attached to his belt. He crawled behind the girth of a fallen tree and peered out above it.

There they were ... so close ... three of them. Two were sitting before the campfire, one with his hands outstretched to the warmth. The other stood, poking at the cinders with a long stick. He could hear fragments of their conversation. "... about an hour's worth of wood ... I ain't going ... tomorrow ..." He stayed there as the evening set to night, watching the three men add wood to the sparkling flame. They were in no worry about being seen. Whatever they were doing out there, they thought they were safe.

Karl readied himself to spring forward, and leaned the rifle over the top of the fallen tree. He peered down the sights. All three men were sitting, barely moving as they talked. His finger brushed the trigger, then paused ... what did they say?

"...no, no, it was Dietrich ... he did what? ... some priest, don't know ..."

Karl's heart beat fast against the side of the tree, and he wished now he'd taken the amphetamines, although his mind was swirling with so much adrenaline that he felt like he'd already taken them. He wanted to see their bodies explode with his wrath, feel the warmth of their blood on his hands, body, face ...

Breathe in.

Exhale.

Focus down the site.

Inhale …

… fire.

Once, twice, a volley of bullets. The entire campsite seemed to jolt, and before he could make sense of what had been hit and what had not, he sprung over the side of the tree, running through the brush, rifle up.

One man grabbed a shotgun from his side and pointed it frantically all throughout the woods. But Karl knew that staring into the campfire would blind them.

He aimed and shot the man below his neck. The man flew backwards, and Karl jumped into the clearing, raving mad, a huffing depiction of cruelty. The closest man lay facedown in the dirt, his head against a rock of the circular campfire, a bloody patch on his back. The man he'd just shot lay on the ground, his hands grasping his throat, unable to breathe, drowning fast. The other was scrambling on his back, his eyes huge, looking at Karl.

"Oh Jes-Jesus Christ!" he shouted, and faltered with the bolt on his rifle.

Karl sprung on him, grabbing the man's gun, and swung his fists down.

Chapter Thirty-eight
Map Maker

The wood crackled as the flames grew low, and the coals shimmered bright orange and red. The two lifeless scouts lay where they had been shot, as silent and unflinching as stumps of dead wood. They wore shoes made of strips of leather with flat soles and tied with a cord to keep them shut, so they would make little noise while traveling and hunting in the woods.

Karl chewed at a rough tear of jerky and took sips from a canteen, with his back against the side of a fallen tree. The heat from the fire had withered to small gusts of warm wind, and Karl closed his eyes as he chewed, focusing on the sensation of the calorie-rich meat on his tongue, filling his stomach. It felt as if his muscles were absorbing the much-needed protein and fat the moment he swallowed each bite.

He opened his eyes and spoke.

"I'm guessing you want me to let you go."

The man didn't answer.

Karl faced him, looking straight into his swollen eyes.

"Am I not correct? Or would you rather stay here, with me?"

"N-no," the man said.

Karl ripped another tear of meat with his teeth and chewed, watching the man out of the corner of his eye. He was not a flight risk, with his wrists tied behind his back, his ankles bound, and a long length of rope looped tightly around his torso to the dead tree behind him.

"Well," Karl said between chews, "I'm going to tell you about your situation. So far, I like the way our conversation has been going. You've been forthright about your intent out here in the woods, and I appreciate your honesty." Karl looked to the pile of papers he'd found in the group's belongings. Roughly drawn maps, trails, and waterways, starting from down in Alice, and ending where they were camped. "That is why you are still alive. And if you continue to be forthcoming with me, your death can be further postponed, perhaps indefinitely. To be candid myself, I will tell you this: if you would like to have an easy go of our question and answer sessions, tell me the truth right away. I have methods of dealing with misinformation and lies that you will not find pleasurable. Understood?"

The man was visibly trembling. "Y-yes," he said.

"Okay then." Karl finished the last bite of jerky, and rummaged through the scout's gear for another strip. "Now, to begin—do you know who I am?"

"Yes."

"What's my name?"

"Karl. K-Karl Metzger."

"On the night of the war, why were my men sick and hallucinating? What did you poison them with?"

"I don't know."

Karl stared at the man.

"Honest to God, I don't know. I know they did something, but I'm not privy to that information. I'm a scout, I'm out here because I can travel in the woods, and I can draw maps."

"Next question: how many of my men are dead? Are there prisoners?"

"I ... some. I don't know how many."

Karl sighed. "You don't seem to know much. Where were you in the battle?"

"I was locked up in the gymnasium until right before the war started. Then we marched out to Nick's mansion. I didn't even fire a shot, swear on my—"

"What happened to Dietrich, and the army coming in from the west?"

"I-I'm not privy—"

"All right, all right." Karl tossed a twig in the dying flame and stood. "You're out here, all alone, except for your two friends here, and yet, you don't know anything about anything. But because you can draw maps, they sent you on a solo mission ... I think not. I think there's more in that head of yours than you're willing to tell. Probably because you're ordered to remain silent, and they know you won't crack easy."

"No. We were sent to draw the terrain, mark the towns that have been destroyed, and the ones that haven't. Find small streams not shown on ordinary maps—"

"Let's be done talking for the night. I'm tired, and I think you'll have a change of heart by the morning. Tonight, I'm going to go easy on you. We have to move out early, and I don't want to drag along a pulverized piece of meat."

The man opened his mouth to talk, but Karl stepped quickly behind him and began untying his ropes. Once the man was free, Karl gripped the back of his neck and pulled him to his feet. The man faltered and limped as Karl pushed him fast to a tree, and slammed his chest up against the hard side. The man made a noise like, "Hmmph," as his bruised and bleeding body rubbed against the bark. Karl made a noose with the rope, placed the open end around the man's neck, then wrapped the free end around the tree, so that his face was pressed up hard against the wood. He then went behind him, grabbing his bound wrists, and pulling them upward so that his shoulders were stretched in the wrong direction. Karl threw another rope over a tall branch, and looped the rope around the man's wrists. The noose had about a quarter inch of slack, and any pulling would result in strangulation.

"Oh, God," the man said. "Cut me down, I'll tell you whatever you want."

"Too late for that, I'm afraid. We'll speak again in the morning."

Karl returned to the fire with a yawn, and unfurled his sleeping bag.

"Please," the man said, but Karl didn't answer.

***

Karl yawned again with the coming of morning, and sat up to stretch his back.

"Hey there," he called to the man. "You still alive?"

The man's words trembled in reply. "Y-y-yes."

"Good. After I have a nibble I'll be sure to loosen your bindings. You hungry?"

"Please, sir … I know things about—"

"After breakfast, please. You've been patient enough. You were quieter last night than I had anticipated. My hat is off to you."

"T-thank you, sir."

After Karl ate from a bag of tasteless granola and nuts, he unsheathed his knife and cut the rope above the man's wrists. His arms fell, and the man shrieked.

"Oh, Christ," he said.

Karl cut the rope at the man's neck, and the man fell to the ground, pale and quivering.

"It will take a while for your arms to feel back to normal. Your muscles are stretched and torn. Give it some time."

The man lay curled like a baby, and Karl brought him a canteen and a strip of dried meat.

"Here," he said. "Drink. You have to drink."

The man grabbed the canteen with shaking hands and drank, then took the jerky.

"Now," Karl said. "Let's begin."

Karl made him stand and retied his wrists before his body, and said, "The more I can trust you, the more comfortable your ordeal."

They sat before the fire and talked into the late morning. The man answered each question in turn, and Karl believed everything that came out of his mouth. He was a scout, trained by Simon Kalispell—who was still alive, and a celebrated war hero. As a part of his training, he had traveled to Hightown on many occasions. The poison that was used on the men was some sort of mushroom, brought in by Brian Rhodes. Both of these men were distinguished for their parts in the war, and were responsible for taking down Nick Byrnes. The soldiers in Nick's mansion had developed rashes due to bales of poison ivy that had been thrown in with their laundry, which was also brought in by Brian Rhodes.

Karl nodded as the man spoke, and they went on to other subjects, going over the names of prisoners. Karl had the man draw out maps and sketches, and was delighted in the detail.

"I can't believe it," Karl said, holding a sketch of Hightown's inner workings. "You know something—I think the two of us will get along just fine."

"Please," the man said. "I've told you everything I know. Please, let me go. You-you promised."

"Ha!" Karl shook his head. "No, no. I never promised. All I said is that you can prolong your life, which you have so far begun to do. But we are far from over. Come now, the afternoon grows near, and we have many miles to cover."

"Where are you taking me?"

Karl *tsked* him quiet and said, "It's time we go over the rules of the journey. First, you do not ask any questions, only answer mine. Understood?" Karl played with a length of rope, pulling it taut. The scouts had packed huge lengths of cord. With a few pitons, they had enough to scale a mountain.

The man looked down. "Yes, sir."

"Good." Karl patted the man on his head.

The noose rope from the night before was tightened around the man's neck, and the supplies were gathered.

"Okay then. We're heading north. You'll have to stay a few steps in front of me. You so much as stumble in any direction that I don't instruct, and I'll make it so you never sleep a peaceful night again. I'll add things like splinters under your nails, sharp things against your throat. So, onward." Karl pointed. "Due north."

He took a step, and then stopped. "One more thing. There was a girl, Bethany Rose. Do you know her?"

"Bethany Rose?" said the man. "It that the girl they found in the basement?"

The skin on Karl's arms turned to goose bumps. "Yes."

"I don't know much about her, other than she seems to be in a relationship with Simon Kalispell. There's rumor that she's related to Albert Driscoll, but honest to God, I don't know anything more. It's hearsay."

Karl's eyes went large. "She's a Driscoll?"

"I have no idea."

Karl believed him. "Proceed," he told the man, and they began their journey to the docks. A smile permeated his lips. *Driscoll ... Kalispell ...*

Chapter Thirty-nine
The General Arrives

The man's leather shoes did little to help him outside of the woods. The streets were a jumble of clutter, with shards of broken glass, rusted and disintegrating soda cans, and various sharp objects of unknown origin that sparked along their path by the full sun.

They stopped to take a break in the shade of a derelict home, and Karl offered the man a canteen. The man shook his head. Karl studied the scout, his bruised face looking solemnly down at his lap, his hands closed in the crook of his folded legs.

"Take a drink," Karl said again.

"I'm fine."

Karl reached out and nudged his shoulder with the canteen. "Take it."

The man looked up.

"Open your hands," Karl said.

He still didn't move.

"Open them."

In the silence, the urgency of an impending fight brought a burst of adrenaline to Karl's heart. He savored the sensation, watched the man's face, his eyes, his skin, his arms and legs, for the slightest tick of an oncoming attack.

But the man just sighed, looked to his hands, and opened his palms. A sliver of sharp metal rested on his palm, the other end twisted and dark.

Karl took a sip from the canteen, then said, "You aim to kill me with that thing?"

The scout didn't answer.

"Just a few weeks ago, I was blown to hell in an explosion that killed several other men. When I awoke, the room where I was lying was ablaze, the whole house on fire. I managed to flee, trailing so much blood my veins were beginning to pump air. For miles I walked, with my wounds covered in duct tape, and managed to get myself in a predicament with one of my closest officers. He had me drugged and trapped in an underground shelter, all the while feeding me roasted slabs of meat that belonged to one of my soldiers, who was kept sedated and restrained on an autopsy table while sections of his leg were removed. The poor bastard. But I'll tell you what; it wasn't half-bad. Greg was his name. Greg wasn't bad.

"The point I'm trying to make is that I've been through hell and back, and I'll be damned if my life is ended by that little toy you got there."

The piece of shrapnel fell to the grass.

Karl offered the canteen again, and the man took it. After a long pull of water he passed it back, and wiped his mouth on his forearm.

"I don't blame you for trying to kill me," Karl said, "Or at least, thinking about trying. Unfortunately, I'll have to make it so you don't pick up any more toys along the way."

Karl stood, and leaned down to grab the man's forearms. The man pulled away.

"I-I'm sorry, Karl—I'm sorry!"

Karl wrestled with the man's thrashing arms and grabbed ahold of his wrist.

"What are you doing? Stop, please! I've told you … I've told you so much. I swear—"

Karl tightened his grip on the man's wrist with one hand and grabbed his pointer finger with the other, feeling the thin little bone between the knuckle.

"Brace yourself," Karl said. "We got nine more to go."

**

The only noise other than the man's feet dragging against the pavement was the gentle melodic chirrup from a small flock of blackbirds, which covered several trees in the properties to their side.

"It's just ahead," Karl said.

The man continued, slumped over, his eyes cast to the ground. Karl tugged at the noose. "No longer talking to me?"

The man jolted at the constriction against his throat, then said, "You gonna kill me?"

"What makes you think that? Just don't do something stupid again, like plan on stabbing me."

"If you're gonna do it, just do it." The man's voice was low, a mumble. "Do it now."

"Ha! Oh, sir, I plan on keeping you around. You're valuable."

"I've told you everything …"

"Not enough. Never enough. There's more in that head of yours, I'm quite certain of it."

"I'll never … never be able to draw you another map." He looked at his hands.

"We have people who can do that for you."

They walked under an overpass that stretched across the highway, and as they came out the other side, the first and then the second ceremonial cannon came into view. There was movement behind the chain-link fence, and after another two steps, a voice called out, "Stop right there!"

The man paused, but Karl continued toward the fence, yanking at the rope for the man to follow.

More people appeared at the gate: soldiers in camouflage pointing machine guns.

"I said stop!" one of them called. "We'll fire!"

"Do you not recognize your superior officer?" Karl said. "Open the gate."

The men behind the chain-link paused, then one said, "Who are you? Identify yourself."

Karl walked to the security booth beside the sliding entrance.

"General Karl Metzger. And this here … what's your name, boy?"

The man opened his mouth, but Karl continued speaking, "Open up, and send word to Captain Liam and Commander Ivanov that I've arrived."

The soldier nearest him lowered his rifle and leaned in, squinting. "That really you?"

"Am I really me?" Karl laughed. "I certainly am."

"We heard you're dead. We heard the war is over. We lost."

"War never ends, soldier. It changes battlefields, but it never ends."

"How do I know it's you?"

"Call up Captain Briggs. Once he recognizes me, you can spend some time in the stockade with my friend here." Karl yanked the rope, making the man lurch forward.

The soldier walked away, talking into a microphone. A minute later he returned, and began unlocking the chains around the entrance. As he slid the gate open he said, "You'll have to leave your firearms at the entrance until we confirm your identity."

Karl walked past him. "I'll do no such thing." He tossed the end of the rope at the man's feet. "Lock him up proper."

As Karl proceeded into the base, a flock of guards studied him as if he was a mythical deity, returned from the dead. The soldiers' uniforms were frayed and patched up, and looked baggy around their gaunt frames. Their eyes were sunken, blinking in their shadowy sockets.

"You," Karl said, pointing to a young soldier with short, springy hair.

The soldier's eyes went large and he pointed to his chest. "Me?"

"Yes, you. Where's Captain Briggs?"

"I, um ... the warship, I presume."

"Escort me there. And call in for a warm meal to be prepared. The last hot meal I had was ..." He shook his head. "Never mind. Just call in for a meal to be made."

"Sir. Yes, sir ... there ain't much in the ways of hot food, but I'll call it in." The soldier took his radio off his belt, and then paused. "That really you, Karl?"

"It's really me, lad. I swear it. Those bastards couldn't kill me if they tried. And believe me, they tried plenty hard."

Chapter Forty

Broth

Karl sipped at a shallow bowl of clear liquid with a few meager cuts of carrot swimming around. He looked out a porthole to the glistening waves of the bay water, which extended far to a thin barrier island on the horizon and then the limitless ocean beyond. The cabin where he sat was a rectangular box, with an oval table in the center and a few dark leather couches to the side. Part of the officers' quarters, he presumed, but he knew nothing about warships. The walls were a drab off-white hue, with thick metal support beams running over the ceiling. Despite the several porthole windows letting in sunlight, he couldn't shake the feeling of being underground again, cut off from the world.

We belong outdoors, he told himself. *Not suffocating behind walls.*

The hinges of the cabin door creaked, and Karl looked up to see Liam Briggs step into the room.

"Karl ... my God ..."

His expression was the same as the soldiers at the gate.

"Yes, yes. I'm alive."

He rushed to the table. "Two soldiers came fleeing here, must have been a day before the battle. They said you were dead, they said they saw Mark Rothstein walk out of a burning house, barely alive."

"I would imagine as such. Sultan was in the basement with the explosives; he would have died instantly. I don't know about Mark. The room where I woke up was burning to the ground as I escaped. I presume his body went with it."

Liam took a seat beside him, and Karl explained the battle in Alice, from what he'd gathered. He stopped before going in depth about his journey with the doctor.

"Why didn't you attack Hightown? The commander promised he'd send a vessel into the bay."

"When word of your death arrived, he rescinded. Said it is a futile gesture."

Karl was quiet in contemplation. He ladled a spoonful of broth and let it trickle back into the bowl. "These are meager offerings you got here."

"The rations are low," Liam said. "Desperately low. Half the boxes that we saw in storage when we first came to town are empty. A few days after you left for Alice, rations went down to half, and it's only gotten worse."

"So, they lied to us, fully prepared to leave behind an army that couldn't be fed. Where are the commander and his lieutenants? Where's Bishop?"

"I sent someone to find Bishop. The officers are on their way."

"How many escaped the battle? How many of our men made it here, to safety?"

Liam shook his head. "Not many. Less than a hundred, I believe. I'll get the exact number, but it was eighty-seven last I heard. Most fled when the fighting began—they were all sick and hallucinating. Ran right off the line and stumbled here, dehydrated near death."

"Less than a hundred ..."

"And none from Dietrich's attachment."

Karl nodded. "I came across three scouts from Hightown on my journey here, and managed to keep one of them alive. He's in the brig as we speak. Dietrich's detachment battled Hightown far from either of the settlements, in what we thought was an ammunition stockpile. Turns out it was a trap. They were slaughtered."

Karl sipped the last of his broth and pushed the bowl away. He went on to explain everything the scout had told him, and then reached to his backpack for the hand-drawn maps.

"Well, I'll be damned," Liam said. "Hear anything from Sergeant Marcus? He make it into Hightown?"

"No. I was about to ask you the same. Tell me, what is the commander's thinking—what is his plan?"

Liam shook his head. "No plan. After news of the war, he spent two days locked in his quarters."

"All the while, his soldiers are starving …"

"Search parties and hunting expeditions go out daily, but they don't turn up more than a handful of cans or a dead bird or two. The fishing's good off the dock, but all they got are some lines, and one or two nets. They're not bringing up enough to feed an army. With proper guidance, they could. But the commander … sure, he can steer a vessel, but actually governing men? Not so much."

"Are his thoughts still on sailing back to Russia?"

Liam shrugged. "To be honest, he hasn't made his intentions known. But I'd imagine his objective will always be to go back to Russia."

"There's a whole army here at the commander's disposal. Is he set on doing nothing with them? Hightown is sending scouts in all directions, surveying, mapping, looking for members of our organization. They're traveling north, south, and west. They'll be on us in a matter of weeks, maybe less; and by then, our defending army will be nothing more than walking skeletons. I sent a scout to Masterson, commanding a full departure. I thought they'd be here before my arrival. Let's hope they weren't discovered by Hightown on their way and engaged in battle. Send scouts to investigate."

"Yes, sir. I'll make the order. There was word that they came under attack after the battle in Alice. The last report stated it was a small melee, but they're expecting a large counteroffensive. By all accounts, let's hope they got out in time."

"Indeed." Karl had expected this. It was only logical that Hightown would follow the Priest's trial. "What about the commander's men? Are they sitting idle, willing to starve while their officers do nothing to ensure their survival?"

Liam cleared his throat and said, "All hope was on you. The men, all they want is to eat, drink, survive. If things had gone different in Alice and Hightown, and the commander and his few Russian counterparts sailed across the ocean, there was no protest over you becoming their new leader. In truth, from what I gathered, the soldiers were happy to have someone in power that displays a willingness to fight, and not simply hide away forever in the boats. They're sick of playing defense."

"Is that so?"

"After the reports of your dying, the attitude changed around here. The men walk around like they're defeated, already dead, when in truth, they still maintain a vast arsenal of weaponry. But under the commander's leadership, there's nothing being done to ensure their safety. I've heard rumors of a few wanting to take power themselves, overthrow the Russians. It might have gone that way if you hadn't returned, and rightly so. To be honest, I was thinking of doing it myself." Liam paused, scratching at his unshaven cheek.

Karl nodded. "Get me a full report of the army's numbers, munitions, and food stockpile. Everything."

"Yes, sir."

Footfalls came from down the hall, echoing through the metal cabin room. Karl spoke fast to Liam, and a moment later, Commander Sergei Ivanov walked into the room in full battle dress, followed by his lieutenants, Ivan and Viktor. His dark uniform held an excess of colorful rank markers and intricate gold embroidery, with shiny golden buttons. His peaked cap was held in the crook of his arm.

"Karl," the commander said through his faded accent. "I don't believe it."

Upon the commander's arrival, Liam stood loosely at attention. Karl leaned back in his chair and put his boots up on the table.

"Commander, sir, you'd better believe it. How about one of those cigars you're famous for sharing and a spot of whiskey? I'm dying for a smoke after such a fruitful meal." He tapped the empty bowl with the side of his boot, and put his hands behind his head.

Chapter Forty-one
Way of the World

Karl was given privacy to bathe and dress while word of his return spread like fire throughout the army, and the men were ordered to meet on the dock in two hours' time for a speech. The excitement was noticeable.

Other than the occasional sponge bath down in the dark recess of Doctor Freeman's basement, Karl had not felt jets of water for … weeks? It was hard to determine how much time had gone by with his consciousness fading in and out through the majority of his trek. But both Liam and Bishop had told him the battle in Alice ended over a month ago. Had the doctor really kept him sedated for that long?

Standing under the stream of water, he leaned against the wall and cut away the final stiches from his leg. The sensation of pulling the threads was not enjoyable, but when he finished, all that remained was a puffy red strip of scar tissue.

Despite there being no hot water, Karl stayed in the shower for a half an hour longer than necessary, re-lathering himself in soap over and over. When he turned off the water and stepped out, dripping on the frigid metal floor, he scrubbed his body with a towel until his skin was red and raw. He felt lighter, if that was at all possible. And then looking at his reflection in the mirror, he picked up the disposable razor he'd been issued, and lathered his face with the soap.

He picked from the meager stockpile of army fatigues a plain set of olive drab pants and a button-up shirt, and fashioned his belt and holster around his midsection.

Karl was not a new man, standing fresh and clean; he was his old self, before the battle in Alice. He was the leader of horribles, the general of all things.

Liam and Bishop waited in the meeting room down the cavernous hall.

"Karl," Liam said as Karl stepped into the room, along with four of his trusted soldiers who had escaped the war. "We just received word; the army from Masterson will be approaching the gates soon. They're only a mile out. There's no indication that they've been followed, but we should assume they were."

"Mister Briggs, that is the best news I've heard in quite some time. Have them march straight to the docks and join the crowd."

"Yes, sir." Liam relayed the message to a guard, and joined Karl beside an ample porthole window, facing the ships. Their warship was at the end, attached to the left lane of the trident-shaped dock. A makeshift podium and stage was being assembled where the three berths converged to a single, wide central road, and the crowd was growing.

A few moments later, the three Russian officers walked into the room.

"Karl," the commander said, "the soldiers are gathering."

Karl had been instructed that they were going out there to tell the people that they had accepted defeat. They were to detail their failed attempt to conquer Hightown and Alice. They were going to explain that they would still survive ...

The commander walked beside Karl at the porthole window, his hands clasped behind his back. "It's time," he said.

"Yes, Sir Commander. It is. Look there." He pointed to the crowd. "In the rear; my army is arriving from Masterson."

The commander leaned closer.

"Your men are impressive," he said. "I thought for sure that Masterson would be defeated."

Karl nodded.

A legion of several hundred advanced onto the docks, mixing with the others, shaking hands, and even hugging some of their comrades. Drifts of smoke wisped into the air as the armies exchanged tobacco, and Karl could only guess the abundance of alcohol that would soon be consumed. His mouth watered.

Despite the arduous fighting in Masterson that saw masses of his men die, and the long march after, his army was in all appearances stronger, larger, and healthier than the near-starved dockworkers. Many were still caked in the mud and gore of warfare, their red handprints freshly painted over their chests in a display of camaraderie. Their weaponry was a mixture of modern firepower along with anything that was sharp or heavy enough to maim and kill. Some wore machetes and swords, spears and sledgehammers, the handles and sheaths adorned with ritualistic artwork and embroidery, made from plunders of war: gold teeth, locks of hair, tanned hides, and sparkling jewelry. Red strips of cloth were tied around their arms, and secured to the ends of spears.

"Dear God," the commander said, his hand held loosely in the fold of his buttoned-up wardress. "They look like demons."

Karl turned, and when he uncrossed his arms, he slid his bowie knife from the sheath in a smooth motion. The blade was sharp and glistening, and Karl aimed right below the commander's lower rib, where the flesh was soft, and the blade could be stabbed upward toward his heart and main arteries.

But the commander was quick to jump back, the blade pierced halfway in. With a terrible shriek, the commander grabbed at his belly with one hand and scratched at his flapped pistol holster with the other. Karl sprang forward, slashing and jabbing at the commander's flailing arms until he had him pressed against the corner of the room. "You're a coward!" Karl issued. "You should have attacked Hightown instead of recoiling away like a whipped dog!"

The two Russian lieutenants leaped forward to help their superior officer, but Liam and Bishop were ready, and grabbed them from behind. They choked them with their forearms, muffling their screams, and stabbed unrelenting down into the men's chests and throats with their knives. The officer's two guards jolted into action, but were subdued by the four Red Hands who had been waiting to pounce.

The cabin door swung open, and two faces appeared. "Commander—" one said before they were yanked into the room and pressed facedown against the cold metal floor. Their eyes were inches away from the widening pools of blood spilling from the officers who lay beside them.

With a final lurch, Karl plunged the knife into the commander's chest, feeling the handle buckle as it maneuvered between two ribs.

The commander's eyes shot wide and his trembling jaw dropped open.

"You've done this to yourself, Commander." Karl spoke through his teeth, his face inches from the man's fading eyes. "This is the way the world works. People in power will always be at odds with impending doom. You never deserved the authority that you held. Your people will rejoice at hearing the news of your demise. They'll rejoice at knowing their fates are now held in the hands of someone capable. Death comes for us all, and now it is your turn to face the reaper. You stopped being the leader to your men the moment you decided that leaving to Russia was more important than ensuring their survival."

He stepped back and yanked the knife free.

The commander made a fluid-filled gurgle and dropped to his knees, then fell facedown.

Karl turned to the two guards pinned to the floor.

"Well," he said, bending down to clean his blade and his hands on the back of the commander's uniform, "in a moment, I'm going out there to address the crowd. I'm going to tell them exactly what has transpired here. I am not and never will give the speech that the commander had intended—to offer defeat, resignation. This war is not over; if anything, my lust for victory has been made even greater. All was not lost in one failed battle, as these men here would make you believe. Under their leadership you all would have died, either by starvation or by the impending fighting that will soon take place once Hightown musters their men to march upon us. They have air power, attack helicopters, and long-range missiles. They'd wipe out half the fleet before we could man the guns.

"However, at the moment, Hightown has little concept of our existence. We will strike while they're still weakened from the melee in Alice. We won't sit back waiting for them to charge our gates. From here on out, we are at total war with our enemies, and I will not stop fighting until all their people are strung up to lampposts. No more trickery to win battles; no more sly maneuvers to work my way inside. We will attack in the fashion that I had implored Commander Ivanov to do." Karl pointed to the commander, who had become still. "This army—his army—was promised to me upon his absence, and I'm here to take it. Starting immediately, the men are issued full rations. They need their strength. They are to begin training at once, ready themselves for battle. We depart when they get some meat on their bones and spirit to their fighting: days, weeks, but not months. We depart for victory, and we will plunder all of the food and resources we could ever need. Gardens. Cattle. No more scrounging for spoiled cans and rotten fish. With victory, we will be the fiercest assemblage of fighting men walking this earth. Oh by God, I swear it."

One of the men on the ground opened his mouth to speak, but Karl continued, "Some will be resistant to what I have done to the commander and his lieutenants. I have been given a list of names of his most loyal men, and my soldiers are ready to eliminate them now, in the gathered crowd outside. The rest will rejoice. Under my leadership, all will prosper. Just ask the men who have fought by my side. Ask the men who have returned from Masterson. Do they sulk at having to retreat from their conquered city? No. They arrive with fresh coatings of war paint on their chests. We will rejoice in the thrill of warfare and the euphoria of triumph. So ask yourself, are you with me? I could have killed you half a step through the door, but I have instructed my men to let all decide their own fates. Choose now the path of salvation, or the path of damnation. What's it going to be?"

Blood had pooled over one of the men from the slain officers, and he struggled to lift his face from the oppressive knee that held him pinned to the ground. "I'll fight," he said. "General, I'll follow you. We all will. No one wants to starve."

The other man issued the same. "I'm with you."

The guards let them go free. With disheveled, stained uniforms, they got to their knees.

"Up now," Karl said. "Join me as I address the waiting crowd. Stand tall and proud."

The guards helped the men to their feet.

"One thing first," Karl said, and pointed to their chests. "If you are to join me, display your loyalty to the brotherhood."

One man stepped toward the dead commander, and then the other followed. They dipped their palms into a pool of blood, and showed their red palms to Karl.

"Do you swear your allegiance?" Karl asked.

"Yes," they said in unison. Then one said, "We serve you, General."

They pressed their palms into their chests and stood tall, members now of the Red Hands, and under the command of General Karl Metzger. King of the East.

Chapter Forty-two
Hightown

Hightown's inner shoreline and docks were protected from the ocean by two overlapping barrier islands. When viewed from over the ample bay, the horizon appeared to be one continuous stretch of land, with the two islands blending into one another. But the gap between them formed a wide channel that had been used for decades as a shipping route to reach the ocean.

High atop the steep banks, a half mile away from the harbor, was a section of Hightown used primarily for surveillance of the waters and the land adjacent to the shore. This was where Hightown's defunct lighthouse still peered out from the top of the incline, along with a number of magnificent homes built to reflect the wealth of the landowners who could afford property with a bay and ocean view. At the bottom of the steep incline, the waters lapped at a shore comprised of boulders and bulkheads, with one small slip of sandy beachfront that once belonged to the county park system. A walking trail stretched along the base, following the shore as it snaked along, with the magnificent homes and the lighthouse high overhead, atop a near-vertical hill of wavering reeds and sections more wooded, with thick bramble and tall trees.

In a home overlooking the bay, a man named Miles was on guard duty in a turret-shaped room, which soared an extra ten feet over the roof of the dwelling. The circular room contained a bed, a desk, and a panoramic view of Hightown. A low sandbag wall circled the windows, and two machine guns rested idle beside ammunition boxes.

Miles sat in a chair, his scoped twenty-caliber rifle leaning against the desk and his binoculars tied around his neck. He was reading a worn paperback noir novel, holding the pages open so that the flimsy spine was further and forever creased. The small flickering light from a candle was his only source of illumination, but with the sun now rising, it would soon not be needed. The candle was in direct violation of his orders, since even the smallest light made his eyesight weak against the nighttime world outside, but after a year on nightshift, not once had a ship approached other than the fuel convoys. No one in Hightown had ever seen a rogue vessel, and most everyone was under the impression that they were the sole possessors of ships and the fuel necessary for sailing the seas, for miles around.

The sun was close to peering out over the distant barrier island, and the sky above was an infusion of brilliant reds, oranges, and yellows. In these early morning hours, it appeared as if the horizon was ablaze, from one corner to the other. Once the sun cracked over the bay, the bright rays shone straight through the glass windows, unhindered in the clear sky, and reflected in colorful sways atop the cresting waves.

Miles blew out the candle, flinching at the spray of hot wax that stung his fingers. He stood and stretched his back, then moved to sit behind the sandbags, in the only spot in the room offering shade in the early hours.

As he stood, a black dot caught his attention far off in the water, and his initial thought was that the fuel convoy had arrived.

Then uncertainty crept into his mind, and he took up his binoculars. He attempted to shield the harsh rays of the sun with his palm, and saw a lone ship entering the channel … wait … was a shipment scheduled this morning? The vessel was following the same path of the convoy … but maybe it wasn't. Instead of veering to its right, toward the docks, the boat was swinging left, its broad side facing the shore.

Miles went back to the desk and picked up a clipboard. He ran his finger over dates and times, looking below the ones with lines crossed through them. There was nothing scheduled for today.

The radio on his belt crackled, and a voice said, "Miles, you there? Over."

He grabbed the radio. "This is Miles. Over."

"You seeing this?" The voice belonged to Alex, in the lighthouse. "I checked the itinerary; there are no deliveries listed today. Over."

Miles placed the clipboard down and looked out over the water. The massive vessel became clear.

He swallowed, then spoke into the radio. "Call it in. Over."

"Affirmative."

Miles grabbed his scoped rifle and rested the stock on the sandbag. He scanned the deck of the boat, and then the barrier island behind, where an observation post and long-range artillery were stationed to guard the channel. Was that a wisp of smoke? It looked like steam ... a white steam. No more than thirty seconds passed before a loud, wailing alarm caused him to jolt.

Holy shit.

If the engineer on duty, John Zur, had sounded the town's alert system, it would be for good reason. The man didn't cry wolf.

Footfalls resounded from beneath the floor as heavy boots came stomping up the stairway, and two men burst into the room. Without missing a beat, they fed the ammunition belts into the heavy gauge machine guns.

"What's going on out there?" one of the men asked.

"Don't know."

The machine guns were put in position, the windows facing the bay flung open, when a thunderous crack made the entire building tremble. The popping noise of small arms followed.

"Jesus," Miles said. "What the hell was that?"

The soldiers peered down the barrels of their weapons, and they all flinched as an even louder explosion thundered from somewhere inside the town, followed by another.

The radio was abuzz, voices issuing commands. He could hear John Zur, his normally subdued demeanor panicked, coughing as if he couldn't breathe.

Miles picked up the radio. "Are we ordered to fire?" he called in. "Are we ordered to fire?" The overlapping voices told him to stand by.

One of the machine gunners said, "Where the hell is our artillery? That ship isn't ours."

The first two motorboats could be seen heading out from the docks toward the ship, and then a dozen more followed, bouncing atop the gentle swells.

The order came in. "Fire with small arms. *Fire!*"

The machine guns opened up from all the various lookouts along the hilltop, and the water circling the ship erupted in jarring sprays of white. Miles scanned the top of the boat through his scope, from left to right and back again, but could see no indication of people.

Then another terrible noise emitted, and the entire top of the ship erupted in smoke. Fast and terrible streaks shot into the air as missiles were unloaded, and a torrent of high-caliber machine gun fire opened up at the approaching small vessels.

The whistling sound of the rockets was near deafening, rattling around that small, circular room. Then a rumble struck the house so intensely that windows shattered, and Miles's book and clipboard flew from the table. A portion of the roof above him cracked and fell in, as a gale of burst shrapnel walloped into the side of the home, and a force struck Mile's side.

A missile had struck the next-door residence, and half the structure disintegrated in a massive gust of fire. The other half crackled like a hundred trees falling at once, then toppled over in a terrible clatter.

"Holy fuck!" Miles shouted. He looked at the machine gunner beside him, who lay slumped over the sandbags, blood pooling beneath his face. He moved to roll the man over, and became aware of a tugging sensation on his midsection. When he looked down, he recoiled to see a shaft of wood, maybe a foot long, implanted in his side.

"Where the fuck is our artillery?"

The second machine gunner was unloading his rounds, when he paused. "Miles—Miles!"

Miles stopped pulling at the shrapnel implanted in his side, and looked forward. "Oh … Christ …"

A swarm of black dots like an infestation of locust issued out from behind the warship in a great horde, a shadow of death extending its ghostly fingers.

Adrenaline kept his mind away from the pain in his side, and he attempted to focus on his breathing. His scope followed the fast-moving tops of helmeted heads jettisoning in their direction, aboard inflatable Zodiac boats, and an assortment of medium-sized attack ships and military landing vessels.

Miles breathed in, then out. Focused. Pulled the trigger. He breathed in, then out. Focused—

The top of the warship erupted again in a cloud of smoke, and a wall of fire issued into the air as the missile systems unloaded.

He did not see the explosion that took his life, or even have time to flinch from the gale of fire. One moment he was there, and in another, he vanished.

***

A voice came in from over the radio.

"We have an unidentified ship. Over."

Iain Marcus stopped in his tracks and put the crate of carrots he was taking to the kitchen down on the ground. He pulled his radio free and listened to the men debate what they were seeing. The lead engineer, John Zur, sounded panicked, which was unusual.

Without hesitation, Iain left the crate on the dusty path and ran across Hightown. When he arrived at an overlook, panting, sweat rolling down his face, his eyes went large.

This is it ...

The ship was moving in direct line to the shore, and he looked up at the magnificent homes not far to his side and the lighthouse a few properties over. This area was the last place where he'd be safe.

He had his orders, but for a fraction of a second, he was powerless to remember what they were. This was plan B, which he went over with General Metzger all those months ago. The war in Alice had failed, and by God ... if the warships were here, the General must still be alive ...

In a flash, he turned and ran toward the center of town. His feet seemed to be moving slower than he wanted, his body aching, his breath coming out in labored huffs, and he cursed the debilitating effects of age on his body. *Ten years ago,* he thought, *hell, five years ago, I could've run a marathon without breaking a sweat.*

He'd made it back to his living quarters when a person on the radio said, "Get to the ships. Send out a squadron." In an eyeglass container, hidden at the bottom of his footlocker, was a tiny amount of C4 explosives. He grabbed the case and swerved around a fellow soldier in the barracks who said, "What's going on out there?"

Iain shrugged and ran past the man.

The air horn blared out from the docks, alarming him, but he didn't miss a step until he was at the edge of a clearing, surrounded by personnel and with a mobile command center to the side. In the center of the clearing were over a dozen long-range missile and artillery systems, with men shouting out commands, and loading the breaches. Shells were being stacked under portable tents, with more locked away in storage sheds to the rear of the clearing.

He could see John Zur inside the mobile command center, hunched over an array of screens and monitors, issuing orders to men nearby.

A soldier appeared before Iain, his face red, with deep furrowed lines cutting across his forehead. "What the fuck's the matter with you!" the officer shouted.

Iain became aware of his sweaty, disheveled demeanor. "Sir, where can I help?"

"Get moving!" The officer pointed to where soldiers were unloading crates of ordnance from the shed to the grass beside the weapons systems.

Before Iain could respond, the officer turned his attention to another soldier, shouting, "Ready artillery!"

Iain hurried to the storage shed, where inside lay stacks of crated artillery munitions. As he neared a crate, he pulled out the glasses case, opened the cover, and flipped a small metal switch implanted in the side, connected to a battery. A red LED light flickered on, and as Iain bent over to pick up a crate, he dropped the case between a stack of boxes. Three other men were grabbing munitions, and one said, "Marcus—hurry it up!"

Iain grabbed a crate, followed the men, and placed the box down beside a lightweight field howitzer. Then he turned and ran, ignoring the sweat stinging his eyes, and the officer shouting, "Fire on my command!"

Someone was calling to him, "Marcus, where're you going? Marcus!"

He was nearing the side of a dilapidated and unused storage structure when the detonator went off, and the succession of explosions were so overwhelming that they all seemed to belong to one giant explosion and not the dozens of crates erupting at once.

Even from his distance, a force of heat pushed him off his feet, and he flew onto his stomach, scraping his chin as he bounced over the ground. He kept his arms over his head as the explosions rippled over the artillery field, with shrapnel soaring in every direction. A blanket of dirt overwhelmed him, shooting into his nostrils and mouth, and he pressed his arms even tighter over the top of his head.

I'm too old for this, he thought, his muscles sore and bruised. The fragility of his body pinged in his mind, sending waves of fear and uncertainty to his thoughts. *If I break something, I'm done for.*

When the waves of heat lessened, he got up and brushed the dirt from his face and eyes, seeing the flaming pit that had once housed the town's artillery. The command center had been ripped in half, and he waited momentarily to make sure the eyes and ears of Hightown, John Zur, had been killed. But then a number of men spared from the explosion, maybe a dozen, were fast approaching, and one was pointing at him.

He heard, "You there!" and he turned and ran.

A shot rang out, and then more followed, with voices shouting, "Stop— Stop!"

Someone must have seen him drop the case, or made some sort of connection when he began to run. But none of that mattered now, because as he ducked behind the crumbling building, he heard the monstrous ignition of the warship's batteries, and within moments, explosions echoed from all over Hightown's line.

***

Karl followed the first wave to shore, ducking low in his Zodiac raft as it bounded over swells. The water was peppered with machine-gun fire, but by all accounts, no artillery was raining down, which meant Iain had done his job. Plan B: Take out enemy defense capabilities at the onset of a naval attack. Plan A would have been the same, only they would have been arriving on land first, after the fall of Alice.

As Karl's boat rebounded over the top of the water, the massive homes on the far hill were burning and exploding. The tall lighthouse that once jutted far over the tallest tree was gone, replaced by a thick trail of dark smoke. But still, the water all around him was being plunked with machine-gun fire, and men were falling overboard. Several boats had erupted into flames or exploded, sending dramatic concentric rings of disturbances in their wake.

The shoreline was filled with vacated rafts as his men flooded the land. When Karl's boat came to a stop, he jumped into the waist-deep water, and trudged with the hundreds of men to the walled bank.

Soldiers were already scaling the steep hill, woven into the eight-feet-tall reeds like lice on a dog. Karl stopped to observe, watching his men near a chain-link fence about halfway up, with rings of barbed wire atop. There were random explosions as mines went off, and grenades were lobbed down from the line of Hightown's soldiers that were amassing at the hilltop.

Karl turned to Bishop, who'd been in the raft with him, and shouted a command. Bishop kneeled, covering one ear while yelling into a microphone. Within moments, the large caliber machine guns on the warship began to rattle, focusing on the hilltop and the section of land just above the fence.

His men crouched low as bullets came perilously close, with many struck down from friendly fire.

Bishop shouted another command, and the bullet fire ceased. A line of snipers on the ship were still taking aim at Hightown's men at the top, and every few seconds, dead bodies came tumbling over the rim.

"Move!" Karl ordered. "Move out!"

He took to the embankment himself, and joined his monstrous swarm up the sheer side, grabbing at thickets of reeds and the occasional large rock to pull himself along. When he reached the top, the men ahead of him had eliminated most of the waiting army. They were quick to further their advance, yelling, shrieking, their minds ablaze and chemically altered by a cocktail of amphetamines the medical staff had prescribed.

Artillery fire from the ship slowed to precise detonations, with areas being called in one at a time. Most of the helicopter pads had been targeted with the first wave, to suppress Hightown's air support. The location of the pads was supplied by Karl's prisoner, who endured hours of torture until every drop of information had been wrung from him. Copies of his map had been made, and the papers were issued to each man. Squadrons were ordered to advance to individual targets and strategic locations.

Largely to their advantage was that a quarter of Hightown's army— including a considerable section of its armored wing—was still down south in Alice, helping repair their line. The Red Hands would have to endure a counterattack once the town was theirs, but if everything went as planned, the majority of Hightown's fortified walls and defenses would still be in place for his army to maintain.

Karl advanced into Hightown, exchanging gunfire with pockets of resistance as his army continued to scale the hill and amass at the top.

As they made headway, Karl and a squad of ten men broke off from the rest of the force, and followed a course previously outlined. Among them was Jacob, his eyes twinkling with narcotics, and smiling like a madman at seeing Hightown's soldiers being blown to pieces. The squad had gone over the layout of the town so many times that they didn't need to use the map to navigate.

The men came around the bend of a building, and stopped short as enemy bullets peppered the corner of the wall.

"Grenades on three!" Karl said over the roar of gunfire. "One … two … three!"

The men pulled the pins on their grenades and lobbed the barrage over the roof of the low building. Following the ripple of explosions, Karl darted forward, his men at his heels, eliminating a scattering of enemy soldiers who were injured or hurt from the explosions.

"That's it," Karl said, pointing to a building ahead. "Move!"

The squad ran to the side of the building and followed the wall until they came around the bend, and to the front of Hightown's Police Department.

The door swung open, and a flash of movement was seen behind the thick plate-glass security window as whoever was guarding the building ran from the front office.

A soldier was quick to plant explosives at the handle of the bulletproof door, and the men swung around a corner. The soldier came running to meet them, holding a small mechanical device. On Karl's instruction he pulled the trigger.

A rush of smoke and debris shot down the hall with the roar of the explosion, and the air became hot and thick.

The squad moved out, and one was shot and fell only a step around the bend. Gunfire was exchanged from both sides, but the sheer pressure of Karl's men to advance caught the enemy off guard, and soon the top floor of the station was clear. A handful of dead enemies lay scattered throughout, and Bishop and the soldiers scoured their pockets, finding several matching sets of keys.

The men were fast down the stairway, using flashlights at the bottom where there was no flowing electricity. The air grew foul as they progressed across a hallway, with no enemy soldiers to be found. At a pair of thick metal double doors, a man in front tried out several keys until one fit, and the army stepped into a prison room. The cells here were large, and dozens of faces peered out from behind the bars. Filthy, blinking, shielding their eyes from the glaring flashlights.

"Open them," Karl said.

"Is that really you?" the prisoners asked. "General?"

Karl didn't stop to greet his freed men, but continued with Bishop and two others to a door in the back. Once open, they went further down a barren hall, and had to unlock yet another door before entering. Beyond were six single cells for the more violent offenders, or those awaiting transfer to larger prisons. Here was where Hightown kept the few officers they had captured, locked behind thick steel doors.

In turn they were opened, with one vacant, and the others containing the battered and half-dead senior officials of Karl's Red Hands. At the last one, Karl himself inserted the key and unlocked the door. So far, everything that the captured scout had told him was correct.

Bishop shone a flashlight as the door was pulled open, and a man sat straight-backed on a cot, facing the wall.

"Dietrich," Karl said.

The Priest turned to face Karl and said, "By the grace of God ... I never doubted you, Sir General."

He stood tall and stepped out to freedom, and joined Karl in the demise of Hightown.

Epilogue
Simon

In the days following the battle in Alice, mass funerals were held for the departed. Flatbed vehicles and garbage trucks collected the dead from the front line, and men in full protective clothing lined the corpses in the zigzagged trenches in the lawn before Nick Byrnes's mansion. The bodies of the Red Hands were tossed inside the damaged home, along with a variety of limbs and parts of unknown origin, and scraps of broken machinery of war. The townspeople gathered to watch backhoes fill in the trench line, burying the dead, and then the mansion was set on fire. The new general of Alice spoke to the crowd in a somber tone as the flames leaped into the air, and the home was reduced to blackened timber. The next morning, work trucks rolled over the destruction, flattening out what was left of the frame. Weeks later, wildflower seeds were scattered atop of the entire front lawn in commemoration.

A large force of Hightown's military stayed in Alice, helping to repair the front line, and sending out expeditionary forces to capture any Red Hands who had fled. The town of Masterson was discovered, where a large enemy force still remained. The expeditionary force fell back, and a full-on assault rumbled into the town, tanks and all. However, the enemy had disappeared before their arrival, and little was left behind to suggest the town was ever inhabited. Scouts were sent to follow their trail.

Simon Kalispell helped spread the wildflower seeds along with a few dozen volunteers. Brian Rhodes was with him, although his knee had been twisted fierce in the fighting, and he had to stop and lean into his cane every few minutes, taking the pressure off his leg.

"Why don't you go back home?" Simon asked, reaching into the large bag of seeds. The tiny grains felt nice in his hand, a living thing not yet come to be.

"Nah," Brian said. "I've spent enough time at home, in bed or on the couch the last few weeks. I need some air. The ground here is bumpy is all. I'm a'right."

Simon shrugged. "Suit yourself."

Off in the distance, his dog, Winston, had his nose pressed deep in the soil. Simon looked up to see him digging.

"Winston!" Simon whistled loud, and his dog's ears perked up. He whistled again, and Winston came trotting over, his tongue bouncing out of the side of his mouth. "Come on, boy. No digging." He scratched at the dark spot of fur on Winston's head, and then said to Brian, "I should have left him at home, with Bethany."

"He needs fresh air too. And Beth's probably working on the front line."

Simon didn't answer to that. Bethany had been working incessantly since her ordeal in the basement of Nick's mansion. She barely slept at night and would wake up before dawn, quickly leaving the house to go help reconstruct the trenches and bunkers. It was her way of coping, Simon knew, not that he could blame her. She'd been abducted, sedated, and made to think that she'd be tortured and brutally killed at any moment. But still, she wasn't allowing herself to process her ordeal.

Simon let the tiny seeds drift from between his fingers, scattering with the breeze. The radio attached to his belt made a muffled noise, and then a voice spoke. *"Simon, come in. Over."*

Simon unclasped the radio. "This is Simon. Over."

"You're needed in North Ward five. Over."

"Affirmative."

Simon looked at Brian, and before he could say anything, Brian said, "Leave Winston with me. I'll take him home."

"Thanks." Simon scratched Winston's head and reached down for his rifle, which was leaning beside a garden rake. As he walked off the lawn, he turned to see Winston lapping at Brian's hand as his head was being ruffled, his tail in a frenzy.

God, that old dog still has so much life in him.

Simon took off in a jog off the lawn, and up the next street toward the northern section of town. North Ward five was a checkpoint close to the trade grounds, just slightly above it.

He jogged near a half mile, and the air expanding his lungs felt good. As he neared the checkpoint, he saw two other Rangers waiting along with the guards. "Simon, sir!" one called out. It was strange being called sir, and Simon wasn't sure if he liked it. After so many of the Rangers died in the battle, he was the logical next in command. Especially with many of the residents looking at him as if he were some sort of supernatural deity after the battle on Nick's front lawn. There was so much death that day ... Simon had killed an abundance ... and he barely remembered doing it. The night was like a dream. He'd fought in the trenches like an animal, his body moving and hacking with the machete of its own accord. At night, when the nightmares came, it was like watching a terrible movie in his thoughts.

"Jack," Simon said, reaching the scouts. "What's going on?"

Jack shook his head. "I don't know, sir. I think it's best you see for yourself. I'll explain on the way."

A jeep was waiting outside of the gates, and Simon sat in the passenger seat as Jack took the wheel, and turned onto the pavement.

"There were three of them, sir. Just came wandering out of the brush. It's-it's a sight."

"What is?"

"Our hunters were out near Partridge Lake, and they saw the first of them. The guy came stumbling out of the brush, his wrists tied before him."

"Who is he?"

Jack swallowed visibly. "A scout from Hightown. It's his eyes, sir. He doesn't have any. Eyes, ears, tongue, nose ... they've been cut away. He's near dead, starved and dehydrated."

"What? Are there more?"

"Three, including the one scout. But he's the only one still alive. The hunters called in a medic and reinforcements—"

"Why wasn't I notified immediately?"

"I don't know, sir. This all just happened. I don't think the hunters knew what they were coming upon, or what was happening."

"Okay, go on."

"They found the second man dead in the woods about a half mile away. His face is cut up the same. The third man was nearby, sitting up against a tree. He was unconscious, but alive. When the medics came and started removing his binds, cutting away his clothing, there was a gash on his side, stitched up, and a bulge. Then all at once the guy fucking blew up."

"What?" Simon's eyes shot large.

"Two medics died."

"Holy shit. What about the other one?"

"The same. Both the one alive and the one dead, they got big bulges in their sides. The medics aren't touching them until a bomb unit arrives. They've been called in, and should be there before us."

"Does the General know?"

Yes, sir."

Jack turned onto a gravel road, the bumps and potholes in bad shape.

"Any idea who the men are?"

Not the one who blew up, or the other one who's dead. It's hard to tell … you know, with their faces how they are. But one of the hunters says he might recognize the one alive. A scout from Hightown, a mapmaker of some sort."

Jack turned again down another gravel road, the woods growing thicker on either side. Ahead were three other jeeps parked off the road. Jack parked next to them, and a soldier walked over.

"Simon," the soldier said. "You'll need to stand back. The bomb squad is there now."

"Is he still alive?"

"Unconscious, I think." The man pointed into the woods, where a dozen armed men stood about. "Just up there. Stay behind those trees."

Simon stepped to the broad side of a maple, and the soldier passed him binoculars. Through the circular peripherals, a man sat with his back against a tree, his hands on his lap. Two men in full protective gear stood before him. The man's face was red with blood, and black with grime. It was difficult to see the extent of his injuries from their distance, yet the dark voids where his eyes and nose should have been were unmistakable.

"One thing more, sir," the soldier said. "His chest is all cut up. Looks like someone tried to write something on him with a knife."

Simon looked away from the scene.

"Here." The man passed Simon a slip of paper. "Whatever it means, it's beyond me."

Simon studied the words. Ante Bellum.

All at once, his radio, along with everyone else's radio, issued a high-pitched alarm. Simon grabbed it from his belt. *"All forces return to Alice. Hightown is reporting an attack. I repeat, all forces return to Alice."* The alarm sound repeated.

Simon turned to the car and ran to the passenger door. Jack started the ignition and turned in the road.

"Take us straight to the General," Simon said.

The window was rolled down, and the warm breeze played over his skin.

Please, Simon thought, *just let this be a false alarm …*

He thought of Brian, injured from fighting. Of Bethany, whose nightmares rivaled his own, and of Carolanne, Brian's wife, who had sewed and patched up hundreds of wounds following the war. He thought of Winston, who now was so old that it took him a pause to sit and stand. He thought about Nick and Tom Byrnes, and the hundreds of people he called friends who were brutally slaughtered during the battle for Alice. All for nothing. He himself had killed dozens, and he would never be at peace with that.

We can't take any more … no more fighting, please, for all that is holy …

But deep down, Simon knew that something terrible was on the horizon.

http://www.BrandonZenner.com
http://www.amazon.com/author/brandonzenner

Thank you for reading *Butcher Rising*. A sequel is coming ... sign up for Brandon Zenner's email list on his website to be kept informed. You will also receive a free short story, "Helix Illuminated," when you sign up. As always, the best way you can support an independent author is by leaving a review on Amazon. Each and every review is read and appreciated by the author, both good and bad. The Amazon link above will take you there. Please read on past the Acknowledgments for a preview of Brandon Zenner's novel, *Whiskey Devils*. For those of you who want more, check out Brandon Zenner's blog site here: https://brandonzennerblog.wordpress.com

From the Author

I mention in the "From the Author" section of *The After War* that this series of books all began when I was sixteen years old. I was walking through a nearby park when the images of a battle formed in my mind, where it fermented and grew into what is still being created to this day, over twenty years later. The first scene, from way back then, was the battle in the woods of Alice Springs Park. Over the years, the story grew and matured, and as I wrote the first draft of *The After War*, I realized that one novel was not enough. The story couldn't end where it left off, and Simon, Brian, Karl, and Winston were not finished yet. The challenge was deciding where to pick up after I ended *The After War*. I typed out fifty pages or so, but didn't like where it was going. What I needed was a story all in its own, and not just a strict continuation of events. To say I felt dejected would be an understatement. I abandoned the fifty pages, and went about feeling sorry for myself, much to my wife's dismay (and annoyance). Then one night, as I was attempting to fall asleep, the first line popped into my head, "In the low of a valley lay a pond ..." All at once it hit me; this book is not only a continuation of Karl Metzger's plight after Alice, the book is in itself Karl Metzger's story. He deserves a novel of his own. After all, he is my favorite bad guy that I have created (sorry to the Russian gangsters in *Whiskey Devils*, and that sharp-dressed lawyer of sorts in *The Experiment of Dreams*). I got out of bed and scribbled down a few lines, then tried to go back to sleep. More of the plot came to me that night, and I had a clear image of the town of Marianna, and the slightly Western tone I wanted for the first part of the novel. In the morning, I typed the first chapter, and had a rough draft completed a few months later. I let the manuscript sit for over a year, then returned to it with fresh eyes. It's a great feeling to see your own work after enough time has gone by to forget some of its nuances.

I still go to the same park where I got the initial idea for this series, and dwell on new concepts. Only now, instead of my mash-up of teenage friends who used to accompany me, I take my four-year-old daughter, and let her come up with stories of her own. And believe me when I tell you, she's full of them. I haven't yet shown her some of my old haunts inside that park, such as the inspiration behind Simon's meditation perch, but we'll get there soon enough. The world is hers, and she'll in time find a perch of her own.

All the best,
Brandon Zenner

Acknowledgments

In no particular order, the following people deserve my thanks and appreciation. You each contributed in your own way, and helped shape this novel into what it has become. Hal Zenner, John Zur, Stephanie Parent, and Deborah Dove. Lastly, my wife, Mallory, for her unwavering support, and my daughter, Sadie-Mae, for always inspiring me.

Preview: Whiskey Devils

"A large marijuana growing operation, Russian mobsters, undercover drug agents, and a biker gang, wraps up with a series of unexpected and shocking plot reversals that brings the book to a violent, surprising, and powerful end." (BookLife Prize in Fiction, by Publishers Weekly)

Chapter 1

Spring, 2003

Weaving through the crowd, I passed my exhausted coworkers, their faces gaunt and ghostly pale in the fluorescent lighting. All of them were salivating before the punch-out clock like a pack of ravenous hounds eager to tear into the flesh of that Friday night. They leaned from one leg to the other, purses in hand, sunglasses dangling from open collars. The din of conversation lessened as I neared the clock, and all eyes were cast upon me.

They were thinking, *Is he really going to do it? Is Powers leaving early?*

The receptionist's sharp stare burned with scorn from behind her blonde bangs, but I ignored her gaze and approached the clock. My time card was in my hand, "Evan Powers" scribbled on top. The paper glided effortlessly through the punch-out machine, making a slight mechanical noise as it stamped out the time, 4:47. The clicking noise echoed in the now-silent room, and I hightailed it to the door, daring my eager coworkers to follow.

Warm air cloaked me in all its glory as I flung the door open. My flesh tingled—honest to God, tingled—like the sun was drawing out some poison from the office's artificial cold air.

As I crossed the parking lot toward my car, I resisted turning to look through the wall-length window of the manager's office. Kim would be staring up from a stack of papers on her desk, watching me in disbelief as she checked the time on her watch. No one left before the clock struck five. No one.

Yeah, I did it. I left early. But fuck it—I quit. So there was that.

The well-traveled engine of my Buick rumbled to life, sputtering out clouds of gray exhaust. I backed out, put the car in drive, and sped the hell out of there.

A cigar was waiting for me in the glove box, and I clamped it between my teeth as I loosened the collar of my button-up shirt.

I laughed out loud, feeling a bit like a madman who laughs alone at the world, thinking, *I'm free, you fuckers—I'm free!* A cloud of cigar smoke was sucked out the window, replaced by the clean springtime breeze.

Traffic was already forming on the highway, but I had managed to beat the mass of cars that would stretch on for miles only minutes after five o'clock. The landscape gradually changed to an immense array of blossoming trees and flat wilderness as I distanced myself from town, driving deeper into the heart of the New Jersey Pine Barrens. My housemate Nick and I rented a nice piece of property: three acres of trees and land, with many more acres of wilderness in every direction. Our nearest neighbor was old Mr. Patrick, or Grandpa, and we didn't cross paths with the man too often. We invited him over whenever we had parties, but Grandpa rarely showed up and never stayed for long. He was cool with us, but when our parties got going, and a handful of ragged hippies turned into twenty, thirty, forty, sixty—whatever—he would take off. Not before schooling us all in a game of horseshoes, of course, and drinking about a six-pack of beer. The man could put them away.

I drove past Grandpa's mailbox and our driveway soon appeared. Nick's work truck came into view as I pulled in, and way out in the back of the yard I spotted him standing beside our massive garden. Nick had been living in the rental house for fifteen years. Our good friend, Darin Long, had been a housemate with us for the past five years, but due to his mother discovering that she has cancer, he had moved back home to Montana. Now it was only the two of us, all alone in that low ranch in the middle of the woods.

Hippie Nick, he was sometimes called, or more recently, The Old Man. It was a term of endearment. The guy had lived through the cultural revolution of the '60s and '70s, which meant that for most of our friends, myself included, Nick Grady was the closest thing to a legitimate hippie that we would ever encounter. The guy followed the Dead, marched at civil rights protests, and did all that fun stuff that made him practically a sage in the eyes of my stoner friends.

I got out of the car and passed Nick's work van on the way to the house. The *G* and *R* in Grady Construction and Repair on the van's side were barely legible, faded with time.

Our front door was unlocked, and I went straight to the kitchen. We had a strict nonsmoking rule indoors, for everything other than herb, so I had to be quick with my still-burning cigar. I grabbed two beers from the fridge and went out the kitchen door to the backyard. Nick was under the apple tree next to the garden, swaying with a beer in hand. The Dead blared from his portable CD player, the extension cord trailing all the way back to the house, lost like a snake in the grass.

Water droplets rained down from the sprinkler over the budding tomato plants, zucchinis, peppers, and everything else we'd planted only a few weeks ago. The corn stalks were already about two feet tall.

Nick moved to the music, barefoot, with his wrapped hemp necklaces and beadwork bouncing on his gray-haired chest. The only article of clothing the guy ever wore at home was a pair of cutoff jean shorts. When he saw me approaching he nodded.

"Hey there," I said.

Nick smiled a crooked smile, a rubber band stuck between his lips as he pulled his long hair out of his face. A cooler was out there next to the few battered Adirondack chairs, and I could tell by the look in Nick's eyes that he was already a few beers in. I handed him the beer I had brought from the kitchen anyway. Sierra Nevada, always Sierra Nevada. It was the only beer the guy would drink if given a choice. However, if he didn't have a choice, he'd drink most anything. Especially bourbon. We went through the stuff like it was water.

The song ended and he yelled out, "Yo, Powers! What's up, man?" He was evidently in a great mood.

"Nothing, Nick." I tried to be nonchalant, but my lips cracked into a smile. "I did it."

His eyes lit up. "You quit?"

I nodded.

"Ha!" He bounced over on quick feet and hugged me with his strong, skinny arms. "I'm so happy for you, brother. I know that job was dragging you down."

"Thanks, man."

"Want to call some people up, get the bonfire going?"

I shrugged. "I wouldn't mind having a few beers."

His face was radiant, and I knew he was swallowing back the question he'd been asking me for years now. The words were trying to burst free from his mouth, but I was going to wait a little while longer before letting him know that I would work for him full time. And I wasn't talking about his handyman service; as good as he was at repairing cabinets, replacing shingles, and even doing some landscaping for a handful of local Pineys. I was talking about his *other* job. His real job.

"You doing some shooting?" I nodded toward the small arsenal on the coffee table: his old Western-style six-shooters. They were a hobby of sorts, first for him, and then for me. After all, we did live in the middle of the woods. Not to mention that the house one over from old Mr. Grandpa's was the fire chief's, and the man was a regular at our parties—as clean-cut as he was—and he kept an eye on the police radio for call-ins about noise. I consider myself clean-cut as well, in comparison to most of the transients who pass through our doors. My hair is short, I wear nice pants and shirts, and I keep myself in decent shape. Ever since I met Nick, I've been trying to get the guy to go running with me, or use the weight bench in the basement. But he always declines. "Look at me," he says. "I'm skinny enough. There won't be nothing left of me." It's true. The guy's a rail: skinny and strong. A lifetime's worth of hard labor made it impossible for him to ever be a pound overweight.

Nick looked to the black powder pistols. "Knock yourself out," he said, and went back to swaying with the music, mumbling along with the words while looking out over the sea of vegetables glistening from the sprinkler water.

As the sun began to set and the beer in the cooler dwindled, we loaded and fired the six-shooters at a wide tree stump across the yard. The process of loading a black powder revolver was tedious, but that made shooting them all the more enjoyable. We had to work for our fun.

While we were shooting, the house phone rang several times, and soon our driveway became illuminated by headlights. A few people showed up with more beer, weed, and various low-grade narcotics and hallucinogens. Ritalin, Adderall—that sort of thing. Most everyone, myself excepted, got stoned the minute they crossed onto our property. Weed was never my thing. I rarely smoked, which was in contrast to the company I kept.

This guy named Mario showed up tripping on mushrooms, sitting a foot away from the blazing flames in the fire pit, his bright orange hair seeming to glow in the flickering light. I thought about asking him for a few caps, but decided against it. Ever since Darin moved out, Nick and I had to be on the lookout for people fucked up on the more serious drugs, like cocaine, heroin, and even speed. That was a big no-no at our home. Darin used to be our enforcer of sorts. He was a strong guy, although his short and stout build made him appear youthful, especially with his long dark hair kept up in a ponytail. Ex Army, believe it or not. But that life wasn't for him. Darin was a feel-good stoner who liked lounging around the house shirtless, just like Nick.

But Darin was gone, so it was up to Nick and me to watch over our guests. Just last party I found a guy taking a line of coke in our bathroom. He was so strung out that he forgot to lock the handle, and when I told him to get rid of the shit he started spewing vulgarities at me through his clattering jaw. Before his erratic mind thought it was a good idea to throw a swing, Nick and I had his arms behind his back, and we did the old heave-ho out the door, holding the back of his belt and his collar. I learned long ago in my bartending days to never let the other guy swing first. Unless of course the other guy was so fucked up that he couldn't hit the side of a wall. Or if the guy was a lawyer. Never hit a lawyer first. But back at my old bar, the local clientele were far from lawyers.

Lucky for us, the crowd was mellow tonight as the alcohol and marijuana flowed. At some point the fire chief showed up, wearing a big grin. He disappeared with Nick inside the house, and when he came back out, he was baked out of his mind.

"Hey, Powers," he said, his red eyes sparkling.

"What's up?"

"Check this out."

The fire chief swung a canvas duffel bag around from his shoulder and opened the zipper. A copious amount of fireworks lay inside.

"Cool, huh?"

"Yeah." I smiled. "Cool."

The night wore on and the fireworks were ignited to thunderous ovation from the enamored crowd. The fire chief kept his radio turned up in case the noise got called into the cops.

Maybe fifteen people were gathered in the backyard when I saw headlights approach from down the driveway and stop short of the house. I checked the time on my watch. It was impossible to see in the darkness, but I knew the headlights belonged to the black Plymouth Fury Gran Coupe that had been arriving at our house at that same time every week, for years now. I looked for Nick in the crowd and spotted him by the fire.

"Hey," I said, approaching.

When Nick looked at me, I tapped my watch and nodded toward the car. His face soured.

"Motherfucker," he muttered, and swilled back his beer.

Nick went to the house, and a moment later he emerged from the front, walking toward the car. He opened the passenger door, illuminating the car's interior while stepping inside.

It wasn't long until the passenger door opened again and Nick got out. The Plymouth reversed out of the driveway, not bothering to swing around the circle. Nick had told me in the past that the man didn't like it when strangers were at our house during his stops. But then he had gone on, "If he makes his stops on a Friday, it can't be avoided. Fuck him."

When Nick got close, I handed him a beer. His face was set in the same crazed anger that always overtook him after leaving the man in the Plymouth. I silently prayed that he wouldn't start hitting the bottle hard, like he often did after the man's visits, and go off on one of his insane rambles. Not now, not tonight. Tonight, I was celebrating my new life. My new path, as twisted as it might become.

"You okay?" I asked.

Nick took the beer and our eyes met. His face softened. "Yeah, man." He patted me on the shoulder, and we walked into the yard to join the circle of people watching the fire chief light off the last of his fireworks.

And there was Becka. Her fair complexion illuminated in bouncing shadows from the fire, her dark, somewhat curly hair pure black in the night.

"Hey," I said, walking up to her. "When'd you get here?"

She turned and smiled at the sound of my voice. "Hey, Powers. Just a minute ago. I was looking for you."

She patted the grass beside her and I took a seat, making it a point for our thighs to touch.

"I did it," I told her. "I quit."

"The office?"

"The office."

"Powers," she exclaimed. "That's wonderful, man!"

She reached over and wrapped her arms around me, burying her face in my chest.

This was good. This is what I needed. I needed Becka, her arms holding me tight all night long. When was the last time we'd hooked up? A week ago? Maybe more. Nick jokingly referred to Becka as my girlfriend, but we were nothing like that. Just friends. Two people in their mid-thirties who had been in terrible relationships, much like all the other loners out there who find themselves still single past their twenties. We just wanted to keep things cool. Sure, we liked each other, but we didn't want to make our relationship something more than it needed to be. For her birthday last year I bought her a small oval locket. Nothing fancy or expensive. I regretted giving it to her the moment I saw the surprise and uncertainty on her face. She did wear it, though, up until recently. She said she misplaced it, put it down somewhere, and that it's got to be around. Probably at home. Probably fell from the kitchen sink. She'd find it, she told me.

But who knows.

Becka had been friends with Nick for years longer than I'd known either of them. I originally thought that Nick and Becka had a romantic past, but Darin later set me straight. Besides, their ages are decades apart ... not that that would stop either of them.

As the last explosion filled the air, the fire chief turned to the crowd.

"That's it," he said, displaying his empty duffel bag. "That's all she wrote."

Nick stood a few feet away from the crowd and we caught each other's eyes.

"Hey, Becka, you gonna be here for a few minutes?"

She looked up at me with a smile and then back to the fire. "I'm not going anywhere."

I hugged her shoulder and stood. "Be right back."

"Hey, grab me a beer while you're at it?" She displayed her near-empty bottle, the light from the fire making it transparent.

"Of course." I smiled, walking toward Nick. "Be right back."

Nick and I stood apart from the group as the fire chief shook out a few stray firecrackers into the fire, turning the duffel bag upside down and shaking it out.

"Hey," Nick shouted over the roar of our friends laughing and jumping away from this madman dumping explosives over the open flame. "We gotta talk."

"Yeah," I said. "I know."

"You give my proposition some thought?"

I nodded, not that he could see me with his eyes transfixed on the fire. With Darin gone, Nick was shorthanded. He'd been asking me to work full time at his operation for years, but I always declined. I was too clean-cut for that life, I used to think. I was better off as a part-time employee. But after spending three years stuck at a cubicle in the stalest environment that I could possibly imagine, wasting away the best and most productive time of the day—between nine and five, when the human mind and body is at its best— I was starting to see things in a different light. Plus, he was offering me more than just hours—he was offering me a management position. Small responsibilities at first, but they would grow over time. But the real benefit, I thought, was that Becka and I would be spending more time together.

"Yeah, Nick, I've given your proposition a lot of thought. I'm in. I'm all aboard."

He turned to me. "Seriously?"

"Seriously."

He extended a hand, smiling like a little boy. "Oh, brother, you are most needed!"

We shook, and then of course he hugged me.

"Man, this is going to be great!" he shouted, arms out in the air, holding his beer aloft to the night sky. The light from the fire flickered dancing shadows all over his body.

"We'll start tomorrow," he said, taking a swig of beer and bouncing on his toes.

I smiled.

He tossed the empty straight into the roaring flame, and grabbed two cold ones from the cooler. He popped the caps and handed me a bottle.

"Cheers, brother," he said.

We clinked glasses.

"Cheers."

He took a long pull, and I again prayed to myself that he wouldn't get too fucked up. I didn't need him screaming crazy shit at our guests, crying, sobbing, and making no sense at all.

"I think it will be best if we start late," he said after a burp.

"Agreed."

Sipping my beer, I watched Becka transfixed on the fire, a smile on her radiant face as she swayed to the music. As much of a free spirit as she was, Becka had something about her. She had class, and an amazing mind that I wanted to keep discovering. She wasn't the type of person to lay her cards out on the table; I had to keep guessing what was in her hand. Her beauty was the type that tongue-tied men, but there was more between us than sheer attraction. We had a chemistry that couldn't be put into words, but only felt as a throbbing heat in my chest. It was intrigue that kept me coming back for more; it was her quiet, pondering eyes that displayed indecipherable emotion. Simple words from her lips carried the weight of the world and affected me like I imagine poetry inspires minds greater than my own.

Her shadowy form beckoned me to approach and sit with her on that lush field of grass for as long as eternity would allow.

Turning, I grabbed two beers from the cooler. I was about to tell Nick that I would be back, but he had seen the rapture in my eyes and had begun to drift away, chatting with the fire chief.

"Welcome back," Becka said, looking up to me as I approached. There was longing in her eyes.

Feeling a bit drunk, I smiled coolly and took a seat beside her to watch the roaring bonfire.

Tomorrow, my life would change—for the better, I thought. I would be managing a productive and quite illegal drug operation. But now, in the present moment, I didn't want to contemplate the future or lament the past. I wanted to stay stuck in time, right where I was.

Continue reading here:
https://www.amazon.com/dp/B01AHI307Y

Or here:
http://www.amazon.com/author/brandonzenner

Or even here:
http://www.BrandonZenner.com